Rapunzel's Escape

by

Bethmarie Fahey

Seattle Serendipity

Rapunzel's Escape

Contact Information: info@thewildrosepress.com

Cover Art by *Tina Lynn Stout*

The Wild Rose Press, Inc.
PO Box 708
Adams Basin, NY 14410-0708
Visit us at www.thewildrosepress.com

Publishing History
First Edition, 2025
Trade Paperback ISBN 978-1-5092-6080-5
Digital ISBN 978-1-5092-6081-2

Seattle Serendipity
Published in the United States of America

Dedication

To the real life Karen and Jan, my best friends and cousins, who were my original beta readers and biggest supporters.

Chapter 1

Melissa Anderson leaned closer, squinting as she studied the human characters on her computer screen and searched for any imperfections detracting from the fantasy world she created. The couples swirled across the screen in time to the soft Viennese waltz coming from the computer's speakers. With a critical eye, she assessed the women's gowns in this ballroom scene. The gossamer gowns floated with each twirl. The player could change the gowns' colors at will to enable the character to blend into the background or stand out as desired. A great feature if the player wants to help the character hide from her enemies or flirt with someone interesting. The gala scene was near the end of the game, an award for successfully slaying dragons and fending off the invading army. Leaning back with a small smile, she attached the new designs to an email, signed her name *Rapunzel*, and clicked Send.

The email zoomed off to the Brothers at Play office in downtown Seattle. No one at the gaming company knew her real name besides the human resource director. Rapunzel was who she was in the world of graphic art.

She stretched her arms out, rolling her shoulders to release the tension. Slowly tilting her head from side to side, she took in the organized clutter consuming her workspace. The area around her keyboard was the only space not covered with piles of draft printouts of her work, ideas clipped from magazines, and numerous rough sketches. Work was done for the day, and she turned off the music she used to inspire the scene.

Swiveling in her chair to look away from the clutter, she gazed at one of Mom's paintings. The oil landscape depicted Lake Union full of colorful sailboats skimming across the waters. Sunlight sparkled on the gentle waves. The Space Needle in the background established this as quintessential Seattle. The blue water and dabs of sunshine yellow in the painting mirrored the colors of the drapes and painted walls above the oak wainscoting. The painting could be in a museum or art gallery along with so many of Mom's works, but she had painted it specifically for the dining room.

Melissa studied how the brush strokes conveyed the movement of the water and rippling of the sails with the same intensity she assessed her own work, noting the delicate touch used to capture the tranquility of a sunny day on the lake. She shifted her gaze back to the scene for the computer game still showing on her monitor. With a disgusted grunt, she clicked Close to erase the image from view.

She glanced back at Mom's painting. Tears pricked at the back of her eyes, threatening to fall. Her grief was still close to the surface. "Enough. Time to get up and moving." Melissa slapped her hands on the arms of her chair.

Her stomach growled. Absently, she reached for the cup of coffee. *Cold. How long has it been sitting here? What time is it anyway?* The clock on her computer read three o'clock. Time to find some food.

Before she could stand, the phone rang. She

winced; her hand hovered above the phone waiting for the name of the caller to appear. *Grams.* She quickly answered. "Hi, Grams." Wiping the last of the lingering tears, she forced a smile and clicked on the video.

"Hi, my dear. How are you doing?" Grams smiled and waved at the phone.

"Oh, I'm fine." Melissa forced a smile.

Grams was silent for a moment.

She doesn't believe me.

"I'm calling to see if you are free to visit me this weekend. I haven't seen you in over a month, and I miss you." Grams's voice had a slight quiver.

Their grief was still sharp, and they relied on each other for comfort. Grams was the one person she was able to be honest with about her pain.

Melissa quickly blinked back the tears starting to form. "Sure, Grams. I miss you, too. I just wrapped up my most recent drawings, so I can come tomorrow. I'll leave mid-morning and should be there by two."

Grams responded with a gentle smile. "Wonderful. I'm working on a new commission and would like you to see it. Stay until Sunday, so we'll have lots of time to be together. Maybe you can give me some ideas of what to include on my tapestry."

"I'd love to come spend time with you, as always. But you hardly need my help on your tapestry."

Grams dismissed her comment with a quick wave of her hand. "Another eye is always helpful. I'll see you tomorrow, and you can catch me up on all you've been doing."

"That won't take long since it's mostly work and more work." Melissa rotated her phone to show the pile of discarded designs scattered across the table.

Grams paused briefly. “Well, then maybe we have to talk about that, too.”

“Grams. Really, I’m fine.” Melissa smiled into the phone, hoping to prove she was okay.

Grams squinted at the image on her phone and slowly nodded. “Okay, so come up and show me.”

“I’ll head out tomorrow mid-morning.”

“Take your time and drive safely. Love you, honey.”

“Love you, too, Grams.”

Grams blew her a kiss and ended the call.

Melissa’s stomach grumbled again, reminding her she needed food. She stood and headed toward the door, still thinking about Grams’s obvious concern. *How to convince her I really am fine? Better yet, how to convince myself?*

****

Minutes later, Melissa entered the park across from her house and started her jog. The sunlight filtering through the dense trees on one side of the path made lacy patterns on the pavement. Last night's rainfall left the air smelling fresh and the grass a little greener. She smiled at the people she passed, letting go of the sadness lingering from talking with Grams. Grief was always there—just off to one side, always ready to envelop her when something or someone triggered a memory.

What she liked about jogging in Green Lake Park was no one interacted with her. No one interrupted her solitude. She waved to a young mother pushing an infant in a stroller, jogged around a group of guys on rollerblades coming toward her, ignoring their whistles, and kept an eye out for kids on bikes whizzing by. She gave a quick smile to an older couple holding hands while they strolled along the path. Her smile became genuine as she neared the snack stand on the far side. The usual small line of people stood waiting for ice cream, popcorn, or hot dogs.

Behind the counter, an elderly man with silver-white hair and the bushiest eyebrows over midnight-blue eyes greeted customers with a smile. Filling orders, he teased the kids, telling them silly knock-knock jokes, and flirted harmlessly with the ladies. The stand had been a favorite father and daughter destination throughout her childhood. They lived on the west side of the park overlooking the lake so the three-mile path around it became a convenient place for their runs. They'd often go for a jog and stop for a hot dog. Mom always pretended she had no idea, and she would tease them that they didn't look any thinner after their run.

Melissa met Howard, the current owner, one day when she was home from college during a semester break. Dad introduced her when they stopped during one of their daily runs. One day, she asked Howard why he decided to take over the stand.

He claimed he was too restless to sit at home after retirement and liked chatting with the steady stream of happy customers.

Howard was busy handing out sodas and snacks as people milled around the stand, laughing and trading jokes.

The first time she returned to the stand after her parents' funeral, she had stood just like this, hesitant. She had gone for a run—grateful the rain hid her tears.

Howard motioned her over. He put a hot dog on the

grill and handed her a bottle of water. When the hot dog was ready, he flipped the sign to *Closed* and sat next to her at the picnic table. He didn't say a word. He just sat there in silence, gesturing toward the hot dog he placed in front of her.

After wiping her face on the sleeve of her sweatshirt, she choked down a few bites and then a few more until the hot dog was gone.

Howard then stood, squeezed her shoulder, and flipped the sign back to *Open.*

She started coming to the stand at least once a week.

Howard never pressured her, letting her pick the times to talk.

Gradually, she began to open up and talk about her parents and her grief.

Over the months, he had gently prodded her to get out more, see friends, and visit Grams more often.

Howard spotted her and waved her over. "So, my fair lady has decided to venture out of her tower and mingle with the masses."

Melissa joined in the playful banter. "Greetings, shopkeeper. What wares do you have for me today?" She curtseyed, pantomiming holding out a long skirt with one hand.

"We're starting to sound like one of those crazy computer games my grandsons are always talking about. All about knights and fair damsels in distress who need to be rescued from dragons and other dangers." Howard gestured with his tongs, lunging forward in a fencing stance. "*En garde*."

"Are you sure the knights are doing the rescuing?" Melissa raised one hand to her mouth, trying hard to stifle her laugh. "In my version of this fantasy, the fair damsels are the real heroes, saving the village and keeping the knights from being eaten alive by the dragons."

"I'm going to have to introduce you to my grandsons someday. You'd have a lively discussion about the fantasy world your generation seems addicted to. In the meantime, what can I get for you today?" Howard wiggled his barbeque tongs and raised one bushy eyebrow.

"I'll take the usual." She wandered over to a nearby picnic table and sat facing the beach. Leaning back against the table, she breathed in the irresistible smell of charcoal-grilled hot dogs mixed with the aroma of buttered popcorn. The sun was directly overhead, just starting to dip toward the west. She adjusted the bill of her cap, shading her eyes, and stretched to release the last bit of tension in her shoulders, letting the sun warm her bare arms.

People soaking up the remaining days of summer before the kids returned to school filled the beach area. She smiled at the sight of children running into the shallow water, laughing, and splashing each other as they played. Two young mothers sat on blankets with toddlers playing in the coarse sand.

At a nearby table, a few teenage girls sat giggling and eating ice cream. A group of teenage boys stood a short distance away, giving them occasional shy glances. Each time one of the girls caught a boy looking their way they'd all giggle even more.

At their age, the interplay between two interested people is so easy.

Now an adult, Melissa struggled to find male

companionship. She wanted what her parents had, the easy back-and-forth where they supported each other's ambitions and dreams. All the guys she dated in college and later were so focused on their own desires, they barely listened to hers, let alone actively supported them. She wished Mom was still around to tell her how to achieve the mutually loving partnership she had with Dad.

Swinging her legs around, she leaned her elbows on the table. Resting her chin in her hands, she took in all the sounds of summer fun around her.

Howard grilled a hot dog just the way she liked it—slightly charred. He piled on mustard, ketchup, onions, pickles, and diced tomatoes. He also picked up two bottles of water. Ensuring no one was waiting to order, he turned the sign to *Closed* and joined her at the picnic table.

Melissa took a bite of her hot dog and closed her eyes to better appreciate the taste. "Perfect." She raised her fingers to her lips in a chef's kiss. "Just what I needed."

"I bet you've been working so hard you forgot to eat breakfast or lunch today," Howard scolded.

She opened her eyes wide in feigned surprise. "What? You mean this isn't breakfast? Why, I just got up and rolled out of bed."

"Well, it would explain the rumpled look, but I don't believe you. I know you too well." He leaned close, shaking his finger. "You've been sitting in front of your computer for hours doing whatever it is you do every day. But seriously, you work too hard, and you need to get out more often. When was the last time you went out to dinner with friends or did something just for fun?"

"Why, I'm sitting here right now having a gourmet meal with a handsome older gentleman." She grinned over her hot dog.

"If I'm the highlight of your social life, then you are in trouble. You need to let someone your age take you out for a nice dinner." His snow-white eyebrows wiggled as he spoke.

She took the last bite of her hot dog and wiped her hands on the napkin. "There's no one like that in my life right now."

"Well, there should be." Howard paused for a moment, glancing around the area.

Melissa held her napkin to her mouth to hide her giggle.

He looks like he could pluck out a boyfriend from the people at the beach.

Howard's eyes twinkled. "I've got a couple of good-looking grandsons I can introduce you to. I bet you'd like John. You're both into those computer games. When he was a teenager, he played them all the time. Then he studied computers in college, and now he does some crazy things with programming and still plays with games." Talking about his grandson, his face lit up.

She smiled at Howard's eager expression. "Sorry, Howard. I'm just not interested right now. And despite the fact I do graphics for computer games, I'm not much of a gamer." She shrugged. "I do just enough to understand the look and feel of the most popular games, but I don't spend time playing them for the sake of the game. I know nothing about programming, so we probably don't have much in common."

His face fell. "But your dad was a programmer?"

"True, but I didn't inherit his computer genius. I followed in Mom's footsteps with my art." She raised her hands in resignation.

Howard cocked one eyebrow. "He's still a nice guy and might be fun to just know."

"I'm sure he is, but I'm not in the right space to begin a relationship. I'll let you know if anything changes." She leaned over and patted Howard's hand.

His face crumpled like someone had just taken his puppy away.

Straightening, he smiled. "I tried. Now, I better get back to my customers. Thanks for stopping by and brightening up an old man's day."

"You're my favorite old man." She stood and gave him a quick hug. Waving goodbye, she continued on the path toward home. She chuckled to herself. *Howard certainly wasn't too subtle about setting me up with his grandson. He's never mentioned him before as a potential date, so, I wonder what prompted him today.* With a shake of her head, she quickly dismissed the thought.

Chapter 2

The next morning, Melissa rummaged in her closet for something clean to pack, making a mental note to do laundry when she got back. Finally, finding a couple pairs of capris and light weight cotton T-shirts, she packed them in the small overnight bag along with a pair of cotton pajamas. Like most homes in the area, Grams didn't have air-conditioning and a quick glance at the weather app on her phone confirmed the weekend would be a scorcher. From the bathroom, she gathered the necessary toiletries and added them to the bag. She didn't need much for her trip north to Grams's house. Doing a quick check around her bedroom, she spotted the phone charger and tossed it into the bag. Pocketing her cell phone, she picked up the bag, headed downstairs, and out the door.

Melissa threw the bag into the back seat of her car and got in. Warm air flowed through the open window. No need for the air conditioner yet. A perfect day for a drive. She first stopped at one of the many drive-through coffee stands dotting the streets. Seattle ran on coffee. Caffeine need met, she merged onto I-5 North for the two-hour drive to the Lummi Nation.

Several weeks had passed since she last made this drive. Yesterday, when Grams called, Grams said she wanted her to see the tapestry she was weaving for the Seattle Art Museum. No surprise the museum had commissioned one of Grams's tapestries. The Lummi Nation was known for their artists, and Grams was amongst the best for creating beautiful woven pieces.

Melissa's own talent came from generations of Lummi weavers, potters, and carvers. While Grams chose weaving and Mom chose paint, her work took the form of graphic design and animation—the perfect blend of Mom's art and Dad's computer skills. With a slight shake of her head, she reminded herself Grams would say they didn't choose an art form, the art chose them. It was what they were born to do.

Pulling into the gravel driveway just under two hours later, she breathed in the salty sea air. Puget Sound was a stone's throw away from Grams's house. The Lummi Nation was on a small peninsula jutting out into the Sound about eight miles from Bellingham and just south of the Canadian border. She happily anticipated long walks on the beach, collecting shells and other treasures washed onto the sand from the sea. Seagulls squawked overhead, preparing to descend on a morsel of food left on the beach.

She parked behind Grams's car, pushed her sunglasses up to the top of her head, and sat for a moment, gazing at what she considered her second home. She spent summer breaks here with Grams, playing in the waves and running up and down the beach. The one-story shingled house was typical of the homes in the area, with a roofed porch stretched across the front and a simple gravel driveway leading to a carport. Flower boxes of red and pink geraniums lined the edges of the porch. The furniture on the porch consisted of two wooden rocking chairs painted in bold primary colors, with a small round table between them.

The front door opened, and Grams stepped out onto the porch, wiping her hands on a powder-blue apron. She was dressed in her usual summer attire—a long multicolored gauzy skirt and white button-down shirt belted at her slim waist.

Melissa took in the long silver-white hair worn in a thick braid down her back, the warm dark-brown eyes, and gentle laugh lines around her mouth and eyes. Grams's appearance reminded her so much of Mom, except for the color of her hair that Melissa's heart ached. She hopped out of the car and rushed into Grams's strong, open arms.

Grams held her at arm's length, squinting slightly. "Come inside. I have iced tea and freshly baked blueberry muffins. You need some fattening up, my dear."

Melissa smiled at Grams's obvious concern. "I'm fine, Grams, really. I've just been busy with work. And I don't need any fattening up, but I'll never say no to your homemade muffins." She looped her overnight bag over one shoulder and, linking arms with Grams, turned toward the house.

"So, other than working day and night, what have you been doing since I last saw you? You look tired." Grams patted her arm as they walked.

"I just finished the work on the graphics for a new computer game. I sent my last few screens off yesterday. So, I have a little break until I get any needed changes. I'm sure there will be tweaks, but for now, I'm free." She set her overnight bag just inside the door and breathed deep, taking in the scent of the baked muffins comingling with the lemon oil Grams used to polish her furniture. Her entire body relaxed as she inhaled the familiar scents of her childhood.

Grams's eyes sparkled. "Excellent. I see you didn't bring your laptop, so I have your undivided attention for the weekend." She gestured to the large loom in the next room. "This is the tapestry I told you about on the phone. The design will tell the history of the Lummi Nation."

Melissa went over to the work in progress and ran her fingers over the salmon leaping across the border of the tapestry. She touched the smooth texture, running her fingers along the threads pulled taut to form the images. In the center panel, she could see the primitive canoes used by the early Lummis to fish.

Grams stood beside her. "I want people to know we are the Salmon People. The Lummi are the *Lhag'temish*, the People of the Sea." She pointed to the partially completed scene depicting the deep-blue water of the Sound. "Since the beginning of the Lummi people, we have depended on salmon to feed our bodies and our souls. I want others to understand our culture and appreciate the beauty and grace we bring to the world, as well as our commitment to protect the environment. So, it can be enjoyed by generations to come."

"This is beautiful. But how can I help? I don't weave." Melissa touched the wooden weaving shuttle on the table next to the loom.

Grams reached out to grasp Melissa's hands. "I don't need your fingers. I need your head." She gently tapped one finger on Melissa's forehead. "You are a storyteller. You tell your stories through your designs on the computer. I tell ours through my weaving. I'll tell you more about your Lummi heritage, and you can help me decide what images best tell our story. The salmon give us life, so we must protect them or soon there will be no more to harvest. Every year, our fishermen's nets are lighter and lighter. This tapestry will honor our past and challenge everyone to act now to save the environment for the future."

Melissa continued to stroke the edges of the tapestry. "That's a tall order. A lot to ask of a piece of art."

Grams dismissed the idea with a wave of her hand. "Pooh. If art doesn't inspire, then what is its purpose? A piece of art needs to do more than just look good. It needs to move the viewer in some way. Sometimes, our art tells a story, or makes us wonder, or fills us with emotion. But at its best, art provokes the viewer to think differently by opening a new window in the mind and letting new ideas in."

"I see what you are trying to do. I'd be honored to help."

"Great, but let's start with some iced tea and muffins. Then you can take a walk to soak in the beauty around us. Later, we'll be ready to add to the design."

Melissa followed Grams to the small kitchen and helped carry the iced tea and muffins out the back door to the patio. The back porch mirrored the front one with an overhanging roof, another arrangement of colorful wood-slotted chairs, and a multitude of flower boxes overflowing with fuchsias, bougainvillea, and dahlias in every color imaginable. The scent of roses drifted by from the trellis along one side of the porch, mingling with the crisp smell of the salty sea air.

The ice tinkled as she set the glasses on the small table. She slid into the canary-yellow chair, melting into the warmth of the wood. Pushing her sunglasses back over her eyes, she gazed out at the calm water. The view always fascinated her. Fishing boats bobbed up and down on the waves in the harbor. Listening to Grams share the latest news about the village and the college where she taught, all thoughts of work, to-do lists, and other distractions disappeared. An extra juicy blueberry from the muffin ran down her chin. Melissa laughed, wiping it off with her hand.

Grams stood to go back into the house. "I'll get dinner started. You stay out here and listen to the water. Let the sea talk to you like an old friend. It's what I do when I need to hear another voice in my head."

Melissa leaned forward to look at Grams and pushed her sunglasses back onto her head. "Grams, do you feel lonely here, living by yourself?"

Grams paused for a moment to gaze out over the water. She turned back with a gentle smile. "There are moments, but in general, no. Whenever I feel the need to connect, I just walk to the community center. I can always find a group of people there. Mostly old folks like me, sitting around sharing stories and doing crafts together. During the school year, I see plenty of people in my classes and around the campus. So, no…I'm not lonely. Sometimes, I just need to hear a different kind of voice to reconnect me to our people and our love of nature and the water."

Melissa searched Grams's face for any signs of melancholy. "I worry about you and feel bad I don't come to visit more often."

Grams's smile was instant and genuine. "No need to worry about me, my dear. But I'd be happy to have you come more often. I worry about you, too. You're too isolated. When was the last time you talked to Karen and Jan?"

"Karen texts me often and comes by occasionally, with pizza. But I haven't seen Jan for two months now. I said I would keep in touch, go out with them, but…" Melissa shrugged and gestured vaguely with her hands.

Grams reached out to place a hand on her shoulder. "I know. It's still hard. But burying yourself in work and avoiding everyone isn't the way to live. I worry the bubble your parents built around the three of you has taught you to isolate instead of engaging in life. Your mom worked hard to keep her public persona from interfering in the family life, but she willingly stepped into the world. She just kept you and your dad out of the spotlight."

Melissa rested a hand on Grams's. Recalling moments with Mom, she couldn't keep her voice from trembling a bit. "I know. People would come up to her in the grocery store or on the street, especially after an exhibit. She used to joke she didn't dare walk outside to get the mail without first getting dressed and putting on makeup. But not me. I like heading out in sweats and not worrying if I remembered to brush my hair."

Grams nodded.

Melissa glanced away, biting her lip. "I like the solitude of working from home and only corresponding via email. I even avoid video chats as much as possible. Karen and Jan have sometimes accused me of being anti-people. It's not that I don't like people—I do. I just want to keep my personal and professional lives separate." She paused, looking out at the water. "When Mom and Dad died, local and national news sources kept asking me to do interviews. I rejected them all. I didn't want public recognition. I knew they only wanted to talk to the daughter of the famous artist Celeste Whitestar and Michael Anderson, the great computer guru. I'm not famous, and I don't want to be." Her voice hardened. "Everyone then thinks they're entitled to a piece of you."

Grams's hand massaged her shoulder. "Those days and weeks following the accident and funeral were hard, especially for you. Many of the press had no regard for the fact you were grieving. All they wanted was the story, to take advantage of your parents' fame for their own benefit."

Melissa's hands gripped her glass, sloshing the small amount of tea left. She set it on the table and stared back out at the water.

Grams continued to rub her arm gently. "I understand why you initially hid away in the house, guarding yourself and your art, and avoided going out in public. But I worry this is becoming a permanent way of life for you. You deserve more. You deserve to be happy again." With a squeeze of Melissa's shoulder, Grams left to go into the house.

Melissa sat back, trying to hear the voices of the water Grams talked about. Instead, she heard Mom's voice pushing her out the door to play with friends or inviting her friends to come to play. Mom made those times special, offering treats and getting out her many hats, scarves, and costume jewelry so they could play dress up. *I miss her so much.*

I know I'm a good artist, but Mom was a great artist. A high standard to live up to, and she believed she fell short. She'd never make the impact on the world both Mom and Grams did with their art. *Theirs hangs in museums. Mine plays out on computer screens seen mostly by teenagers. By comparison, I'm invisible, and I'm okay with that.*

She let the sound of the waves relax her. Closing her eyes, she took a big breath in, then slowly released it, in-and-out, in-and-out. The tension gradually eased away, and the ugly memories receded.

Grams's voice drifted out, softly singing an old classic in harmony with the sound of chopping vegetables. Melissa stood to go inside to help with dinner preparation. The evening was spent quietly with Grams sharing more about the Lummi traditions while Melissa sketched out the images the stories provoked.

****

August mornings came early in the Pacific Northwest. Melissa's day started with breakfast with Grams at the table on the back porch and then a run. Afterward, she wandered the beach area, picking up random shells and other small treasures washed ashore with low tide. She searched for unusual shells and stones. Using her cell phone, she took a few pictures of bleached driftwood and boats bobbing in the water. Sometimes, a random image could be helpful in creating a scene for a computer game.

Melissa entered through the back door and found Grams making a small salad and turkey sandwiches. "Yum, this looks great. I'm starved."

"Then wash up and set the table. We'll eat soon. How was your run?"

Talking over her shoulder as she washed her hands, Melissa described her run. "After completing my three miles, I walked back slowly, searching for treasures."

Grams stopped for a moment and regarded

Melissa. "You used to come back from a walk on the beach when you were little, pockets loaded with the stones, shells, and other items you found. You had a shoebox I gave you where you stored your treasures to take home and show your mom and dad. Remember?"

Melissa grinned and nodded. "Yes, I do. I wonder what happened to the box. I might need a new one for all the pieces I picked up today." She emptied her pockets and laid the items on the table. Then, she pivoted to get plates from the cupboard.

Grams carefully examined the items one by one. Holding a large iridescent shell in her hand, she motioned to Melissa. "Oh, this one is special. It's a pinto abalone shell. This is the only abalone found in Washington State and only in the area around the San Juan Islands. Finding one is rare, but occasionally, the sea will drop one on the beaches along the reservation. This one is unique since it's intact. Most have chips from being bounced around. To get an intact one like this, you usually need to go diving," she explained. "The sea has given you a very special gift."

Melissa took the shell and rotated it in her hand, watching the colors change as the light hit it. "I thought it was beautiful and hope it gives me inspiration."

Once at the table, Grams announced a tribal meeting was scheduled for that evening. "They want to talk about a recent development affecting the salmon population. Protecting the salmon is especially important to the Lummi people, and as an elder, I'm obliged to attend today's meeting. You should come, too. This would be an opportunity to learn more about your heritage."

Melissa hesitated. "I've never gone to one before,

and I'm not sure I'd know what to do."

Grams chuckled. "There's nothing you need to do other than listen. Like any community meeting, there will be lots of talking, some discussion, and disagreement. But eventually, everyone will agree on what to do. Last night, I shared some of the Lummi history, and this will give you a chance to see how, in times of trouble, the tribe always comes together to find solutions."

This was important to Grams, so she quickly agreed. "Okay, I'd love to come."

After lunch, they returned to the tapestry. Melissa noted the sketches she had made last night depicting the net fishing traditionally used by the Lummi fishermen and women gathering plants and berries next to Grams's loom.

Grams picked up her shuttle and gestured to Melissa's sketches. "These images will guide my hand as I weave our story. I have another story to tell you. This is the story of Duh-hwahk."

Melissa picked up her sketch pad and nodded that she was ready to listen and draw.

"The myth says Kulshan had two brides—the beautiful Duh-hwahk and the kind Whaht-kway. Over time, Duh-hwahk grew jealous of Kulshan's attention to Whaht-kway and decided to force him to choose by threatening to leave him. She believed her great beauty was enough to have him choose her, but instead, he consented to let her leave. As she wandered away, she continued to look back to see if he was chasing after her, begging her to return. He never did. Eventually, she wandered so far, she could no longer see her village, so she rose on her tiptoes to see farther. She grew taller and taller as she searched to see him waving his hands for her to return, but Kulshan never called her back. Today, you can still see the two brides—Whaht-kway in the north as the white-capped Mount Baker visible from our home and the towering presence of Duh-hwahk in the south as Mount Rainier."

Melissa furiously drew images of the two brides and the mountains they became.

Grams clapped when Melissa showed her the images. "I love these. I will add them to the very center of my tapestry. It's a core myth of our people."

Feeling her cheeks flush, Melissa set her sketch pad and pencil aside. "Grams, how did you become a member of the tribal elders? You lived much of your life outside the reservation, and Mom never lived here."

"True, I left as a young girl to pursue my art and traveled the world studying tapestries from all cultures. I returned to the tribe only after your grandfather died."

"But they welcomed you back and made you an elder despite your absence?"

"Yes, Lummi blood is Lummi blood. In our culture, you speak for your ancestors, and they speak for you. Our family goes back to the beginning of the tribe. That makes me an elder, even though I only returned in my later years. We respect and honor those who came before us."

Melissa sat, absorbing the information. "Through you, they would see me as Lummi, too?"

Grams nodded. "Yes, through me, through your ancestors, they accept you as one of them. You are a member of the tribe no matter where you live."

Melissa studied the sketch pad in her hand. She had covered the page with Lummi images from Grams's stories. She knew of her heritage but never lived it. In her mind, she was an outsider or an interloper. *But am I?*

****

That evening, Melissa stood in the back of a large room used for meetings at the Tribal Community Center. Grams had already taken her place at the head table. She tentatively smiled at people who made eye contact, trying to act like she belonged. She had been to the center a few times during her summer visits to do arts and crafts with the other kids. Looking around, she spotted a few she recognized now as adults. These were her people, according to tradition.

The room buzzed with conversation. The members were all alarmed at the potential impact of an oil company's decision to build a new pier just north of Bellingham. The pier would be near the reservation and would affect their fishing waters. People continued to enter the room. Voices began to build in intensity and volume. Small clusters formed. Many people gestured animatedly. Their faces were grim. They greeted each other with curt nods. Many stood with hands on hips, shaking their heads. The air crackled with the intensity of the emotions. But it didn't feel angry. She didn't hear harsh words or cursing. What she heard was determination. A definite sense of urgency filled the air. The need to act and to do so quickly was the focus of most of the conversations around her. She stood, soaking it all in. It was a physical force drawing her closer to the people gathered.

A young woman with straight, jet-black hair, in her early thirties and balancing a toddler on her hip, walked over, smiling warmly. "Are you Melissa?"

Melissa frantically searched unsuccessfully for the woman's name. She was one of the young girls she had played with when visiting Grams. "Yes, hi. It's good to see you again."

"I'm sure you don't remember. I'm Jessica. I saw you come in with your grandmother, so I assumed you were Melissa. I haven't seen you in many years."

As the memory came back, Melissa blushed. "Jessica, yes, it's been a while. I still come to visit but usually just spend my time at Grams."

Jessica resettled the squirming toddler. "I was so sorry to hear about your mom and dad. The whole village mourned their loss. I didn't know them but would see them around when you visited your grandmother. We all saw the grief on your grandmother's face when they died. I'm glad you both are together."

The council leader signaled the meeting was about to begin.

Jessica must have seen him, too. "I should join my husband, but I am so happy to see you here. Welcome back." She hurried over to sit next to a man near the front of the room.

At the bang of the gavel, voices stilled, and everyone hurried to take their seat.

Melissa sat toward the back, where she could watch the people.

The room grew quiet.

The leader addressed the assembly. "I appreciate the passion and energy everyone here has for this issue. This is not the first time we've had to fight back against the wishes of industry, and it won't be the last."

Everyone nodded at the leader's words.

"We need to approach this problem like we do all crises, with deliberate and thoughtful action. We have fought big business before and won. We've even taken our cause as far as the Supreme Court of the United States of America and won. Not only because our cause was just, but also because we prepared and knew how to present our side in a way that resonated with the hearts and minds of the judges. I've asked Doctor Robert Julius from Western University to tell us more about the potential impact this proposed pier will have on the salmon population."

She studied the crowd.

Most everyone leaned forward, listening intently.

While the speaker stood and moved to the microphone, there were whispers. "This is important." "A matter of survival for some." "It's our birthright to protect the salmon." "It's our purpose."

A middle-aged man wearing khaki pants and a plaid shirt strode over to the microphone. He carried a laptop. Standing tall, he took out a pair of round-rimmed glasses and put them on. Consulting his notes, he began his presentation.

Melissa found herself carefully following the facts.

Dr. Julius showed the results of a recent study done by Washington State. The new pier would lead to an increase in potential oil spills, causing environmental damage and disruption of the traditional fishing grounds of the Lummi. The charts he showed estimated the oil spills could increase by twenty-six percent in just four years, polluting the waters. The scent of the oil would interfere with the salmon's ability to sense the presence of their home stream or river and interfering with the annual migration. Additionally, the increase in oil tanker traffic would endanger the salmon traveling through the waters.

The hall was silent. Everyone paused to absorb the facts presented.

She let the facts sink in. Left unchecked, the salmon would die off and never return. Based on what Dr. Julius had shared, this had already happened to the steelhead. Concern about the environment wasn't a new issue, but somehow sitting here, hearing the potential impact this new pier would have on this community made it personal.

Dr. Julius turned off his laptop and slowly wiped his glasses on his shirt sleeve. Peering out at the group, he opened it up to questions.

The man sitting next to Jessica stood. "Dr. Julius. Thank you for coming tonight. My name is Joseph. I'm a fisherman. These waters are how I feed my family." He gestured to Jessica and the child sleeping on her lap. "If what you say is true, in just a few years, I could lose my livelihood. How do we stop this?"

Dr. Julius returned his glasses to his face. "That's the key question. There are options. A final decision has not been made. The city council in Bellingham will have to grant permission to build this pier. I suggest we start there. Petition the council to allow your concerns to be heard. Then you need to educate the people of Bellingham, so they demand the pier is denied. You have friends outside of the reservation, use them. This isn't just the Lummi Nation's problem. It's everyone's."

The phrase landed deep in Melissa's heart. *It's everyone's problem.* Everyone needs to be involved in the solution. *Does it mean me, too?* She was connected to this, in part because of her Lummi blood, but also because the issue went far beyond just this moment, or even this pier. What she realized from Dr. Julius's presentation was the environmental damage had already begun and would spread unchecked unless people chose to change. The proposed new pier was the current challenge, but not an isolated one. If people continued to turn a blind eye to the situation, things would only get worse until nothing was sacred or protected. The tribe would fight the pier and might even win this battle. But it would take much more than just this tribe to win the war.

She sat back in her chair and slowly twisted the end of her ponytail.

All around her, people stood to ask more questions and propose actions. A plan began to form. Some would work on petitioning the city council. Others suggested a visible protest in the bay around where the proposed pier was to be built. Jessica's husband volunteered to organize it.

Ideas and commitments to action swirled around her. Caught up in the fervor, she asked herself, *how can I help?* She was startled when Grams put her hand on her shoulder.

"You look engrossed. I'm glad you came to hear this."

"So am I." Melissa's mind continued to reel from the information. On the way back to Grams, she continued to ponder the situation. *Why has this affected me so deeply? Why do I suddenly care? If I heard about this on the news, would I have even paused for a second to think about the impact? No, I would have shrugged and moved on. So, why can't I now? Maybe it was the wave of emotions and commitment flowing through the room that swept me up and along with it like the powerful tug of a riptide. Or it's my Lummi blood connecting me to the powerful force of an ancestral promise to protect the salmon. Whatever it is, it's now mine. The only question left was how.*

****

Sunday morning, Melissa helped Grams cook and bake many of her favorites, knowing full well she was going home with most of the food. She sat at the kitchen table, listening while Grams mixed a new batch of muffins and talked more about the Lummi traditions and their commitment to the environment. Her pulse suddenly quickened as an idea started to form. She leaned forward, letting the words stumble out as the idea took shape. "Grams, I'm thinking about what you said the other day. You know, about how this tapestry's purpose is to share the Lummi story and teach people about the importance of saving salmon here in Puget Sound. I'm wondering if maybe a computer game could do the same thing."

Grams stopped and turned. "I'm listening."

Melissa paused, mentally visualizing elements of the game. "It's just an idea. I don't know if anyone would be interested in it. But here's what I'm thinking." She took a deep breath. "In the fantasy game I'm drawing now, the players need to meet certain challenges to save the kingdom. They face lots of dangers and situations requiring conning to escape. What if instead of fighting dragons and scaling castle walls, they fight pollution and other dangers to save the salmon?"

Grams stood silently for a moment.

Melissa searched her face for her reaction.

Beaming, Grams pulled her into a warm embrace. "I love the idea. You're the perfect person to do this."

Melissa glanced away briefly, rubbing her hands on her crossed arms. "You don't think it's silly? A game to teach about the environment and the importance of preservation?"

Grams's eyes sparkled. "No, I think it's a beautiful idea."

Melissa bit her lip, glancing at Grams's loom in the other room. "It's not as beautiful as your tapestry, but maybe it can be a way to reach younger people."

Grams crossed her arms and tapped one foot. Her eyes grew serious. "Melissa, listen to me. I know some people have unkindly compared your work to your mother's."

"And to yours, Grams." Melissa gestured toward the unfinished tapestry. "This will be beautiful. It will hang in a place of honor for people to see." The piercing stab of pain from past critiques still lingered just below the surface. She gripped her arms tightly across her chest, fighting to keep the pain from showing.

Grams gently placed her hands on Melissa's arms. "And maybe to mine. Your mother was called to a different art form than I was, but it didn't mean her art was any less valuable. She made her work unique by using her own gift. She excelled once she fully embraced her gift. Now, you have a different gift, equally valuable. This is an opportunity for you to show the world your unique talent. You know she was always so proud of what you did and the beautiful designs you created. In her eyes, you were a shiny star."

"I know. I'm trying to remember that." Melissa blinked back the tears threatening to flow.

"Good. Maybe this is the universe saying this is your time to soar."

Melissa released her grip, lowered her arms, and smiled.

Grams stepped back and placed both her hands on Melissa's shoulders. She looked her directly in the eye. "Welcome to the fight, my young warrior."

Sunday evening, Melissa headed home feeling renewed, with a full stomach and an even fuller heart. Her head spun with possibilities, and she was eager to start sketching out ideas for her game. This was a whole new direction.

Chapter 3

Monday morning, Melissa woke to the sound of her phone chirping. She stretched herself awake, sat up, and fumbled for the cell phone that was never too far away. The chime indicated an email from Brothers, likely a list of suggestions for the scenes she submitted last week. A quick glance showed little tweaks and minor adjustments, enough to keep her busy for several hours. It was time to get showered, dressed, and to work, but coffee first.

Hours passed before she leaned back from her computer screen. After she carefully checked the changes, she decided she was satisfied with her work and ready for a break. Bright sunlight flooded the room beckoning her to go enjoy the beautiful day. *Time for a jog around the park for a visit with Howard.* By the time she got there, the lunch rush should be over, and he might be eager for a chat. Before she took off, she stored a couple of her collected sea treasures in her pockets to show him.

Coming around the bend in the path, she started to call out a greeting but stopped in her tracks.

The man behind the counter was not Howard.

Her heart raced. *Something's wrong.* She ran the last few yards and skidded to a stop, grasping the counter to steady herself.

The top of a man's head was just visible. She could

see he was rummaging through the cupboards under the counter, muttering to himself.

Two teenage boys standing nearby backed away.

"Hey. Who are you and where is Howard?" she yelled.

A man in his early to mid-thirties popped up and smiled. "Hi, I'm John, and Howard isn't here today. Can I help you?"

A hand to her chest, she gulped in air. She dropped the volume of her voice but not the sharp edge. "Yes, you can tell me where Howard is, and why you're behind the counter of his snack stand." She reached into her pocket for her cell phone and waved it in front of her. "With one button, I can have the police here in minutes."

The man raised both his hands to shoulder height, palms forward. A bag of chips still clasped in one hand. "Whoa, there's no need for that. I'm his grandson, and I'm just managing his stand for him today."

She lowered her cell phone but kept it in her hand. "Grandson?"

He handed the bag of chips to one of the nearby boys and extended his hand. "Yeah, I'm John. Say, are you the Melissa I've heard so much about?"

She glanced around, blinking rapidly.

The two teenagers just shrugged.

She stepped back, clutching the phone in front of her like a shield. "Yes, I am. How did you know my name?"

John ran his hand through a mop of light-brown hair and smiled. "Pops has talked about you. Says you're one of his favorite customers."

She continued staring at John. "You said Pops?"

The words came out in a stutter.

"That's what all we grandkids call him."

The realization finally hit, and Melissa let her muscles uncoil. Putting her phone back in her pocket, she flexed the fingers of her right hand. She hadn't realized how tight her grip had been. She took a deep breath. "So, is Howard around?"

"No, I'm managing his snack stand for a little while. He fell the other day and broke his hip. I'm helping him out while he recovers."

She gasped; one hand covered her mouth. "He broke his hip? How is he and where is he? Is he going to be okay?" The words tumbled out in a torrent. A broken hip at Howard's age could be serious.

John reached into the cooler, picked up a bottle of water, and held it out. "Here. Have a seat, and I'll give you all the details." He gestured toward the closest picnic bench. "Just let me get these guys their dogs, and I'll join you."

Melissa accepted the water bottle and backed away, lowering herself to the nearby bench. No longer panicking, she could see the resemblance.

He has the same midnight-blue eyes. Actually, he's kind of cute—tall, lean build, light-brown hair that falls over his eyes until he shoves it back with his hand. This is the grandson Howard told me about and hinted, not too subtly, that I should meet.

John added the condiments and handed the hot dogs off to the boys. "On the house," he said with an exaggerated wink.

The boys smiled their thanks and moved away, giving the table where she sat a wide berth.

She covered her face with her hands. She could

feel the heat rise on her neck. "I must have looked utterly crazy, rushing up to the stand and brandishing my cell phone like a weapon," she muttered out loud.

John strolled over to the table with a grin and sat on the bench opposite her. "Nah, not utterly, just a little crazy."

She gave him a sheepish smile, continuing to study him. He appeared to be close to her age. Twisting open the water bottle, she took a quick swallow and lowered her eyes to stare at the table. "What happened? How did Howard break his hip?"

"Pops was stubbornly cleaning out his gutters. I'd told him my brother and I would clean them for him this weekend, but he wouldn't wait." John pursed his lips and shook his head. "He slipped coming down the ladder and landed on the driveway. Fortunately, his neighbor saw him fall and called 911 immediately." He paused to push back the hunk of hair that threatened to cover his eyes. "My mom and dad are the emergency contacts in his phone, so the hospital called them. They called my brother and me, and we all got to the hospital in time to talk to the surgeon before they took him into the operating room. They repaired his hip with a few screws. He'll be fine after several weeks of rehab. Right now, he's still at the hospital for a few more days, then he'll be moved to a rehab center."

Melissa released a long breath. "I'm glad he's going to be okay. Do you think it would be all right if I went to see him?"

"I'm sure he'd love to see you. He came through the surgery fine and is already complaining about the food. Apparently, there aren't any hot dogs on the hospital menu." John grinned.

Melissa glanced back at the stand with a laugh. "Sounds just like him." Mirroring John's position of elbows on the table, she twisted the water bottle in her hands, avoiding eye contact. "You said you're going to run his stand for him. Can you do that? Don't you have a job?" She glanced away quickly. "Oh, that sounds rude. Sorry, you don't have to answer." She continued to fidget with the water bottle.

"No worries. I don't mind explaining." John waved his hand dismissively. "Yes, I do have a job. My brother and I own a small company, so I can take time off and pitch in here. My brother will also take turns when I need to work on something in the office. There are enough cousins I can get more help if needed. But I'll manage the stand for the most part."

"That's wonderful you can and will do this for him." She set the water bottle down and finally dared to look at him directly.

"Of course, it's what family does." John shrugged away the compliment. "Plus, I know he'd never stay put and do the rehab needed if he thought the stand was just sitting here empty. Keeping it open means a lot to him, and he wants to be here for his regulars, like you." He gave a playful grin. "I've been expecting you to show up some afternoon. He said you tend to hole up in your tower and forget to interact with the world."

"Oh great, guess there's no secrets in your family," she groaned.

John smiled, shaking his head. "Nope, but he only talks about people he thinks are special. So, consider it a compliment."

"Thanks, I think." She stood. "I'd better let you get back to managing the stand. What hospital is he in?"

"He's at Northwest, room three twelve."

"Thanks, I'll go by to see him tomorrow. Nice to meet you, John." She gave him a little wave and strolled home, thinking about Howard. She didn't think of him as old, but any type of injury and surgery at his age was a concern. *Hopefully, John's right when he said he would be fine.*

****

John stood there for a moment, watching Melissa walk away. *Pops is right. She is special.* He liked her feistiness and that her first instinct was to protect Howard's stand. He had no doubt if she hadn't liked his answers he'd be in handcuffs by now.

Based on his grandfather's description, he assumed she was about his age. He was fascinated with the long, dark-black hair she wore in a ponytail under a battered baseball cap. Pops had said she was part Native American, and he could see the characteristics in her hair and cheekbones. The green eyes were a surprise. He wanted to get to know her better. Hopefully, knowing Pops wouldn't be here wouldn't stop her from coming by often.

****

The next morning, Melissa sat in her car in the hospital parking lot, sweaty hands gripping the steering wheel. She stared at the building, her heart racing. The sound of a siren transported her right back to the day her parents were in a fatal accident. Fortunately, this wasn't the same hospital. Still, her heart pounded, and her ears rang. *I need to do this for Howard. Just open the door and go. It'll be okay.*

She hurried through the front door and headed directly to the elevators, not looking left or right.

Already knowing his room number, she didn't stop at the information desk. She pressed the button for the elevator and took a deep breath to slow her heart rate. By the time she arrived on the third floor, she felt a little better. The hallways were a maze, but after a few detours, she found the right room and gently knocked. A familiar voice called out for her to enter.

Howard sat propped up in bed, dressed in a hospital gown. "I hope you're here to rescue me and get me out of this place," he grumbled.

Entering the room, she was surprised at the bright and sunny space. Since her parents' deaths, hospitals had been dark and foreboding. Melissa rubbed her sweaty hands on the rough surface of her jean skirt. "I am but a fair maiden and left my dragon-slaying sword at home." She fell naturally into their typical verbal game. "I'm afraid the dragons at the desk outside your door would stop us in a second." She gave Howard a smile as she approached his bed.

"You're right about that," he muttered. "Those nurses might look sweet, but they've given me the head dragon, and she breathes as much fire as any of those in your games."

The door opened, and in strode a very capable-looking female nurse.

"How are we feeling, Mr. McDonald?"

Howard harrumphed. "I don't know about you, but I'm feeling lousy cooped up in this bed like an invalid."

With an amused grin, the nurse started to straighten out the sheets Howard had managed to tangle. "That's a great sign. It means you're feeling better, and we'll have you up and walking again soon."

Howard continued to scowl. "I've been up already.

Your head torturer was here earlier and made me walk the hallway using a walker. I've never used a walker in my life." His voice was gruff.

The nurse regarded him with a half-smile. "I know. It's a bit of an inconvenience, but we don't want you to fall again. Until you've fully regained your strength, the walker will be your constant companion." She turned to Melissa. "Are you his granddaughter?"

"No." She shook her head. "I'm a friend. I came to cheer him up and see if he needs anything."

"Yes, I need to go home," Howard groused.

"Soon enough," promised the nurse. "But first, we want to keep you here for a few days to make sure all is well. I'll be in later with some more pain medicine, unless you feel you need it now."

"No. I'm fine for now," Howard replied in a more polite tone.

"Okay. Enjoy your visit." The nurse smiled at Melissa and left the room.

Howard gestured for Melissa to sit. "I gather you went by the stand and met John." His eyes twinkled.

She adjusted the chair, so Howard could see her without having to turn in bed. "Yes, he was the one who told me about your fall and broken hip. At first, I was worried he might have been robbing your stand, so I tried to scare him off." She told him about pointing her cell phone at John and threatening to call the police.

"I knew you were really the hero of the story and not a helpless fair maiden. Good for you. I'm sure that set him back a bit." Howard's face crinkled with laughter. "How is the place? Did it look like he's doing a good job managing my empire?"

A flush started to spread across her cheeks, so she

gazed out the window for a moment before responding. "Um, he seems to have it well in hand. It's great he can take time off and step in for you. He also said there are lots of cousins and his brother to help if needed." Melissa continued to stare at her hands in her lap for a moment before looking back at Howard.

"Yes. I'm happy he agreed to take over for a while. I know I'm lucky I only broke a hip. It'll heal, but it will take time. Enough about me. How are you doing?"

"I'm fine." The nurse had closed the door to Howard's room, blocking out the usual cacophony of noises in a busy hospital. She could forget where she was except for the IV hanging next to Howard's bed and the overall sterile feel of the room. "I went to see Grams over the weekend. She's working on a new tapestry to tell the story of the Lummi Nation and its connection to the environment, especially the salmon. She wants it to help people see the need to act now to protect what we have before it's gone."

"I always knew your grandmother was very wise." Howard sat for a moment, staring off into the distance. "She's taking on an honorable and noble cause. I wish her the best of luck with her project."

"Grams would say luck has nothing to do with it." Melissa shook her head. She imagined what Grams's response to his statement would be. "It's what the spirits of her ancestors are telling her to do with her talents. It's an obligation."

Melissa slid a little forward in her chair and pressed her hands together between her knees. "While there, I went to a tribal meeting with Grams."

Howard tilted his head, raising one eyebrow. "Oh, must have been interesting. What was the meeting about?"

Melissa described what to her was a moment of awakening, explaining the reason for the meeting. "The discussion at the meeting and the conversations with Grams about the connection of the Lummi people to the salmon got me thinking maybe I can do something."

"Ok, I'll bite. What do you mean?" Howard shifted his weight in bed, leaning a little more on his good hip.

Melissa started to stand to help.

He waved her off and gestured for her to continue.

She hesitated, staring down at her hands. "It's just an idea…but I'm playing with the possibility of creating a game about protecting the environment instead of another fantasy game. It might just be crazy, but I plan to work on it and see what happens."

Howard's reaction was immediate. "That's not crazy. I think it's a great idea. As a grandfather myself, I like the idea of my grandkids playing something like that instead of slaying dragons and other mythical creatures. I never could understand the attraction to those games, but I know you young people love them."

Seeing his enthusiasm for the idea, she straightened and sat back. "I brought some things home I found on the beach and hope will serve as inspiration." She laid out her collection on the bed tray.

Howard picked up each one at a time, examining them closely. "I especially like this shell. It reminds me of the sun on the water." He held the small shell up to the light, watching the shades of purple, pink, teal-green, and pearl-white dance as he turned his hand.

"Grams said this is a pinto abalone shell. She said it's a special gift from the sea since it's rare to find one without chips."

Howard handed the shell back. "So, where are you with your game idea? Have you started?"

"I have some ideas I need to start building out further. I think my first step is to learn more about the salmon and how and when they migrate."

Howard paused for a moment, tapping his chin with his finger. "A good place to start is the salmon ladder at the Ballard Locks. You can see the salmon swim through the locks. It's a good time to go since they are returning to the rivers and streams around Puget Sound to spawn about now."

Melissa straightened and leaned forward in her chair. "Great idea. I don't have anything I need to do this afternoon. Maybe when you're ready to nap, I'll go there."

Howard stared out of the window for a moment and then turned back, eyes twinkling. "You know, my grandson John is really into those computer games. Maybe you can talk to him about it, too."

Melissa hesitated. "I…well, I'm not ready to share it with anyone else yet. It's still just an idea in my head." She noted his look of disappointment. "But I'll definitely keep it in mind."

After promising to come back to see him soon, she left the hospital and drove to the Ballard Locks. In late August, there should still be salmon migrating up the rivers through the locks. Driving into the parking lot, she realized she had been here years ago with her parents. A nice memory—though the details weren't clear. Lately, more and more happy memories were popping up, rather than just those heart-wrenching images of her parents after the accident.

She crossed the bridge leading to the viewing

building, pausing midway to watch the water spilling through the drainage pipes. Just inside, she stopped to let her eyes adjust to the greenish light permeating the tunnel. The green hue emanated from the glow of the water on the other side of the large glass windows where visitors could watch the salmon swim upstream. The sensation was like being in the water with the salmon. A group of elementary school children were just starting a tour, so she tagged along at a respectful distance. Soon, she was caught up in the teacher's explanation of the migration process.

She learned three types of salmon species passed through the locks to travel forty to fifty miles upriver to spawn. Taking a notepad out of her purse, she sketched the salmon working their way through the locks. While all the salmon were long and cylindrical, she noted subtle distinctions in each type. The most commercially available were the Sockeye, also known as redfish. She had seen this species many times in the fish market. Typically silver, while spawning, their heads turned green, and their bodies were scarlet. The Chinook were the most prevalent in the lock at this time. They had changed from silver to their spawning colors of olive-brown. They were also two to three times larger than the scarlet sockeye. The third type swimming through the locks is the coho. Unlike the sockeye, they were only red on their sides, and the rest of the fish was black. She would have to study more about their colors and other distinguishing marks when in the ocean to portray them accurately in the game. Today at least, she had a better image of what they looked like while moving.

She decided to visit Grams again very soon to learn

more about the Lummi Nation's solutions for protecting the salmon and how she might incorporate some of those ideas into her game. The game was becoming more real. The challenge was how to balance any remaining work she had on Brothers' *Den of Dragon* and her increasing desire to develop this new game.

****

When she returned home around four that afternoon, she immediately opened her computer to begin mapping out a storyboard for her game idea. She decided to call it Save Our Salmon, or SOS for short. For the next few hours, she immersed herself in research, taking notes on the various environmental hazards affecting the salmon population. Regrettably, most were human-generated.

The ding of an incoming text broke the silence. The phone chirped again while she groped around, scattering the piles of paper while she tried to find the device. "Oh well, I'll catch it later. Probably just someone wanting to sell me insurance." When it chirped again, she unearthed it from the chaos on her desk. The name *Karen* appeared on the screen. She hesitated before opening the text. She had a good idea why Karen was texting. Closing her eyes for a second, she clicked it open.

—Melissa, you must have lost my number. Haven't heard from you in ages. This is your BFF, Karen. Jan and I want you to come to brunch on Sunday. Call me.—

Melissa stared at the phone for a moment. *I can't keep avoiding them.* She took a deep breath, squared her shoulders, and hit the button to call Karen back. She put it on speaker, picked up a pencil, and began doodling on a scrap piece of paper.

"Hello? Melissa, is it really you?"

Melissa smiled. Karen sounded like she had dashed to answer the phone. She always had half a dozen balls in the air, juggling furiously. Melissa cleared her throat. "Hi, Karen. Yes, it's really me. Sorry, I couldn't find the phone when you texted."

Karen's laughter burst through the phone. "Hidden under a pile of papers, right? I'm so glad you called. How are you? I mean really, how are you doing? Are you burying yourself in your work as usual?"

She cringed at the accuracy of the comment. "I've been pretty busy on this new project. But I don't know about meeting this Sunday. I'm really swamped." Hopefully begging off because of work sounded genuine and not just another excuse to avoid going out.

"Melissa?" Karen paused. "Melissa, you need to get out of your tower and have some fun. You need to start living again."

"I know…but I'm really busy right now." She swallowed, feeling the tears start to form. The doodling continued, filling the page.

"Seriously? Too busy even for brunch with us while it's still warm enough to eat outside, down by the water. By the way, you haven't seen Jan since she announced she was pregnant, and she's popped. You've got to see her. She's so cute with her little baby bump." Karen paused again. "What would your mom say if she was here? Do you really think she'd want you to be locked away in your house, avoiding everyone? Especially your best friends?"

Melissa met Karen's question with silence.

"Melissa?"

A lump formed in the back of Melissa's throat. She swallowed it down. "I'm here…I-I know you're right. She would be the first one to tell me to get out and have fun. She'd probably push me out the door."

"Yes, she would. So, how about it? Just the three of us. We haven't all gotten together for two months."

Karen's sigh was audible.

Melissa paused to wipe her eyes with her free hand. "Okay, I'll think about it."

Karen moaned. "No thinking. Sunday, one o'clock at the Dockside Café. I'm making reservations."

Melissa closed her eyes. *I know Karen won't accept a no or even a maybe*. "Okay, Sunday. I can meet you both there." She stifled a sigh as she agreed.

"I'm holding you to it, even if Jan and I need to come over and drag you out by your hair. And you know a pregnant person shouldn't be doing any heavy lifting, so you need to come on your own."

Melissa smiled at the idea of a pregnant Jan dragging her out of the house caveman style. "Okay, I promise. Sunday, for sure."

"Love you. See you then."

"Bye, and, Karen, thanks for calling." Melissa slowly put down the phone. *Karen is right. Mom would definitely be pushing me out the door. It's time.*

Chapter 4

Sunday mid-morning, Melissa got ready to meet Karen and Jan at a restaurant on the waterfront for brunch. The cloudless and powder-blue sky promised a perfect day for dining outside. She chose a casual sundress in a bold floral print. A nice change from the ubiquitous capris and T-shirts she usually wore each day. The advantage of working remotely was no one cared about her appearance. She ran a brush through her hair and decided to leave it loose for a change.

The place Karen chose had a relaxing view of the water. Getting out of her car, Melissa stood for a moment to watch people and cars exit the large ferry at the nearby dock. They all had places to go and things to do. Lately, she had limited her life to the house, Howard's stand, and Grams. All safe places. Melissa gave a little shudder at the idea of hopping in her car, boarding a ferry, and heading off on an adventure. Mom often planned small family trips when she was young. She'd pack a picnic, and they'd all get in the car and take off exploring.

Taking a deep breath, she smoothed out the skirt to her dress and headed into the restaurant. Entering the restaurant's patio, she spotted Karen and Jan seated at a table outside overlooking the marina.

Karen jumped up to wrap Melissa in a huge bear hug. She held Melissa at arm's length and squinted her hazel-brown eyes. "Welcome back to the real world. I'm so glad you agreed to come today."

Melissa returned the hug, smiling at Karen's enthusiastic greeting. "Thanks. Between you and Grams, I couldn't refuse even if I wanted to, which I don't."

"Hey, don't forget me." Jan pushed her chair back enough to stand.

"Never. You look amazing. You literally glow."

"At least I have an excuse now to eat for two." Laughing, Jan placed her hands over her on a very small bump at her waist. She gently rubbed her stomach, her cornflower-blue eyes sparkling.

"Like you ever needed an excuse," teased Karen. She turned to Melissa and gave her an exaggerated wink.

"Tell me everything. What's new? What are you both doing?" Melissa leaned forward, propped her chin in her hands, and glanced back and forth between both women.

"Whoa, this might take some time. It's been a while." Karen raised one eyebrow and snickered.

"Don't listen to her. Yes, it's been a while, but it doesn't matter. What's important is we're all together now." Jan reached across the table to squeeze Melissa's hand.

"Obviously, married life is agreeing with you. How soon is the baby due?" Melissa asked.

"Not until after the first of the year. Somewhere around early February. I'm just a little over three months now but starting to feel this is real. I finally had to break down and buy maternity clothes since I can't quite zip up my pants without squeezing the baby and cutting off my breathing." She patted the slight bulge of her stomach.

"Breathing's a good thing." Melissa smiled at Jan. "And, what fun, buying new clothes. Have you and Derrick picked out any names yet?"

Jan's eyes popped open wide. "Oh no. We've barely wrapped our heads around the fact we're going to be parents." She softly caressed her stomach. "Plus, we don't know if we're having a boy or girl yet."

"Do you want to know? I know some people like the suspense of waiting," Karen asked.

Jan's blonde bob swung as she shook her head. "You know how good I am with suspense. I always need to read the end of a book to make sure it ends happily before I get too far. Plus, I want to do the nursery appropriately. Pink and ruffles for a girl or blue and animals for a boy."

"This is so exciting." Karen shifted to grin at Melissa. "We're going to be aunties. I can't wait."

"You need to wait another six months. This little one has got some growing to do yet. Ugh, I can't believe I just said that. I am already starting to feel like a walrus, so what will I be like in nine months?" Jan pantomimed an expanded stomach and puffed out her cheeks.

"Don't ask us." Karen held her hands up in front of her, palms up. I plan on it being a long time before I personally know the answer to that question."

"Same here. I understand this is a partnership project, and right now, I'm still a solo act," added Melissa.

The girls all burst out laughing.

Jan was the first to compose herself. "Fish and

chips for me. I'm not sure how the baby will like fried food, but I've been craving it since I smelled it on my way in."

Melissa put down her menu. "Same for me."

Karen groaned. "While driving here, I told myself I was having a nice, healthy salad and shrimp. But there's no way I can sit here eating lettuce while you both devour crispy hot cod, tartar sauce, and French fries. I'm in, too." She caught the server's attention to indicate they were ready to order.

Melissa swiveled toward Karen. "We know what Jan has been up to lately." She winked in Jan's direction. "How about you? What's going on in your life?"

Karen sat back, pushing her curly, shoulder-length, chestnut-brown hair behind her right ear with one hand. "Not a lot. Mostly the same old, same old. But things are starting to pick up. I know it seems early, but the holiday season is fast approaching, and people are planning their holiday galas. We've got a couple of company parties on the books already. And the Adamses always do this enormous Halloween bash, so planning has already begun."

Jan frowned, shaking her head. "It seems the holiday season is starting earlier and earlier each year. School hasn't even started again, and I'm already seeing Christmas decorations in the stores."

Karen gestured dismissively as she pouted. "That's the problem with being an event planner. You're always a season or two ahead of the general public. By the time the actual holiday arrives, I'm sick of it."

Jan lifted a hand to her forehead and struck a dramatic pose. "Oh, woe is me. The tragic life of one of

Seattle's most sought-after party planners."

Karen further exaggerated her pout. "It's hard work planning all these glamourous events."

Melissa and Jan glanced at each other and burst out in unison. "Yeah, but somebody's gotta do it."

The server approached the table with their food.

The three had tears running down their faces from laughter. They each whisked their napkins from the table, wiping their eyes.

He placed the dishes in front of each of them. "I'd say enjoy, but I think you all beat me to it."

Melissa quickly recovered and picked up the malt vinegar to sprinkle over her fish and fries. "Don't make me laugh anymore. I'm famished, and this smells too good to wait. A nice change from Grams's casseroles, which are delicious, and Howard's hot dogs."

Jan paused, her fork suspended in the air. "Okay, you know what I've been doing, and we've heard about the poor, tragic life of Karen rushing from party to party, so it's your turn. What have you been doing these last few months? Have you seen Howard or your grandmother lately?"

Melissa observed her two best friends, noting how eager they were to hear she had been doing more than just hiding away in her house working on her graphic designs. Both had stopped eating, waiting for her to reply. Avoiding direct eye contact, she played with a French fry, dredging it through the ketchup. "Well, I've been doing exactly what you both assume I've been doing—working and not much else. I've been busy with my freelance artwork."

"I suppose you're still working as Rapunzel, too?" Karen rolled her eyes.

"Yes, I'm still Rapunzel." She caught the look exchanged by Karen and Jan, but they didn't say anything further. "But I did go to see Grams last weekend. I attended a tribal meeting with her on Saturday." Melissa made it sound like she had done something positive.

"Oh, tell us. Anything interesting?" Jan asked.

Melissa perked up. "Actually, yes. The meeting was to address a new project proposed by a local oil company. They want to build a new, much larger pier in Bellingham, which would do serious damage to the salmon population. The tribe intends to fight it."

"Yahoo, good for them." Karen pumped a fist into the air.

"Yeah, I agree. I was impressed with the members' commitment, and it got me thinking, maybe I could do something, too."

"Really, like what?" Jan put down her fork and leaned forward.

"What I'm thinking about is a new computer game. It would focus on a series of challenges the player would need to solve to save the salmon. They'd earn points by doing things like cleaning up the environment or protecting the routes the salmon take each year to migrate upstream to spawn." The pitch of her voice rose as she explained her idea. "I'm calling it *Save Our Salmon,* or *SOS* for short. It's still just an idea. I haven't worked out the specifics yet."

Karen and Jan both grinned.

"What a fantastic idea!" Karen exclaimed.

"I love it. I can see kids getting into it and even teachers using it as a teaching tool. You need to develop it," Jan added.

Melissa beamed. She put her fork down and leaned in. "You think it's good?"

"Good? It's freaking brilliant." Karen waved her fork in the air for emphasis.

Melissa leaned back and pressed a hand to her heart. "Whew, I was worried people would think I was crazy, or it would be too goody-two-shoes for young people to want to play."

Jan raised a hand in a stop motion. "It's a super idea, and if there are interesting challenges and opportunities to advance levels, kids will play it. They love anything that looks like an adventure. You know how to do that. You've already done several other games, so this is perfect for you."

Melissa straightened and shifted forward again. "So far, Grams, Howard, and you two are the only ones who know about it. I need to develop it more before I share it with anyone else."

"So, what did they say about it? I bet they loved it, too," inquired Jan.

"Grams said it's my way of honoring my Lummi heritage. Howard also liked the idea when I visited him in the hospital."

"Hospital? Is he sick?" Jan gasped.

"No, he's not sick. He fell and broke his hip last weekend and is recovering from surgery. Now, he's more concerned about his snack stand than his hip. His grandson, John, is running it for him."

"That's nice. Have you met John?" Jan leaned forward, her chin in her hand.

Melissa fiddled with her napkin and glanced out at the water for a moment. "Well, um, yes. I met him the other day when I went to see Howard at the snack stand to tell him about my weekend at Grams. I was concerned he was stealing, so I confronted him."

Jan put down her fork and gasped. Her eyes widened. "You confronted a complete stranger, alone?"

"I had my cellphone in my hand ready to call 911 if needed," Melissa protested.

"Oh yeah, that's a real deterrent. But go on. Obviously, he wasn't stealing." Karen crossed her arms and narrowed her eyes.

Melissa shook her head. "No, he wasn't. We didn't talk long then, just long enough for me to find out how Howard is and where he is, so I could go visit him. I did the next day." She moved a few French fries around on her plate without looking up. "He suggested I talk to John about the game. He said something vague about John also liking computer games." She paused to stab two French fries. "I went by to see John again yesterday…just to tell him I visited Howard." She popped the French fries into her mouth and slowly swallowed.

Karen and Jan turned to each other, then back to Melissa with mischievous grins.

"Please continue." Karen gave a dramatic wave of her hand.

"That's it. The stand was busy, so we only chatted for a few minutes between orders." Melissa fought to keep her voice even.

Karen wiggled her finger at Melissa. "Oh, no. There's more. Come on, spill. You like him, don't you?"

Melissa pushed the remaining food on her plate around and didn't meet Karen's gaze. "I, um, well, he's kind of cute."

Karen and Jan high-fived each other.

"Yay, Melissa has a boyfriend," they began to chant.

Melissa glanced around, noting people at the nearby table smiling. "Stop, stop. This is embarrassing. Besides, I just met him."

Jan leaned forward. "But you'll see him again, won't you? You'll have to go back to get updates on Howard's recovery." Her face radiated with excitement.

Melissa sat still for a moment, pondering the possibility. "I guess so. Yes, I will see him again."

At that point, their server returned to refill water glasses and asked if they'd like anything else.

"Yes," Jan replied at once. "We need the most decadent chocolate dessert you have."

"With ice cream," added Karen.

"And three spoons," concluded Melissa. Melissa outstretched her hands to clasp both of theirs. "Thank you. I needed this. I've missed our talks. We've always been each other's support group, urging each of us to take a chance and try something new. I love you guys."

"Back at ya." Karen squeezed Melissa's hand.

Jan returned Melissa's squeeze. "And we're not going anywhere. We're all right here and will always be." She let go of Melissa's hand and leaned back with a Cheshire cat smile. "And we need constant updates."

"We'll see." *We'll see is right. Between Howard and now Jan, I might just have to go back and see him. But just about the game, to get his opinion as a gamer.* A quick twitch in her stomach belied her rationale.

Chapter 5

The next few days flew by as Melissa worked on the final round of graphics for Brothers. Every day, she woke to a series of emails from Sarah requesting subtle adjustments to a character's costume or a new scene the developers decided was needed to enhance the game. Thursday afternoon, after sending off the latest batch of changes, she decided to visit John at the snack stand. *I'm only going to check up on Howard. He might have moved to a rehab center by now, and I need to know where so I can visit him.* "*Sure*," mocked the voice in her head.

The early September weather had cooled, and the trees showed hints of the coming fall. Out on the still lake, a couple of kayakers raced each other. Their laughter rippled across the water.

John glanced up and smiled.

Her stomach did a little flip.

"Hey, I hoped you'd come by again." John paused in the process of restocking the bags of chips on the counter.

"I wanted to hear how Howard's doing. Is he still in the hospital?" She casually put her hands in her pockets and feigned nonchalance.

John put down the empty box and gave her his full attention. "No, we moved him to a rehab center Tuesday. The last I checked, he was settling into the routine of physical therapy, mealtime, followed by more therapy."

Melissa gestured to the vacant area. "How are you doing managing the stand? How's business?"

John leaned one hip against the counter. "So far, so good. It's quiet right now. Do you have a few minutes to sit and chat for a while? I can offer you a bottle of water or a soda?"

"Water would be great."

John picked up two bottles and gestured toward the closest picnic table. "It was so busy when you were here the other day I didn't get a chance to fully reassure you I'm not a thief." He sat on the opposite bench and held out one of the waters.

Melissa raised a hand to her flaming cheek. "Don't remind me of what a fool I made of myself."

John grinned. "No, I thought it was wonderful the way you stormed in, ready to defend Pops's stand—just like Joan of Arc of Green Lake."

Melissa laughed. "Howard always accuses me of living in a fantasy world, playing the heroine rescuing the village and besieged knights. All I needed last week was a broadsword to complete the picture."

"I like that image. What prompted him to think of you that way? He's not exactly the Knights of the Round Table kind of guy. He leans more toward chess for his entertainment." John came forward a little and studied her closely.

Staring down at her hands, she debated how much to tell him about herself. Anonymity had become a habit. But there didn't seem to be any harm in answering his question. "I draw graphics for a variety of gaming companies. Since so many have a Medieval theme, we sort of fell into a shopkeeper and lady of the castle game of banter."

John opened his eyes wide. "You do computer graphic art? Interesting. Any games I might know? I'm a bit of a gaming enthusiast."

She hesitated. "One I did a little while ago was *The Dark Forest*."

John leaned forward, his finger poised in the air. "I know it and played it. It's from a company called WizKids out of California. Did you used to live there?"

Melissa shook her head. "No, I've always lived here other than when I was in college at Berkley. I freelance, so I work from home."

"Gotcha. The graphics in the game are impressive. I'll have to play it again soon to see your work."

Melissa waved away his praise. "I mainly did the non-fighting scenes. The witches and wizards and those sorts of things."

"Fun. I'd love to hear more about the other games you've done. You probably can tell I'm a bit of a nerd when it comes to computer games." He leaned his elbows on the table and rested his head in his hands.

Melissa paused again. Off to one side, she spotted a group of joggers coming down the path toward the stand. "Sure, but right now it looks like a crowd is headed your way, and they look hungry." She pointed to a group of joggers.

John jumped up. "That's my cue to get back to work. Can't have you reporting to Pops I'm slacking off. He's in the St. Francis Home in Edmonds. I'm sure he'd love to see you."

Melissa stood and nodded. "I will go see him soon."

John headed toward the stand. “Come back soon. Next time, I’ll even grill you a hot dog.” He called out over his shoulder.

She gave a little wave, even though he was already focused on his customers. *I will come back and not just for the hot dog.*

****

Saturday afternoon, she headed out to see Howard. A cool breeze ruffled the leaves in the trees as she walked from the parking space into the rehab facility. The leaves had started to change to their autumn colors of burnt-orange and scarlet. After checking at the nurses’ station, Melissa found Howard in the dining room, playing chess with one of the nursing assistants. Sunshine poured in through a wall of windows facing out onto a garden, belying the cooler temperature outside.

Both Howard and the young man were absorbed in the game, heads bent over the board.

The young man jumped to his feet and offered her his chair. “I should get back to my duties. Thanks for teaching me more about the game of chess, Mr. McDonald.” With a nod to both Howard and Melissa, he started to leave the room.

Howard held up his hand in a stop motion. “You’re getting there, lad. You just need some more experience. I’m here every afternoon and available for a game any time.”

“I’ll remember, Mr. McDonald.” He glanced down at the chessboard and then at Melissa. “I need to go online tonight and see if I can find some strategies to let me at least have a fighting chance of beating him. So far, he’s killing me. He seems to know what I’m going to do even before I do."

Howard's gaze followed the young man as he left the room. "He's a good kid. Working here and going to school part-time at night to get his degree in nursing. He's going to go far. Now, have a seat and tell me what you've been up to lately."

Melissa sat in the chair vacated by the young man.

Howard gestured at the game board.

Laughing, she declined. "You'd have me in three moves or less. I know nothing about chess."

With a shrug, Howard returned the pieces in preparation for another game later. "Fine, I'll be fresh for when one of my grandsons comes by this evening. Speaking of, have you been by the stand recently? How is John doing holding down the fort?"

"I saw him yesterday, and he seems to be doing just fine." Melissa brushed the nonexistent lint from her denim jeans and bit back the smile that threatened to spread.

Howard stared at the queen he still held in his hand and then at the chessboard. One finger curled around his mouth while he studied Melissa. "John gave me an update when he helped me get settled in here the other day. But I'm not sure I quite trust him." Howard set the queen down.

Melissa gasped. "You don't trust him? You can't mean he might cheat you?"

Howard waved away her concern. "No, no. He's as honest as the day is long. But he might lie a little. I know the whole family is determined to keep me here to recover, so he might skip over a few details." He paused and tilted his head to one side as he studied Melissa. "Say, I have an idea. You can be my spy. Just casually stop by for a hot dog now and then to scope out the place. Maybe hang around for a while so you can see if the business is as good as he says it."

She laughed at the idea of spying for Howard. "Should I wear my deerstalker hat and carry a magnifying glass? Maybe adopt a British accent?"

Howard slapped his knee and chortled. "That would be something. But maybe a little more subtle approach. Just out for stroll and getting a little hungry. That will do."

"Gotcha. I'll be nonchalant."

They both broke up laughing.

"What about your new game idea about protecting the salmon? Have you worked on it some more?"

"I've been busy with work lately, but I've been doing some research. I learned a lot more about the environmental hazards impacting migration and spawning." Her voice sparkled with excitement. "What I need to do now is figure out how the player interacts with the game. How I can make it a challenge, so they keep playing." She leaned back and stared off into space.

Howard leaned forward and tapped her knee. "Why don't you talk to John about it? He's into gaming and might have some good ideas."

She nodded. "He mentioned he's a bit of a gaming nerd yesterday. I'd love to hear what a player thinks about my idea. He might have some thoughts on what makes a game addictive. It can be part of my cover for checking out the stand." She leaned forward and gave him a conspiratorial wink.

Walking to her car later, Jan's and Karen's words that she needed to go back to see John again floated into her head. *Now I have a reason. Thanks, Howard.*

****

Monday morning started with the expected email from Sarah at Brothers with another list of tweaks. The list got shorter each day, so they must be getting closer to the final version. She knew from past projects the testing phase would likely mean more graphic edits. She worked for a few hours and then sent today's graphics to Sarah. This might be a good time to follow through on her promise to Howard and go check out the snack stand. A hot dog sounded rather good.

A small group of teenagers waited at the stand while John scooped ice cream. Kids were back at school, so the beach area wasn't as crowded during the week as on weekends. This likely was a late afternoon crowd on their way home and stopping by for an after-school snack.

She stood back to observe John's interactions with the boys. He had Howard's sense of humor, teasing them about being back in school and having less time to hang out.

"Sorry to disappoint you gents, but summer's over and all the young ladies have gone back to school. You'll just have to wait until next year."

"No way, man. We just need to come back on Saturday," countered one of the group members.

John laughed. "That's a good plan. I'll see you on Saturday. Then you can buy some ice cream treats for the young ladies, too. It's what a true gentleman would do."

The group of boys ambled away.

John turned and gave a big smile. "Hi, stranger. I was wondering when I'd see you again. I wasn't sure if the attraction to the stand was the great hot dogs or Howard. But since you're here, it must be the hot dogs …or maybe Howard convinced you to spy on his behalf, so you're here for nefarious reasons?" He cocked his head to one side and grinned.

She laughed. "Is everyone in your family so suspicious? I might just be in desperate need of nourishment, and this is the closest place."

"In that case, I'm happy to oblige. You like your dog slightly charred with all the works, right?"

Melissa tilted her chin down and stared. "Right. How did you know? I didn't have a hot dog when I was here before."

John just grinned over his shoulder and placed a hot dog on the grill. "I visited Pops last night. He mentioned you might be stopping by soon. He also told me how you like your hot dogs, so I didn't mess up with his favorite customer…and now mine." He winked.

Melissa fumbled with her baseball cap and avoided direct eye contact. "Was that when you figured he might have asked me to spy for him?"

"I knew something was up. He had that twinkle he gets when he's plotting. So, I figured it was something like that. He thinks I won't tell him the truth about the business, so he won't worry or come back too soon."

"Your suspicions are correct. He said pretty much the same thing when I visited him yesterday." She leaned against the counter to watch him cook her hot dog.

John turned the hot dog on the grill, letting it char on all sides. He continued to talk over his shoulder. "Well, he's right. I wouldn't tell him if business was bad, but it's doing just fine. You can assure him I haven't given away the goods or closed up shop."

"Whew. He'll be relieved." Melissa feigned wiping her brow with one hand.

"Let me monitor your hot dog before it goes from charred to burnt. Help yourself to a soda or water if you'd like. It's quiet now so I should be able to sit with you for a while. We can trade notes on how we think Pops is doing." John turned his attention to the grill.

She took a bottle of water from the cooler and headed to the closest table. She sat facing the stand for an opportunity to study John more. He had an easy, relaxed way about him. He went about grilling with a confident air, even though she doubted this was what he did professionally.

Once the hot dog was charred to perfection and topped with everything, he flipped the sign to *Closed* and brought the hot dog to the picnic table.

"We got cut off the other day, but it looks like we might have a better chance today." He set down the fully loaded hot dog and swung his legs over the bench to sit opposite her.

"That would be great. Howard suggested I talk to you about something." She nodded her thanks.

"Oh? Yeah, sure." John reached his right hand up to rub one eyebrow. "Anything I should be concerned about?"

Melissa took a bite and savored the mixture of garlic and sugar that gave the hot dog its irresistible taste. She quickly shook her head and waved her free hand no. "Oh no, not anything bad. Howard said you're into computer games, so I hoped you might be willing to listen to an idea I have and tell me if you think it has any merit."

"I'd be happy to. I noticed the T-shirt you had on when we first met had some game characters. I was going to ask then, but you left so quickly once you heard about Howard I didn't get the chance."

"What shirt was that?" Melissa paused for a moment, trying to remember what shirt she wore that day, then shrugged when nothing came to mind.

"Had characters from a game called *Den of Dragons*." John lifted his eyebrows and checked out his fingernails.

"Oh, yeah, that one. I have a bunch of different T-shirts with game characters from my work. It's from a game I worked on for a local company recently. I'm currently doing the sequel so will likely have another T-shirt soon. Nothing but the latest fashions." She laughed and pointed to the local sports team T-shirt she wore today.

"I'm guessing you did the graphics?" John leaned forward with his elbows propped on the table. This time, he looked her in the eye.

"Yes, are you familiar with the game? Have you played it?"

John hesitated briefly. "Um, yes, I've played it quite a bit. It's got some awesome graphics."

"Thanks, I was part of a team so can't take much credit, but it was a fun game to do." Melissa reached up to twist a lock of hair that had come loose from her ponytail and then quickly pushed it behind one ear. "That leads me to what I wanted to talk about. I have an idea for a new game. I'd like feedback from a gamer's perspective to see if it's lame or could be interesting."

"Go ahead. I'm intrigued." John cupped his head in

his hands and leaned closer.

Melissa gave him a quick overview of how she came up with the idea at the Lummi tribal meeting, explaining how she wanted to make the game fun to play, but also educational.

John sat back, his fingers curled around his chin and stared into space. Finally, he leaned forward again. "I like this. I think you have a good idea for a game. The challenge is ensuring it's fun to play and doesn't seem like you're beating the player over the head with the environmental aspect."

Melissa released her clenched fingers and spread them out flat on the table. "Yes, that's my concern, too. For as much as I want the environmental message to be prominent, I know if the player is bored or turned off, they'll stop playing, and I've lost them. Do you have any ideas?"

John was silent for a moment, tapping his chin with his index finger. "Yes, I have a few. But I'd like to think about this more before I just spout out random ideas." He paused again. "Can we get together again sometime to discuss this? Maybe over dinner instead of squeezing in a few minutes between customers here?"

She twisted her napkin and then laid it on the table to smooth it back out. Her immediate reaction was to decline. She was still reluctant to add new people into her life. Ever since her experience with reporters and a few so-called friends after the funeral, she didn't quite trust people's motives. *But this is Howard's grandson. Howard wouldn't have encouraged me to talk to him if he wasn't trustworthy.* "Yes, that would be nice, I guess." She gave him a small smile.

"Okay, how about Thursday night? We can meet at

the restaurant. Say, seven at the pizza place nearby on Green Lake? Santora's. Does that work for you?" He leaned back with his hands on the table and smiled.

"That works. I'll see you then, thanks. I should let you get back to work." Standing, she pulled out a five-dollar bill.

John waved it off. "Today's dog is on the house. It's a thank-you for caring so much about Pops you're willing to spy for him."

"Thank you, but next time I pay." She smiled at John, then headed up the path toward home. A little way off, she stopped and turned to glance back at the stand. *Was the invite for pizza a date or just a friendly offer to help since I'm a friend of Howard's? And what if it is?* She hovered a hand over her stomach as it did a flip-flop.

****

A group of young mothers with jogging strollers strode up. They ordered a couple of hot dogs and a bag of popcorn to share and stood laughing and chatting as they waited.

Melissa's comment about doing the artwork on *Den of Dragons* toyed with John's brain.

We use several different contract artists at Brothers, but I don't recall a Melissa. Dan handles the talent, so maybe he'll recognize the name.

Watching the mothers head off to enjoy their hot dogs, he pulled his phone from his pocket. He was just about to text his brother when he paused. He realized he didn't even know Melissa's last name. He'd have to remedy that when they met on Thursday. He noted she appeared skittish when he first mentioned getting together. *Odd since she seemed comfortable enough with me here at the stand. A mystery lurks behind those green eyes.*

Shaking his head, he texted Dan.

—Hey, do you know of a graphic artist we used on the Den of Dragons game named Melissa?—

A minute later, his phone buzzed. "Hey yourself, bro. No Melissa that I know of. Want me to check with human resources?"

John hesitated for a second. "No, thanks. I'll do it later."

"Still on for burgers and a visit to Pops tonight?"

"Sure, see you later." He pocketed his phone and gazed in the direction of Melissa's departure. *Maybe I can ask Pops more about his favorite customer tonight.*

Chapter 6

Later that evening, John met Dan at their favorite hamburger joint.

Dan ambled over to the table in his usual casual style. His T-shirt was only partially tucked in, and he sported his favorite baseball cap worn backward. He slid his six-foot frame into the booth and leaned back with a grin. "Greetings, bro. How's the hot dog business?"

"You'd know if you'd ever stopped by. Why don't you tell me what's happening at the office instead?"

Over burgers and fries, Dan filled John in on the projects at Brothers at Play. "*Den of Dragons Part Two* is progressing nicely and should be ready for beta testing in just a few weeks. So far, we've only encountered minor glitches. Although the testers will do their best to break it." Dan paused to take a sip of his beer. "Now that you're up to speed with the company, what's up with your text about a graphic artist named Melissa?"

John told him about Howard's friend, Melissa, who came by the snack stand, and how he noticed her wearing a T-shirt with characters from *Den of Dragons Part One*. "I thought she might have been a gamer, but she told me she did some of the game's graphics. So, I was curious about her. I don't interact with the graphic talent like you do and thought you might recognize the name."

Dan shook his head. "Nope, no Melissa I know of. But we do have a few freelance people we use periodically, so maybe Sarah called on one to help. I can ask her."

John waved off Dan's offer. "No thanks, I'll ask Melissa myself. I'm having pizza with her on Thursday."

Dan put down his burger and grinned. "Don't tell me the lone wolf of programming has actually asked a woman out on a date? Hold the presses. Call out the media. This is breaking news."

"Calm down, Romeo. It's not a date. She has an idea for a new game she asked my thoughts on. We tried talking at the stand, but we kept getting interrupted by customers. I invited her to have pizza, so we can talk more."

Dan sat back and continued to grin mischievously. "Yeah, sure, I buy that. Wait to tell Pops. He's been hounding you about your lack of female companionship for a while now."

John scowled and wagged his finger in a warning gesture.

Dan ignored John's gesture. "So, she wants to talk about a new game idea. Do you think she knows who you are?"

John sat back, rubbed his earlobe, and then shook his head. "I don't think so. She didn't give any indication when she told me about her game idea. I think she's clueless. She thinks I'm a gamer, not a gaming company owner."

"Interesting," Dan dragged out the word. Well, let's go see Pops. I bet he has the chessboard set up, ready to trounce us both, as usual." He took the last bite of his burger and snatched the last few fries off John's plate as he stood.

Shortly afterward, both brothers strode into the community room at the rehab center. As Dan predicted, Pops sat there ready to go.

"Which of you two hooligans wants to take me on first?"

Dan plopped down opposite with a loud sigh "Might as well get it over with. But I warn you, Pops. I've been studying some new moves."

Pops laughed. "The only moves you've been studying are ones designed for the pretty ladies you meet. And if my observations of your dating life are correct, they aren't very effective."

"Speaking of pretty ladies." While Dan positioned his first pawn, he told Pops about John's recent encounters with Melissa. "Seems he's even asked her out on a date."

Pops glanced at John, his eyes gleaming. "Good for you. It's about time you had a real date."

John gave Dan a look that said his time would come for retaliation. "It's not technically a date. We're just having pizza to talk about her game idea. Did you know she's done graphic work for us?"

Pops muttered something under his breath and stared at the chessboard. "I do know she's an artist, just like her mom."

"Neither Dan nor I remember a Melissa on our graphic team."

Pops continued to study the chessboard. "Um, I know she works from home, so maybe she never comes into the office."

John noted Pops didn't look him in the eye, nor had he answered his question fully. He appeared engrossed with the game in front of him. *But that doesn't ring true. Pops could beat us both with his eyes closed.* Intrigued, John leaned forward, elbows on his knees. "What can you tell me about her? I don't even know her last name, and you've known her for years."

Pops straightened and smiled. His eyes glowed. "Now it's her story to tell, not mine. You'll just have to get to know her in your own way. All I'll say is she's worth it."

An hour later, Pops had managed to cream them both. "Time for this old man to retire."

After they accompanied him back to his room, the brothers headed out.

Outside, Dan faced John. "Well, Pops was certainly cryptic about your new friend, Melissa. Not like him not to share information about people he knows."

John glanced back toward the center. "I know. I wonder what he's up to?"

"Up to? You think he has an ulterior motive?"

John just laughed and slapped his brother on the back. "Nothing about Pops would surprise me."

****

Thursday evening, Melissa parked in front of the pizza place where she agreed to meet John. She sat for a moment, debating how much to share with John about who she was. *He's likely to ask more questions about my work.* When she told him her most recent project was with Brothers at Play, he seemed a bit taken aback. *Does he know something about the company?* She had done her due diligence and had her lawyer check out the company.

Her lawyer confirmed Brothers was legit and highly regarded as an up-and-coming video game studio.

As she entered the restaurant, she spotted John at a nearby table.

He smiled and waved her over.

Her stomach did the little flip-flop that happened each time she saw him.

He pulled out her chair and waited for her to sit. "Pops said to say hi. I visited him the other night."

"I plan to go by and see him soon. I can show him my new graphics for *SOS*."

John nodded. "He'd like that. Now, what do you like on your pizza? I'm an everything but anchovies guy."

After a brief consultation about pizza topping preferences, they placed an order for the house special, loaded with lots of vegetables, pepperoni, and Italian sausage.

When her wine glass was placed in front of her, Melissa twirled it in her fingers, then took a sip to loosen the lump in her throat. The slight taste of cherry lingered on her tongue.

John cleared his throat and swallowed a sip of his beer.

"Sorry, it's been a while since I've been out with anyone." Melissa stared at the tabletop for a moment. "I guess I'm just a little nervous." *We're both nervous, it seems.*

John let out a deep breath. "Same here. Let's start with the basics. You already know I'm John McDonald, but I only know you as Melissa. I assume you have a last name.

Melissa let her muscles relax and took a sip of her wine. "Yes, it's Anderson. I'm Melissa Anderson."

John extended his right hand across the table to shake. "Greetings, Melissa Anderson. Tell me about yourself. I know you're a graphic artist. Pops mentioned your mom is an artist, as well. But that's all he said."

Melissa's hand trembled. She carefully set her glass back on the table. The tension returned to her shoulders.

John jerked a hand through his hair. "I'm sorry if he shouldn't have said anything. I don't mean to pry."

She shook her head, took a deep breath, and released it slowly. "No, it's fine. Howard has known my parents, mostly my dad, for a few years." She stared down at her hands clutched in her lap, twisting her napkin. "My parents died a little while ago, and I still…well, it's still hard to accept."

John gasped and quickly set down his beer. "Oh my God…I-I'm so sorry. I mean…" he stuttered and started to redden. He rubbed a hand across his mouth and stared at the tabletop.

She blinked back the tears that threatened and gave John a brief smile. "Thanks, it's okay. There's no way you would have known. They were killed in a car accident almost a year ago. It's been hard to deal with, but Howard has been a huge support over the past months. I'd stop at the stand. He'd feed me hot dogs and let me talk when I needed to."

John leaned forward, his head dipped, and he offered a weak smile. "I'm glad he was there for you. Pops talked about the accident. I know he really liked your dad and looked forward to their chats. I just didn't realize they were your parents." He paused to gaze off in the distance for a moment. "I can't imagine losing both your parents. I admire your strength in dealing with it."

The heaviness in her chest lessened, and her breathing slowed. "Thanks. My dad used to love to stop and talk with Howard on his daily runs. They became good friends. That's how I got to know Howard."

John sat back, his eyes twitched back and forth. "Anderson? Anderson?" He paused for a moment. "Your last name is familiar."

She released a small laugh. "It's a pretty common Scandinavian name here in Seattle."

"True, but I met an Anderson once, Dr. Michael Anderson, the renowned computer genius. He lectured a few times at the University of Washington when I was an undergrad. My degree is in computer science."

She lowered her head and replied in a whisper. "He was my father."

"Wow, I'm really dredging up sad memories." John slapped a hand to his forehead. "I'm sorry."

John's voice conveyed a sincere tone. She stared down at her empty hands briefly and then shook her head. Avoiding eye contact, she motioned for him to go on.

"I admired his work. He inspired me to take risks and try new things in programming. He would say, 'There's no such thing as bad code…'"

"Just lousy users," John and Melissa finished together.

"Yes, it was his favorite line any time he gave a lecture to computer programmers." The memory helped her heart stop pounding, and she could breathe again. "You're a programmer, too?"

"Nowhere near your dad's level, but I like to think I'm competent. So far, so good. My brother and I are doing well enough to pay a small staff."

"I'd ask what kind of programming you do, but I must admit I'm not computer savvy—other than graphics. I didn't get my dad's brains for that." Melissa shrugged.

John nodded. "But according to Pops, you got your mom's artistic talent. Did she go by Anderson?"

"No, she used her birth name, Celeste Whitestar. She already had a reputation by the time she married my dad."

John sat back. He clapped one hand to his chest and silently mouthed the word *whoa*. He shook his head slowly. "Wow, you do come from incredible roots. I know some of your mom's work. My mom loves art and occasionally would drag me to showings at the Seattle Museum Your mom's work is phenomenal."

Melissa bit her lip and stared at the tabletop before she looked back. "Thanks. Yes, she was amazing."

John leaned forward again and placed a hand on the table. "I admit I was curious after you told me you did graphics for computer games. I looked up the credits for the first game you mentioned but didn't see a Melissa Anderson or any Melissa listed."

Melissa fidgeted with her wine glass. *What to say?* She shifted her gaze to study his face.

He raised an eyebrow and tilted his head slightly to one side. His eyes never left her face as he sat silently.

She took a deep breath. "You wouldn't. I use an alias for my artwork."

"An alias? Why?" he blurted out. He waved a hand in the air. "Oh, never mind. It doesn't matter. It's your right and none of my business."

His fluster was obvious. Melissa smiled. "It's okay. Let's just say I have my reasons for staying anonymous."

When the server placed their pizza in front of them, the tension was broken.

They both carefully took a bite of a hot slice and ate in silence for a while.

John set his pizza slice on his plate and wiped his fingers on a napkin. "We got together to talk more about your game idea. I told you I'd think about ways to make it exciting for the player. I have a few ideas if you're open to hearing them."

Melissa also put down her slice and leaned forward. "Yes, I'd love to hear any ideas you have."

For the next hour, they slowly ate pizza and discussed several options for challenges to keep the players involved.

John talked about the importance of creating both incentives and penalties for the players as they advanced levels, using examples from *Den of Dragons*.

Melissa took a notebook and pen from her purse and scribbled notes in between bites of pizza.

The pizza gone, John out of ideas, and Melissa out of questions, they headed into the warm night.

He accompanied her to her car, and after an awkward moment hovering between a hug and a handshake, he opened her car door and wished her a good night.

Once home, Melissa fought the urge to sit at her computer to immediately work on the suggestions John proposed. Instead, she shut off the lights and headed to bed. Her brain buzzed with ideas for *Save Our Salmon.* As she dozed off, a question flashed in her brain. *Did I ever tell him the name of the game? Oh well, I can do it when I see him next.* The fact she really wanted to see him again was a warm glow.

Chapter 7

The next week, Sarah let Melissa know the graphics for the current project were complete. Minor edits might be needed after the beta testing, but for now, all the screens had been approved and were in the hands of the programmers to complete the final build. She also hinted Melissa might hear from Brothers soon with an invitation to create graphics for the sequel to the fantasy game she just completed. The setting would be several months later with the kingdom facing a new potential disaster. This time, the kingdom would be invaded by a neighboring kingdom coveting their rich resources.

Melissa devoted her new free time to *SOS*, as she now called *Save Our Salmon.* Days and evenings were spent huddled over her computer, sketching out rough drafts of different scenes, or standing in front of the wall she used as a brainstorming space to lay out the possible sequence of actions and challenges for the players. John's advice rang through her head while she considered rewards for creating safe spaces for spawning and penalties for leaving potential dangers behind. The game had come alive under her fingers. Her excitement about the possibilities grew with each new scene. She eagerly anticipated John's reaction when she returned to the stand to show him her work.

Mid-week, her body demanded she get outside and

move instead of staying glued to her computer. A quick run to the stand to see John was the perfect solution. The weather was cooperating for a change, and the day looked promising.

Orange, scarlet, and yellow leaves crunched under her feet as she walked. She told herself she was only seeking his opinion of her designs for the game, but her stomach continued to flip-flop.

John gave her a big smile as she neared the stand.

She held up her tablet to let him know she had new scenes to share.

He held up his tongs and cocked one eyebrow.

Waving away his silent ask, she sat at the nearest table and gestured for him to join her.

John flipped the sign to *Closed* and ambled over. He swung his legs around the bench and slid close.

Melissa's breath caught as he inched closer. She quickly diverted her gaze to the screen and pointed to the new images. "I took your advice and added some challenges." She explained what the players would need to do to protect the salmon.

John nodded.

Out of the corner of her eye, Melissa carefully observed his reactions. *So far, so good.*

He continued to smile.

Once she walked him through the new scenes, she turned to face him. "So, what do you think? Is this challenging enough to hold a player's interest?" She twisted a lock of hair that worked loose from her ponytail.

John took the tablet and slowly flipped through all the scenes, studying them intently. "These are good. I like what you did here." He pointed to one of the obstacles. "What about incentives? What do they get when they solve these problems?"

"I worked out a system where players earn points they can later redeem for supplies to use in future levels."

John propped his elbows on the table and leaned forward. "Great idea. Players like getting the opportunity to acquire new tools as they go."

"I got the idea from the recent work I did on the latest version of *Den of Dragons*."

John sat back and laughed. "Thought it sounded familiar."

Melissa tilted her head to one side and pursed her lips.

The tips of John's ears turned red. He coughed. "It's a typical approach to incentives in many of the games I've seen, and it works."

After chatting for a few minutes about Howard, Melissa stood to leave.

A few people headed down the path, so John went back to the stand and flipped the sign back to *Open*.

With a wave, she meandered toward home, thinking about her relationship with John. He always acted excited to see her, and they chatted for a while in between orders for hot dogs and popcorn. *Could we be moving toward more than just casual friends? If yes, how do I feel? Am I ready to trust someone?*

****

Over the next few weeks, they quickly evolved into the same routine Melissa had with Howard. She stopped to see John once or twice a week. Sometimes, she'd stay long enough to have a hot dog, especially when John could sit for a while between customers.

Mostly, they talked about *SOS* and her desire to make it a success. John now knew who her parents were and that she used an alias for her art. Some of the walls she had erected came down. She shared more about her life, her grief over the death of Mom and Dad, and spending time with Grams.

John also revealed more about his family and his relationship with Howard. She learned Dan was his only sibling, but he had several cousins he was close to. He also told funny stories about working with Dan and the other programmers in their company. He made it sound like controlled chaos, surviving on late-night pizza and crazy brainstorming sessions.

She had no clue what they ultimately produced. It sounded like the kind of project work Dad had done. He clearly loved what he did. That made it even more meaningful that he willingly stepped away to work at Howard's stand.

They met regularly at the stand and exchanged texts frequently in between. Most evenings, when she wrapped up, she'd send him images of new scenes for *SOS,* and he'd send back his comments. The text conversations quickly morphed into little insights into their days and random thoughts about likes and dislikes. When she compared their text chats to the scenes from *You've Got Mail* with Meg Ryan and Tom Hanks, Melissa laughed. The difference was she and John knew who the other one was. She hoped he'd ask her to dinner again, but he seemed hesitant for some reason. *I hope I'm not misreading the signals, and he also is looking to develop a real relationship beyond friendship.*

At the end of the month, she received an official

request from Brothers asking her to work on the new game. The financial compensation for the project was very generous, more than what she had been paid for the previous game. The email was also full of glowing praise for her work.

Melissa reread the email, one finger tapping lightly on her chin. Her emotions churned. She told herself she should feel wonderful about this new opportunity. She was being acknowledged as a talented artist, and they were willing to pay her handsomely to do more. *Why aren't I excited?* The answer came quickly. All she had been thinking about lately was *SOS*.

She flashed back to a recent call with Grams. Grams shared some of the actions the tribe engaged in to help influence the decision before the Bellingham City Council. The protest at the proposed pier site had been a tremendous success. The Lummis arrived in their fishing boats, and other tribal members were on shore with signs. Many Bellingham residents and people from nearby communities joined them, creating a presence that was hard to ignore. And the local press didn't. Melissa had even seen footage on the Seattle news. The tribe's efforts fueled her desire to make this game a reality. She swiveled in her chair to study the scenes on the wall she created to tell the story of the salmon and the Lummis' commitment to protect them. Melissa was more determined than ever that her work would do more than just entertain. It would make a difference.

She bounced her gaze back and forth between the email from Brothers and the expanding graphics for *SOS* on the wall in front of her. With one last glance at the email, she closed it. She stood, circled the table, and stopped in front of the very rough storyboard she had started. With a finger, she gently traced the images on the wall. She needed to do something to help sort everything out in her head.

An hour later, Melissa pulled up to the rehab center. When she entered his room, she saw Howard gazing out of the window.

He erupted with a huge smile. "Come to rescue me, my fair maiden?"

"Only from momentary boredom." She returned his smile.

"It's a start." He shrugged.

"How are you doing today?"

"Antsy to get out of here and back to my stand. The weather is still nice, so business should be good for a little longer." He gestured out the window at the sunlight illuminating the gardens.

She sat in the chair opposite Howard and smoothed the orange paisley skirt she paired today with a yellow long-sleeved T-shirt. Looking around, she noted the room, while compact, was comfortable and cozy. The window overlooked a garden still in bloom with fall flowers. The riot of colors dancing in the breeze captured her attention. The scene was reminiscent of the type of paintings Mom favored.

When she turned back to Howard, she saw his knowing smile.

"Reminds me of some of your mom's paintings, too. I enjoy sitting here. But I'm ready to see my own garden."

Melissa smiled. "It must be tough to be stuck here, but you'll be home soon. What does your doctor say?"

"The goal is to climb three stairs and walk down

the hall and back. I can do the walk, but the stairs are still a bit of a challenge. I think I need another few days, and then they'll let me go. But enough about me. What's new with you?"

She hesitated for a moment and stared out of the window. "I have a conflict."

"Oh?" Howard leaned forward. His eyebrows twitched.

She explained about the offer from Brothers.

Howard listened with one bushy white eyebrow cocked. "So, what's the conflict? Are you unhappy working for them? Have they mistreated you?"

She quickly shook her head. "No, nothing like that. I've enjoyed the previous projects, and Brothers has been very easy to work for. My heart's just not there." She brushed a nonexistent piece of lint from her skirt. "When I did the first game, I loved my characters. But now it feels like just another version of the same thing." She squirmed in her chair and scraped one hand through her hair.

Howard inclined his head and gestured for her to go on.

"I keep thinking about what Grams told me about honoring my heritage and using my talent to make the world a better place. I want to make a difference. The concerns about the salmon population are real, as are all the other environmental issues destroying nature. I think my idea for *Save Our Salmon* could be my opportunity."

"It sounds to me like you have found your answer and your purpose. Now, you need to find a way to make it happen."

Melissa sighed. "Easier said than done. I have the

idea, but I don't have the resources to make it real."

Howard's eyes began to twinkle. He leaned back in his chair and crossed his arms across his chest. "And who do you know that does?"

She sank back into the chair. "I've worked for two different gaming companies." She held up two fingers. "Either might be interested since they know my work."

Howard gave her a piercing look. "Hmm. Isn't one in California and the other one local?"

She nodded. "Brothers is local. But they do fantasy games, and I'm not sure how willing they'd be to consider this idea when they want me to do the sequel to *Den of Dragons*. I considered showing it to them, but they're devoted to the fantasy realm. Even their website is a version of *Den of Dragons* and some of their other games. I'm not sure they'd be interested in something like this."

Howard sat with his fingers steepled below his chin while a slow grin formed.

His expression resembled that of a cat lapping up cream. Melissa propped her head in her hands, resting her elbows on her knee. "Any thoughts?"

Howard leaned forward, pointing his finger.

He quickly assumed the stance of the lawyer he was. He looked like he was about to make the clinching argument to the jury.

"Didn't you tell me before they encourage their people to come up with ideas for new games? I think you should approach them about your idea."

Melissa straightened and shook her head. "But I've never met anyone there. I don't know any of the designers in person, only by email, and just Sarah, the head designer on my last project."

Howard sat back and crossed his arms over his chest again. He gave her a crisp head nod and a smug smile.

"I suppose I could approach her," Melissa stammered.

Leaning forward again, Howard slapped his hands on his knees. "I say skip the designers. Take this straight to the top. Ask to meet with the owners. Be bold."

Her eyes widened. "That's pretty bold."

Howard sat straight and waved a hand in front of his face. "The worst is they say *no*. Then you work on the fantasy game and earn a bunch of money. But I have a feeling they're going to like this." He tapped the side of his head. "Call it an old man's hunch. Have you talked to John about your idea yet?"

Melissa hesitated and rubbed a hand on her skirt. "Yes, he and I talked a few times about it. He's given me several ideas on how to ensure the game is fun to play. He's got a good perspective as both a gamer and a programmer and has been a big help."

"Good, glad to hear he's helping you. That should give you some more encouragement to pursue this further." His eyes twinkled as he slouched back in his chair.

"It does. I'll talk to him about my dilemma, too. As a business owner, he might have some perspective on how to approach Brothers. By the way, all seems well there. It looks like John is taking good care of your empire."

****

John glanced up and waved as Melissa neared the stand. He grabbed a bottle of water and placed it on the counter. He also held up a hot dog with his tongs.

Melissa nodded. She bit back her grin as she walked to the stand.

John tossed her the water bottle and gestured to an empty table. Once the hot dog was done exactly how she liked it, he added the works, took a second water bottle, and joined her at the table.

No one else was around, so she hoped they could talk for a while. She took her tablet out of her backpack and set it on the table.

John gestured toward it with a raised eyebrow. "Show and tell time?"

When she took a quick bite of her hot dog, Melissa gave him a thumbs-up. Grinning, she wiped the dab of spicy mustard that dripped down her chin. "Yes, I wanted to show you the more recent designs I created using your ideas. I really like the direction and hoped if you had some time, I could get some player feedback."

"Sure." John ran a hand through his hair to shove it back as the wind blew it forward. "I'm excited to see what you did with my suggestions. May I?"

"Please, scroll through, and I'll explain if needed."

John scrolled from screen to screen, commenting on the details she put into each drawing. Occasionally he'd touch an object on the screen or nod. "The salmon look alive as they swim through the polluted waters."

In between bites, Melissa explained the tasks the player would have to perform to remove the debris and clear the waters. Each successful series of actions would allow the salmon to swim farther upstream toward their spawning place.

John switched back and forth between scenes, pointing out the subtle changes as more obstacles were removed as the game progressed.

Melissa studied John closely while he was engrossed in the graphics. She smiled at how he absentmindedly shoved his sandy-brown hair back with one hand as it fell into his eyes when he bent over. Those hands appeared strong, though she could well imagine them flying over the keyboard, creating new codes. He was tall and lean with a runner's physique. *If he's a runner we might have one more thing in common.* Melissa sat with her hands over her mouth and anxiously awaited his reaction.

John finally handed the tablet back.

Lowering her hands to take the tablet, she could feel the flush reddening her cheeks. "Sorry. I'm so nervous and wanted to jump in to start asking what you thought." She sat still for a moment. "So, what do you think?" She blurted out her question.

John raised his right hand in a high-five. "I really like what I see so far. No surprise, your graphics are amazing."

Melissa opened her mouth without speaking. Then she lifted her hand to meet his gesture. As their hands met, she morphed her tentative smile into a grin. "They're not finished. These are just rough drafts so you can get the idea."

John pushed back a lock of hair that had fallen over his eyes while studying the graphics. He then leaned forward, resting his elbows on the table. "Rough drafts or not, your artwork is excellent. I also like the tasks the player needs to complete to clear up the pollution. I like how you built in some penalties. It will keep the game interesting. Nothing like a setback to keep you playing into the wee hours."

Now more at ease, Melissa outlined some of the other new game activities she was working on. It included breaking down barriers preventing the salmon from migrating upriver to spawn or cleaning up oil spills poisoning the salmon. Their level of success was determined by how many salmon they saved. The more salmon they saved, the more tools they earned to continue to protect the environment and the salmon population.

John commented on a few and offered suggestions to make the tasks more challenging.

After capturing all his suggestions, she closed her tablet. With a glance at the darkening sky, she put the tablet back in her backpack. "It seems the weather forecaster was right. We're likely to get rain after all."

John glanced at the sky and frowned. "Looks ominous." He shifted his gaze back to Melissa. "So, what's your next step? You aren't a programmer, so how do you plan to build the game?"

Melissa leaned forward, resting her head in her hands. "That's a great question. I talked to Howard about it the other day, and he suggested I take my idea to Brothers. They were pleased with my work on my last project, so they might be open to listening. The thing is, I have no idea who to approach. Howard seems to think I should go directly to the owners."

John squeezed his eyes shut briefly. The smile was gone. When he opened his eyes again, he stared off into the distance.

"John?"

John rubbed his face with his hands and took a deep breath. "Huh, oh sorry. Guess I got a little lost for a moment. Melissa, there's something I should tell you before you do that."

"Okay?" She placed her hands palms down on the table and studied John's face. This was the second time he reacted when she mentioned Brothers.

Just then, a group of young boys dashed over to the stand. "Hey, man, you open or what?"

John acknowledged them and stood to take their orders. He stopped for a second, looking at her. "Melissa, wait here, please. I really want to talk to you about this some more." John dashed back to the stand and quickly filled the boys' orders.

Something is definitely odd about his behavior. Does he know something he isn't telling me? She had her concerns about taking her idea to Brothers, too. She waited for John to return and quickly held up her hand before he could speak. "There's a possible problem about talking to Brothers."

"Oh? What's that?" John stumbled as he swung his leg over the seat, gripping the table.

"I'm flattered to have them say they value my work. But if I say *yes* to the offer, working on the new game will consume my time, leaving little for *SOS*. I do have some personal savings, so I can afford not to take any other work for a little while. Enough, maybe, to see if *SOS* is viable. But the other reason I feel I need to take it, is I'm afraid if I turn down their offer, then they might not be receptive to my *Save Our Salmon* idea."

John rubbed his chin. "Could you do both? If they value your work and like this new idea, they might be open to working out something."

She shook her head. "I thought about it. Even though I'd mainly be doing the graphics for both, it's a serious time commitment. I generally only work on one major project at a time to ensure I'm doing my best work. Plus, I know my heart is with *Save Our Salmon,* which means I might not be as devoted to the other game. And that's not fair to Brothers."

John nodded.

Melissa stared down at her hands, lying flat on the table. "I want to do more than the graphics for *SOS.* I know I don't know how to build the game, but I want to be involved in the creative aspect, helping to develop the tasks and the overall look and feel of the game. That's an even greater time commitment."

John ran a hand through his hair. "I see. You do have a dilemma. So, what are you thinking?"

She raised her hands in a surrender motion and shrugged. "I'm stumped. I'm going to take a day or two and think this through more. I don't need to respond to them right away, but I also don't want to leave them hanging. It's not fair to them, and they've been very fair with me." She started to stand.

John held out a hand. "Melissa, I've wanted to tell you something for a while. Do you remember when you told me you did graphic work for a local gaming company?"

"Sure?" She sat again, wiping her hair off her face. The increased wind whipped it around her head.

"I told you I recognized the characters on the T-shirt you were wearing, and I was familiar with the game. I wanted to tell you then—"

A loud clap of thunder rumbled through the air as rain poured down in sheets.

They both jumped up and ran to huddle under the meager shelter of the stand's awning. It did little to keep them from getting drenched.

Clutching her backpack, Melissa stared out at the rain. “Yikes. I’m soaked and freezing. I need to run home and get into some dry things.”

John wiped away the rain on his face. “Yeah, and I need to close the stand before everything inside gets soaked, too. Can we get together tomorrow?”

“I’ll try to come by. I want to develop the game a little more before I decide what I want to do next.”

“Good idea.” He leaned back against the counter and farther out of the rain. “You stay focused on building out the rest of your salmon game. No matter what you decide about Brothers, you should continue to pursue your idea for *Save Our Salmon.* I think you’ve got an innovative and exciting idea.”

She gave him a bright smile and lightly touched his arm. “Thanks, John. I really appreciate your support and feedback.”

Melissa ran off into the rain. *Am I reading him wrong? I think he likes me, but then he pulls away at the mention of Brothers. Maybe he did some work for them, too, and had a bad experience. But they’ve been great to me. Hopefully, he trusts me enough to tell me whatever his concern is.*

Chapter 8

That weekend, Melissa invited Karen over for pizza and wine. Promptly at six, she greeted her at the door with a hug.

Walking through the dining room, a bottle of pinot noir in hand, Karen glanced around at the work in progress.

Melissa grimaced at the usual clutter of papers on the dining room table that served as her workplace.

Suddenly, Karen stopped and pointed to the wall of graphics. "Are these for the new game you told Jan and me about? The one about protecting the salmon?" She walked the length of the wall, looking at each scene.

"Yes, I've been playing around with some ideas, and I'm trying to create sort of a storyboard for the game." Melissa jammed her hands into her pockets to avoid pointing out the different ideas.

Karen stepped closer, taking time to study each sketch. "I like this. I can see where you're setting up potential hazards for the players to solve. Very clever."

Melissa released the breath she had been holding. "Thanks. I've had some help from John. He's given me several ideas on how to make the game fun to play." She pulled her hands out of her pockets and gestured at the images. "I'm learning there's a lot that goes into designing one of these games. Not as simple as it might seem from the outside."

At the mention of John's name, Karen raised an eyebrow.

Melissa felt the flush on her cheek and resisted the urge to rub the spot.

But Karen didn't comment. Turning back to the game images, she nodded. "I can see that. I've never been much of a gamer, but I have played a few cooking-related games. The one I've done most keeps adding new restaurants with new cuisines just when I think I'm done."

Melissa stood with her hands on her hips, her head cocked to one side. "I never knew you played computer games. I think I know the one you're talking about. But you don't like to cook. Why did you choose that game?"

Karen gave Melissa a wide grin and a playful swat on her arm. "You don't like to cook either, hence pizza for dinner tonight. I might not be too handy in the kitchen, and I don't know the difference between a sauté and a sauce, but the game is fun."

They were interrupted by the doorbell.

"Speaking of pizza." Melissa chuckled and went to the door to get the delivery.

The two friends chatted about what they had been doing since they last were together while they ate pizza and sipped wine. They also discussed whether Jan was having a boy or a girl.

Karen had a theory that since Jan was gaining weight at a similar rate as her sister did, it must be a boy. "But I hope she has a girl. It will be so much fun to buy cute little outfits for her." She paused between bites of her cheese and pepperoni pizza.

Melissa picked off a pepperoni dripping with

melted cheese and popped it into her mouth. "I agree, but as long as the baby is healthy, that's all that matters. I just can't quite believe one of us is now going to be a mother. Where did the years since college go?"

Karen gestured with her pizza slice. "I don't know. It doesn't seem that long ago, but since then we've been busy building our careers." She counted off on her fingers as she recited what each had done since college. "I'm working for one of the top event planning firms in the city, and you're creating incredible graphics. Jan's been teaching full-time for several years now, and even Derrick is busy with his new medical practice. It was so great he stayed in Seattle for his residency and was offered a job here when he finished. Otherwise, Jan would have moved away."

"I know, we would have really missed her and missed becoming aunties. We've all grown up."

Karen lowered her hand and narrowed her eyes. "Speaking of growing up, why are you still using an alias for work? Don't you think it's time you take full credit for your talent?" She gestured toward the graphics taped to the wall in the dining room. "What you do is fantastic. You deserve to be known."

Melissa swirled the wine in her glass, avoiding eye contact. "It's hard to explain. Well…not hard so much as embarrassing." She paused and glanced at the ceiling briefly. She took a quick swallow and faced Karen. "I started using the name to avoid comparisons to Mom and Grams, and it just became easier to stay anonymous."

Karen put down her wine glass, pursed her lips, and studied Melissa. "Okay, girlfriend, it's time for a serious chat. I know you've had a few bad instances where some small-minded, stupid people who think they're God's gift to the art world said nasty things about you. But…that's the past, and like I said, they're stupid and so very wrong. You're incredibly talented in your own right."

"I believe that *now*." Her voice pitched higher as she ended her declaration.

Karen gave Melissa a hard look and wrinkled her nose. "Do you really? I get why you hid at first. You were just getting started then, and it was scary. But now, you've proven yourself as an artist. You can stand on your own merits and welcome the comparisons to your mom and grandmother as compliments, not criticism. And face it, there will always be someone who will try to put you down. They do it to make themselves feel bigger, and it has nothing to do with you." Karen waved a hand in the air.

"When did you get so wise?" Melissa stared at Karen and shook her head.

"The first time some society grand dame criticized me for using beige napkins instead of the ecru ones she requested. Seriously, beige is beige. I was fortunate enough to have a boss who told me not to pay attention. Our client probably had no clue what color ecru really was but had heard the word somewhere and probably thought it sounded sophisticated. I learned to roll with the punches." Karen sat back and raised her wine glass in a salute. "Here's to silly people trying to act all-knowing." She went on, gesturing again toward the graphics. "Seriously, your art is amazing. Tell me, what are you doing about finding a way to get your game made? I don't care what name you use, as long as you continue to work on this."

With the change of subject, the knot in the pit of Melissa's stomach went away. She relaxed back in her chair and sipped her wine, letting the tart taste coat her tongue. "I'm thinking about approaching people at Brothers. I'm not sure how to do that. Do I go as myself? I have a reputation as Rapunzel, so it's complicated."

Karen shook her head. "Anyone who knows you as Rapunzel will happily accept you as Melissa. Besides, I want to brag on my best friend, and it's hard to do so when you use an alias. I can't say I'm besties with Rapunzel because they'd be like, who's that? Isn't she like a fairy tale or something?"

Melissa laughed at the exaggerated Valley Girl impersonation. "I see your problem. I'll think about it."

"As a wise, short alien said, don't think, do."

"You need to update your movie references."

Karen chortled. "Don't blame me, blame the reruns on late-night TV. They're addictive."

Melissa was silent for a moment, looking off into space. "I suppose if people would accept Rapunzel is Melissa, then maybe people would accept Melissa is Rapunzel. I might try with John." She spoke slowly as she continued to gaze off into the distance. "He already knows I do graphic art for games, and he said he couldn't find my name on the credits for the other games I told him about."

Melissa chuckled as Karen waved both of her hands in front of her like a pinwheel in a windstorm.

"Whoa, whoa, change of subject. This is the second time you've mentioned John tonight. Spill. Sounds like you've seen quite a bit of him." Karen cocked one eyebrow and gestured for Melissa to talk.

The heat started to creep up her neck. “I, well, um, yes. I’ve talked to him a few more times. About the game,” she added in a rush. She told Karen about the times she visited the stand and that John had asked her out for pizza.

A wide grin spread across Karen’s face. “In-ter-es-ting.” She leaned back in her chair, observing Melissa over her wine glass. “So, you’ve been out on a date.”

Melissa continued to twirl her wine glass. “It wasn’t a date. We talked about the game. We kept getting interrupted at the stand, so he suggested we meet somewhere we could talk longer.” She kept her tone casual, attempting to downplay the significance of their time together.

“Yeah, I can see why you just had to go and spend time with John. After all, you needed to talk to someone about the game.” Karen continued to grin.

Melissa squirmed in her seat. Karen’s grin reminded her of the Cheshire cat. She took a fortifying sip of her wine. She swirled the glass slightly, releasing the oaky fragrance before setting it on the table. Placing her hands on the table, she straightened. “Well, yes, he’s a programmer, so he can tell me if my ideas are doable. I also wanted to talk to him about maybe approaching Brothers about the game. He seems to know a lot about what games are popular. We didn’t get a chance to finish the conversation because it started to rain, and I dashed home to get dry.”

“I guess you’ll just have to go back again to talk to him.” She gave Melissa an exaggerated wink.

She returned Karen’s grin and stared her down. “I guess I do.”

Karen poured the last of the wine into their glasses.

"Seriously, it sounds like you really like this guy. I haven't seen you interested in a guy for a long time. What makes him special?"

Melissa sat back and stared into her wine glass. "Well, first, I'd say his devotion to Howard. He's willingly taking time away from his own business to run the stand, so Howard doesn't fuss and stays committed to his rehab. He's been a great sounding board for my ideas for *SOS*. He listens when I talk and supports my ambitions with this game. Reminds me of the way Dad used to listen to Mom when she was brainstorming a new project. It feels good." Her stomach did the now-expected flip-flop as she talked about John.

Karen smiled, one hand resting on her heart. "I think you're falling for this guy."

"Falling?" Melissa gasped.

"Yes, falling in love." Karen nodded.

Melissa vigorously shook her head. "No, no. I mean. I don't know. I like him, but I'm not sure how he feels about me."

Karen hesitated, then cocked her head to one side. "Oh? Why's that?"

Melissa set her wine glass on the table and rubbed the back of her neck. "Well…it's odd. When we're together, he seems interested, at least in *SOS*. But then, suddenly, he pulls away. He gets this strange look and mutters something about needing to tell me something. But he never does."

"Maybe he's shy?"

Melissa shook her head. "No, he's definitely not shy. He's very outgoing with all the customers. He talks all the time about his family, working with his brother, and lots of stuff. But anytime I mention taking my game to Brothers, he gets quiet and acts weird. I don't know."

Karen rested her chin in her hand and tapped one finger against her cheek. "That is strange. Do you think he had a bad experience with them? You said he's a computer programmer. Maybe he worked for them once, and it ended badly."

Melissa sat back, letting Karen's idea roll around in her head for a moment. "I had the same thought, so maybe." Suddenly, she slapped a hand on her forehead. "Duh, I'm such a dummy. I bet I know what's up. He's a programmer. What if he'd like to do the programming for the game, and I'm hurting his feelings when I keep mentioning Brothers? He's probably concerned I'd feel obligated to use his company since he's Howard's grandson, so he just clams up." She grinned at her realization. "That's got to be it."

"You might be right. Do you know what kind of programming he does?"

"Actually no. Just that he has a small company with his brother. It sounded like contract work, maybe."

"Well, that's easy to fix." Karen removed her phone from her pocket and started tapping the keys. "We can just check him out online…hmmm…John McDonald. M-C, not M-A-C, right?"

"You're not serious?" Melissa nearly choked on the words.

Karen shrugged and kept tapping on her phone. "Sure, I do it all the time. I look up everyone."

"Seriously, everyone?" Melissa stared at Karen with her mouth open.

Karen blushed. "Well, not everyone. Mostly

clients."

"Clients I get. But not friends. You don't search online for information on friends. Friends you get to know by spending time with them, not investigating their life history."

"For someone who makes a living working with a computer, you certainly act like a Luddite. You don't even have a website."

"I don't need one. And if I did, it would be under Rapunzel, not Melissa Anderson."

Karen continued to ignore her and kept tapping on her phone. She glanced up, shaking her head. "This is weird. I don't see any mention of a John McDonald working as a programmer. I see Howard and Paul, both lawyers. There's a website for their law firm, and Paul shows up on some society pages with his wife. Paul must be his dad. But no John. It also shows Dr. Natalie McDonald, a child psychologist. Hmmm, that's cool. I'm guessing she's his mom. She has a website." Karen held out her phone to show Melissa.

Melissa considered the possibilities. "He probably uses a company name for his work. I'll have to ask him."

"Yeah, when sleuthing doesn't work, try the direct approach. Say, you should tell him who you are, both Rapunzel and Melissa. Maybe it will prompt him to tell you why he seems to dislike Brothers."

Melissa paused for a moment. "You're right. If I'm serious about building a relationship, I need to be honest."

Karen clinked wine glasses with Melissa. "Here's to honesty."

Later that night, Melissa fell into an uneasy sleep,

thinking about telling John she was Rapunzel and finding out why he reacts each time she mentions Brothers. She tossed and turned in bed as snatches of her past played like a movie in her mind.

She had handed in her artwork for the new ad campaign an hour ago and sat at her workspace, absentmindedly working on another project while anxiously awaiting feedback. Her nerves were on edge since this was her first solo assignment. Until now, she had always worked as part of a team of designers. The account was important, and she wanted it to be perfect. At the sound of stiletto heels bouncing off the walls like ricocheting bullets, she looked up to see Mad Maddie stride across the room.

The other graphic artists all glanced up, waiting to see who Mad Maddie intended to skewer now.

Melissa's heart raced. She realized Mad Maddie was heading directly to her desk. She smiled weakly and straightened in her chair.

Ms. Madeline, as she insisted on being called by all her underlings, stopped at Melissa's tiny workstation, held the papers away from her body, and wrinkled her nose.

Melissa knew it was her artwork.

"Melissa." Mad Maddie spoke just loud enough to capture the entire room's attention.

Heads swiveled to see to watch the impending slaughter.

"Melissa." A dramatic pause followed to ensure she had an audience. Waving the papers at Melissa, she continued, voice dripping with fake honey. "Melissa, darling. I'm assuming you hit your head or got drunk at lunch and decided to play a little game. Because this work can only be described as a joke. It's certainly not art."

Melissa blanched at the criticism and sank lower into her chair.

"When I hired you, I had such high hopes. I hoped you would bring an element of sophistication and style to this dreary place. That you would bring me elegance and class. Or, at least, art. Instead, you give me cartoons. Cartoons no better than what I'd expect from my three-year-old niece. I figured the daughter of the great Celeste Whitestar would have more talent in her little pinky than this entire room of misfits could ever hope for. But alas, I was wrong. Oh, so wrong."

Melissa continued to cower, every word a wasp stinging over and over again.

Waving the papers around, Mad Maddie pivoted in a circle, ensuring everyone was now hanging on to her every word.

Melissa hunched down further at her desk, head in her hands, feeling all eyes on her.

"Is this the work of the only progeny of the great Celeste? Are you sure you're not adopted?"

The accusation hung in the air like a poisonous cloud.

Mad Maddie leaned in. "Tsk, tsk, tsk, your poor mother must be so disappointed. Thank goodness you aren't using the name Whitestar. You're a disgrace to your family's legacy."

With an evil laugh worthy of a B-rated movie villain, she tossed the papers onto Melissa's desk and pivoted, searching for her next victim while everyone ducked, trying to look busy. Over her shoulder, she delivered her final barb. "You can try again to produce something maybe halfway approaching art, or you can quit now while you're ahead." She cackled like a demented witch. "Or do I mean already behind?"

Melissa sat, feverishly creating new design after design, until her computer monitor began to smoke. In the background was the persistent sound of clicking heels and cackling laughter.

Mad Maddie towered behind her. "Cartoons, cartoons, they're all cartoons."

With each point of her red-lacquered finger, the graphic on Melissa's screen exploded, covering her in multicolored confetti. Soon, she was drowning in the shards of her own artwork.

Melissa sat up in bed, gasping for air. Looking around, she half expected to find her bed covered in confetti. Taking a deep breath, she calmed herself. When her heart rate returned to normal, she laughed at the absurdity of the dream. "They might be cartoons, but they are darn good cartoons," Melissa proclaimed to the empty room. "*Save Our Salmon* will prove Mad Maddie wrong."

Chapter 9

Monday morning, Melissa awoke to dense fog shrouding the area. She could barely see across the street. The park on the other side was lost in the gray mist. A typical fall day for Seattle, but not a great day for heading to the snack stand to see John. She decided to put in a few hours on the storyboard for *Save Our Salmon*. The hours flew by as she sketched out ideas for different environmental issues causing potential harm to the salmon population. Each issue would be a separate level in the game, progressing from easy, like clearing logs blocking a river used to spawn, to more challenging ones, like cleaning up an oil spill from a leaking fishing vessel returning from Alaska after the summer season. Noting the rain had stopped and the sky had gone from menacing black to dreary gray, she decided to go see John. Despite the earlier weather, she hoped he would be there.

She pulled her ponytail through the back of her favorite baseball cap and put on an old college sweatshirt of Dad's. It still carried a faint scent of his preferred aftershave. The memories no longer hurt as much as they had a few months ago. Eager to see John again, she took off in an easy jog once she entered the park. Nearing the stand, she could see John was behind the counter.

He was alone.

The fallen leaves crunched under her feet as she picked up her pace.

John glanced up and waved. He closed the box of bags of chips he was adding to the display and put it back under the counter.

Breathless from the pace of her jog, she leaned against the counter and waved a hand in greeting. The flutter in her belly intensified when he smiled.

Without asking, John handed her a bottle of water after twisting the cap loose.

She nodded her gratitude and took a long drink. "Hey, hi. Wasn't sure you'd be here today given the lousy weather this morning."

"Yeah, it was a bit rainy. I took the morning off, but I decided not to lose the entire day's profits."

"Howard would approve."

"Pops's theory is as long as there isn't a foot of snow on the ground, he's open."

"That sounds like him. Given this is Seattle, the possibility of a foot of snow on the ground is pretty remote, even in January. So, I guess that means the stand is open fifty-two weeks a year, no matter what." Melissa laughed as she gestured to the empty tables.

John joined in the laughter. "Well, he does shut down for Christmas. Have you created any new challenges for *SOS*? Are you still working on it?"

"Practically day and night. One wall in my dining room is plastered with rough drafts of scenes I'm considering. I'm creating a storyboard to outline the general flow of the game."

"Great idea, but why the walls of your dining room?" His head tilted to one side as he leaned in closer.

Melissa paused to take a sip of water. "Does sound odd, doesn't it? I use my dining room as my workspace. The wall functions like a giant mind map. It helps me see how ideas might connect." She pantomimed the scope of the wall project with expansive hand gestures.

"Interesting." John grinned. "I use whiteboards myself to work out programming ideas. Our office space has multiple whiteboards all around that the different teams use to sketch out ideas and share comments on ongoing projects. To an outsider, it would look like a chaotic mess, but to the nerds in our company, it's their playground. People don't fully appreciate how much of the software development process is done standing at a whiteboard or flip chart, colored markers in hand, drawing out a problem, and brainstorming possible solutions."

"I get it. I often find myself standing in front of the wall, staring until a new design image emerges in my mind. Then I rush back to my computer to capture it before it disappears."

"I guess we're both sort of nerds. Though you're definitely the artistic kind. I'm just the bits and bytes kind of coding nerd."

They both laughed at the shared visions of cluttered and chaotic walls of ideas.

John leaned back against the counter and crossed his arms across his chest. "On a more serious note, have you given any more thought to the offer from your current gaming company, or if you're going to approach them with your idea?"

Melissa noted the change in his tone of voice. It morphed from light banter to serious business. She took a few steps back and sat on the bench at the picnic table and leaned against the tabletop. She gestured for John to join her.

After a quick look around at the empty space, John ambled over and straddled the bench facing her.

"Yes, the more I work on *Save Our Salmon*, the more I realize it's where my heart is." In a steady voice, she explained her current thinking. "I want to make this game work and get it developed. I don't think it's ready to go to anyone about producing it yet. A key part of my interest in the game is to honor my Lummi heritage, but I didn't grow up on the reservation and have only gone there periodically to visit Grams. I don't know the traditions and stories, so I feel somewhat inadequate to represent them."

John's body tensed, and he rubbed his hands on his jeans. "I assume your grandmother can help you."

"True, and she has told me stories all my life. But I don't think of myself as Lummi. I wasn't raised in that world. I don't want to dishonor them or make a caricature of their commitment to the salmon. Before I share the game with anyone at Brothers, I feel I need to get the tribe's blessing."

The tension visibly flowed out of John's body.

His hands stilled. "So, you'll wait a while before you make a pitch?"

What does he have against Brothers? He prickles whenever I mention the possibility of going to them with SOS. "Yes, but in the meantime, I also need to decide if I take the offer for the new version of *Dragons*. I can survive for a little while on savings, but eventually, I will need to earn money."

"I still say you could do both." John straightened and smiled for the first time since the conversation started.

Melissa shook her head. "No, I know myself well enough to realize it's not a good idea. I need to take a hard look at my finances and decide how long I can pursue *SOS* before I have to either find a company to help me develop it or take a new paying project. I just hope if I tell them no, I'm not burning bridges."

"It will work out." John glanced away, scraping a hand through his hair.

"You don't sound too certain." Melissa frowned and crossed her arms across her chest. "You've hesitated before when I talked about Brothers. Do you know something I don't? You said the other day you had something to tell me. Is it about the company or is it my idea? You think it's bad?"

"No, no, I think it's a great idea." John jumped to his feet. "I think they will love it. They'd be crazy not to jump at the opportunity to do this with you. I just need…I need to tell you something I should have said before." Rubbing both hands through his hair, John paced back and forth.

"John, whatever it is, just say it. I'll handle it."

"Hey, mister. Are you open?" Three teenage boys approached the stand.

John hesitated momentarily, looking back and forth between Melissa and the boys. "Yeah, I am. Be right there." Turning back to Melissa, he held his hands together in a plea. "Wait, wait just a minute for me to come back. We need to talk."

Melissa slowly nodded and sat back with a deep sigh. *Finally, he seems willing to share whatever is bothering him, and we get interrupted again. If he wants to do the programming for SOS, we'll talk about it.* She preferred Brothers since they were already in the gaming business but was open to John's potential request.

No sooner had John gotten snacks for the boys and started back to Melissa than a group of runners jogged up to the stand. "Great, you're open. We're hoping you'd be. We need some dogs."

John gave Melissa a hopeless gesture.

She motioned for him to attend to his customer and continued to sit patiently waiting. Within minutes, the afternoon rush had begun. Another group of school kids came around the bend.

John dashed back to Melissa. "It doesn't look like I'm getting a break for a while. But I really need to talk to you. How would you like to go out to dinner with me soon? And not just pizza. We'll go something nicer."

She felt the familiar flutter. *This sounds more like an actual date.* "I'd like that very much."

He glanced over his shoulder to indicate to the group at the counter he'd be right there. "I can't do it tonight. I need to see Pops. But maybe tomorrow?"

She fought to hide her disappointment. *The sooner we talk about whatever is on his mind, the better.* "Oh, I should visit my grandmother tomorrow and see if I can talk to the tribal elders. Could we meet this weekend, or is that a busy time for you here?"

"I'll make it happen. Saturday. I'll text you to set a time and place."

John hurried back to the stand to take orders. His attention quickly fully focused on the growing line of customers.

Melissa sat for a few moments, watching John. His serious tone had disappeared and returned to friendly banter as he joked with his customers.

He glanced her way, shrugged, and gave a small smile.

She waved goodbye and stood to head home. *Whatever he needs to say will come this Saturday. And I'll tell him my alias. No more secrets.*

Once home, Melissa called Grams to ask if she could visit for a few days and if she could talk to some of the elders.

Grams enthusiastically agreed and said she'd start a new batch of muffins right after she made the call.

Melissa sat and stared at the designs on her wall. *Talking to the elders and getting their blessing to continue work on SOS solves one issue. John, though, is an entirely different problem. Hopefully, Saturday will bring a solution or at least an honest conversation about whatever is bothering him.*

****

That evening, John went to see Pops at the rehab center, sneaking in two hot dogs fixed just the way he liked them, with lots of bright-yellow mustard.

"Quick, close the door. I don't want anyone to see or smell these, or they might just confiscate them and hold them for ransom."

"Is the food that bad here you expect to be ambushed for a couple of hot dogs?" John chuckled as he closed the door and crossed the room to sit next to Pops. He opened the bag, pulled out one of the hot dogs, and handed it over.

Pops smiled as he inhaled the aroma before responding. "No, the food's pretty good, but it's all healthy stuff. Nothing beats a juicy hot dog loaded with mustard." He closed his eyes as he took a bite. "You look like you could use one yourself. You seem pretty glum."

Setting the bag with the extra hot dog on the small table between them, John slumped in his chair. "I've got a problem, and I'm not sure how to get out of it."

"Okay. Tell me." Pops gestured while he focused on his hot dog.

"Well, I told you Melissa has been stopping by the snack stand a few times a week since you've been gone. Initially, it was to spy for you, but lately, we've been spending more time together." John noted Pops's quick smile before he shifted to a more neutral expression.

"And that's a problem how?" Pops asked.

"The problem is she's been talking to me about her idea for a new game called *Save Our Salmon*. I like it, and I think she might have something special there. I've encouraged her to keep working on it and have even given her a few ideas. Recently, she told me you suggested she talk to the owners of the gaming company she's been working for to see if they'd be willing to produce it."

Pops grinned and pointed with what was left of his hot dog. "That's right. I think her game is a great idea. You and Dan should jump at the chance to get involved."

John jolted up and gaped at Pops. "What? How? You know she works for Brothers?" The words came out in a stuttered rush.

Pops sat back and crossed his arms across his chest. His grin grew even wider. "Yep, have known for a while now. I see you finally figured *it* out."

John sat in stunned silence for a few moments. He shook his head in disbelief. "The first time we met, she wore a T-shirt with images from one of our games. I asked her about it the next time she came to the stand, and she said she did some of the graphics for the game. Afterward, I asked Dan if we had an artist named Melissa, but he said *no*. So, I checked with HR and found out Melissa and Rapunzel are the same."

Pops sat straighter and assumed what he and Dan always referred to as his lawyer stance.

"Good. Now, I trust you to be fair with her when she approaches you about her game." Pops gave him a brisk nod.

John sat back and ran a hand through his hair. "You know I'll be very fair, and I'd love to produce it." He dismissed Pops's demand with a quick wave of his hand. "She seems to trust me. But the issue is, she only knows me as your grandson, not as the founder of Brothers at Play. I'm not sure how she'll react when I tell her who I am. She might think I have an ulterior motive if I encourage her to approach us with the idea."

"Hmmm." Pops steepled two fingers in front of his mouth. "You don't think she knows you own Brothers with Dan?"

John shook his head. "If she does, she's one heck of a great actor. She's never indicated she does. I assume she might have looked us up when we hired her, but our real names aren't on the company website."

Pops scowled, tapping the arm of his chair, and glared. "All you young people with all these crazy aliases. Doesn't anyone use their real names anymore? It just mucks up the system with all this secrecy."

"It's not about secrecy. It's how the gaming world works. Our website isn't about us. It's about their games. And player names are what all gamers use."

John sagged back into his chair. “It’s more complicated than just the aliases. Her contract with us stipulates we keep her real name secret and only refer to her as Rapunzel.”

Howard leaned forward in his chair. He scrunched his bushy eyebrows together. “How did you not know her real name in the first place? It’s your company. I figured you’d both put two and two together when you first met her and got past this silly alias stuff ages ago.”

John sighed. “I wish. Sarah hires the graphic talent, and Dad handles our contracts, so I didn’t need to know Rapunzel’s real name. HR has it on file for her payments and tax purposes and such, but I don’t see those documents unless it’s someone I hire. I knew Melissa used an alias but never asked what it was. It didn’t matter. Everyone at Brothers, even Dan and Sarah, only knows her as Rapunzel.” John sat, his shoulders slumped and hands between his knees. “Seems she has a very strong desire to keep her professional and personal lives separate.” He continued to think out loud. “If I break the agreement, she might decide she can’t trust me enough to work with us, and worse, she might sever all connection with me personally, as well.”

“What’s harder to take, the loss of the business opportunity or her?” Pops spoke softly.

John didn’t hesitate for a second. “I dread losing her. I really like her and think we might have a future together.”

“Good answer.” Pops stared out the window for a long moment before turning back. “You need to be honest with her about both issues. She needs to know who you are and that you have feelings for her. She’s a smart woman. She'll understand the truth when you tell her."

John hung his head, his hands still dropped between his knees. "I hope so. I know you're right about telling her, and I started to a couple of times but always got interrupted."

Howard waved away John's comment. "You're a McDonald," he growled. You just need to make this happen. Don't let anything stop you."

John nodded his agreement. "I asked her to dinner, but Saturday is the first night she's available."

Pops's face brightened. "Good, take her to Mario's. It's a nice, romantic place, and the food is great. Don't tell Mario I said that, or he'll never stop reminding me. Now, if you won't eat the other hot dog, give it to me."

John stayed a while longer to play a game of chess until Pops began to yawn. He stood to leave.

"One last piece of grandfatherly advice. Bring her some flowers. Then, after a glass of wine and some antipasto, you can tell her the whole truth. I hope she doesn't toss her wine at you and walk out. But either way, she needs to know."

Once in his car, John sat, staring out the window. *How will Melissa react? Will she understand? Will she even stay long enough for me to convince her I was trying to respect her desire to maintain her alias? The wine will have to be Mario's best.*

****

Mid-afternoon the next day, Melissa stepped into Grams's house and called out a greeting.

Grams answered from the kitchen.

The smell of freshly baked muffins filled the air. "Yum, smells delicious in here." Melissa stopped in mid-step.

Jessica sat at the table, bouncing her toddler on her lap.

"Jessica, what a surprise."

Grams lifted the whistling teapot from the stove. "I invited Jessica. I thought it might help to talk about *Save Our Salmon* with her before you meet with the elders later today."

Melissa quickly hugged Grams and then sat next to Jessica.

The baby smiled and held out his hand.

"He certainly has got a strong grip." Melissa smiled at Jessica. "What's his name?"

"Donald, after his paternal grandfather. We call him Donnie."

After pouring three cups, Grams set the teapot on the table. "Now tell Jessica about *Save Our Salmon*."

Jessica nodded. "Yes, please. I've been dying of curiosity since your grandmother called me yesterday." She handed Donnie a toy, so he'd let go of Melissa's finger.

Melissa explained how the recent tribal meeting triggered the idea. She took out her tablet and showed Jessica and Grams the graphics she had designed.

They both "oohed and aahed" over the vivid images of salmon in their bright spawning colors, moving through the streams.

Melissa explained how the players would interact to clear paths and protect the salmon on their journey.

Even little Donnie clapped when she finished.

"What do you think?" Melissa watched Jennifer's face for her reaction.

Jennifer grinned. "I think this is amazing. I love

that you're creating a game to teach people about conservation, and you're focusing on the salmon population. It's taking our tribal commitment and bringing it into the modern world."

"Do you think the elders would approve?" Running a finger across the image on the screen, Melissa hesitated briefly. "I know I'm Lummi by blood, but I was raised in the non-Indian world. One that hasn't always been kind to Native Americans. I don't want to be seen as exploiting my heritage."

Jessica reached over and took Melissa's hand. "Inside you are Lummi, no matter where you were raised. It's not a place. It's a heritage passed down from generation to generation, and it's yours as much as mine. What you have done here honors your heritage, and that is all that matters. The mother in me wants my son to have things like this that teach him to respect his heritage."

Melissa clasped Jessica's hand in both of hers. "Thank you. Your words mean so much to me. I love this game and what it can do. I want it to be seen as a gift. This is my gift back to my ancestors."

Jessica bounced Donnie on her knee and looked back at Melissa's tablet. "Say just that and the elders will be thrilled. You understand more than you believe you do."

"It also doesn't hurt that Jessica's grandfather is our current council leader." Grams chimed in. "I know he has a soft spot for his new great-grandson. If Donnie's mommy likes the game, he will, too."

Jessica smiled. "I've convinced Grampa of all sorts of things over the years. He's why I went to college in San Diego when my parents wanted me to go here in

Bellingham. But I won't have to this time. He'll see the value of what you're doing."

The time passed quickly while Jessica and Melissa got caught up on life.

Grams soon put on another pot of tea and announced the elders on the council would be here shortly.

Jessica stood and gathered all of Donnie's toys and other baby paraphernalia. "Don't worry. They will love this idea." She hugged Melissa. And I'll just happen to walk past Grampa's on my way home." She picked up Donnie and left, with Donnie waving goodbye over her shoulder.

Melissa helped Grams lay out teacups and the tray of muffins in the dining room.

Soon, the room filled with members of the council leadership.

Joseph, the leader, took Melissa aside. "Jessica talked to me before I came over. She tells me your idea for a game to help protect the salmon is wonderful. I trust my granddaughter. She's the smart one in the family." He gave a wink.

Seeing him up close, Melissa was struck by his regal stance. His proud stance projected an aura of confidence and strength.

Joseph stood at the head of the table and called the meeting to order. He presented the reason for the impromptu meeting and handed it over to Melissa.

Like she had done earlier with Jessica, Melissa explained her motivation and intentions for the game.

Some council members said their children and grandchildren were avid gamers, so they understood how the games could influence their thinking.

After answering questions, Melissa turned to face Joseph. "I humbly request your blessing for me to continue to develop this game and find a producer to make and distribute it. I want this to respect and honor the Lummi heritage, my Lummi heritage."

Joseph nodded his acknowledgment. "All in favor of giving our blessing to Melissa and *Save Our Salmon,* please say aye."

Melissa held her breath as she waited.

"Aye." The group responded unanimously.

Melissa smiled and slowly released the breath she was holding.

The meeting ended. Each member wished her great success and expressed their eagerness to see the final product.

Before leaving, Joseph put an arm around her. "What you are doing would make your mother proud. I know your grandmother already is. I appreciate you coming to us to ask for our blessing. If your game turns out to be half as good as what you showed us today, it will be dope, as my grandkids say."

Once they all left, Melissa collapsed on the couch in the living room.

Grams sat beside her and wrapped her in a warm hug. "I'm so proud of you. What you're doing is a wonderful gift. You are sharing your talent in a way that will make a difference. Now sit here for a moment to catch your breath, then join me in the kitchen to help finish dinner prep."

Melissa sat there briefly, contemplating the enormity of what had just happened. The next step was hers to make this a reality. She couldn't wait to tell John.

First thing the following day, Melissa drafted an email to Sarah at Brothers, before she lost her nerve. She briefly explained her idea and asked if Sarah thought the owners would be open to hearing about her new game. She read through the email three times to make sure it sounded professional and not too desperate. She included she lived here in the Seattle area, so she could be flexible with the timing of a meeting. Satisfied it hit the right notes, she clicked *Send*. Now, she just had to wait. She pressed a hand to her stomach to reassure the butterflies circling wildly.

Melissa spent the rest of the morning talking to Jessica and her husband about the status of the fishing season.

Robert described several ideas for ways the players could protect the salmon.

Jessica majored in marine biology in college, so she had more information on the impact of pollutants and how they could be cleaned up.

After an early dinner with Grams, Melissa headed back home.

Thursday morning, she was eager to do more work on her storyboard, just in case she heard from Sarah and the owners at Brothers were willing to meet. Opening the file of ideas and graphics for the game, she reviewed what she had put together so far. She organized the images to show the game's sequencing and how the players earned points. In addition to removing obstacles to the salmon's migration, she added opportunities to build protective environments to shelter them. She would also design it, so players lost points for poor decisions like overharvesting. Hours flew by in a flash. Now, she had a comprehensive storyboard with options for each level of the game.

Mid-afternoon, the eagerly awaited email arrived, confirming a meeting at Brothers for tomorrow at ten a.m. She'd have lots to tell John over dinner on Saturday. If all went well tomorrow, she could say that she had a company interested in producing her game.

Chapter 10

Thursday night, John parked and ambled into the rehab center to find Dan and Pops hovered over the chessboard.

Pops glanced up with a wicked grin. “Can you believe I already beat him once, and he’s such a glutton for punishment that he demanded a redo? As they say, there’s a sucker born every minute.”

Dan frowned. His eyebrows scrunched together. “Hey, enough smash talk from the opposition. I’m thinking.”

“Think away. In the meantime, John, you can give me an update on my stand. How’s business lately?”

For the next few minutes, John filled Pops in on the business flow and which customers had asked about him.

Pops quickly dispensed with Dan’s feeble attempts to capture his king and ended the game with a checkmate.

Dan slumped back in his chair. “I give up. It’s impossible.”

Pops just chuckled. “Okay, Dan, it’s your turn. What’s happening at Brothers?”

Dan sat up and smiled. “That’s at least a topic I can happily say is going along just fine. We’re working out the last of the kinks in the game, and it will be ready for launch in just a few weeks.”

"That's great news. Anything else going on? How are we set for the sequel?" John inquired.

"Good, actually. We won't start working on it until we wrap up part two, but Sarah's putting her graphic team together. Oh, that reminds me. You know our new artist, Rapunzel?"

John felt his stomach drop. His back stiffened, and he stared at Dan. "Yeah, what about her?"

"I have a meeting tomorrow morning. She has an idea for a different type of game, so Sarah asked me to meet her to discuss it."

Dan had barely finished his sentence when John shot to his feet. "What? What meeting? Why didn't you tell me you set up a meeting with Melissa to talk to her about her new game idea? What are you doing?" John ran his hands through his hair as he paced. "I was going to talk to her, and now, you pulled a fast one and jumped in front of me."

Dan leaned away from John's clenched fist. "Whoa, bro, calm down." He raised his hands in front of his face.

"Don't bro me. I want to know what you were thinking." John hovered over Dan, his hands clenched at his side.

Dan sat there, staring wide-eyed. "First of all, who's Melissa? I don't have a meeting with anyone named Melissa."

"Rapunzel, that's who. You have a meeting tomorrow with Rapunzel, and she's really Melissa." He paced back and forth in the small room like a caged animal.

"Hold on a minute. You're saying Rapunzel is Melissa?" Dan looked back and forth between John and

Pops, scratching his head.

John threw his hands up into the air. "Don't you ever listen to what I tell you? I told you one of Pops's customers at the snack stand is Rapunzel."

Dan tipped his head back to stare at the ceiling for a moment. Shrugging, he turned to face John again. "Yeah, but you never said she was Melissa." His eyebrows shot up. "Wow, what a small world. You didn't tell me anything about this new game idea, either. Did you know she was working on it?"

John rubbed his forehead as he continued to pace. "Yes, she's been talking to me about it for several weeks. I like it. You will, too." He gestured vaguely in Dan's direction as he slowed his pacing.

"Great, why don't you get someone to cover for you and come to the meeting, too? It might put her more at ease to see a familiar face." Dan slid forward in his chair and nodded.

"She doesn't know who I am." John stopped pacing and slumped into a chair, lowering his head between his hands.

Pops loudly cleared his throat.

John jerked up his head and pointed his finger. "Don't say I told you so. I was going to tell her Saturday at dinner. I had a plan."

Dan opened his mouth and sat blinking rapidly. "Pops, you knew?"

For once, Pops kept silent, simply nodding.

Dan looked at John with one eyebrow slightly raised. "Wait. You never even told her your name? What does she call you, *hey you?*"

John just glared. "No, dummy, of course she knows my name. What she doesn't know is you and I own

Brothers." His words came out through clenched teeth.

"Wow. You never told her you're kinda her boss?" Dan slapped a hand on his forehead. "Why not?"

John used both hands to rub his forehead. "I tried, but we kept getting interrupted whenever I broached the subject. Plus, it's complicated." He raised both hands in a hopeless gesture. "And now, it's too late. I know I blew it. Now that she's meeting with you, she's bound to make the connection as soon as you tell her your last name."

John buried his head in his hands again. "She'll never want to see me again," he mumbled.

"Hold on, big brother. There's more to this than just the game, right?" Dan's voice softened.

John slumped further. "Right. I really like her, and maybe she's starting to feel the same way about me. But if she thinks I lied, I'm doomed."

Dan approached John and placed a hand on his shoulder. "This *is* a mess. What do you want me to do? Should I cancel the meeting?" He continued to speak softly.

John shook his head. "No, that's not fair to her. She deserves to have her idea heard. But I think you're right. I need to join you tomorrow." He sat straighter and pressed his hands on his knees. "Time for the truth. How about I meet with her first to tell her in private? Then you can join us to hear her presentation."

Pops stood and patted John on the other shoulder. "It will work out. I have faith in both of you."

"Thanks, Pops, but I have no idea how best to tell Melissa the truth."

Dan continued to pat John's shoulder. "I'm sorry, bro. I had no idea. Hey, I'll buy you a beer, and we can talk more."

John shook his head. "Thanks, but I need to go home and work out how to handle this tomorrow."

****

The next morning, John paced the floor of Dan's office. "What am I going to say when she gets here?"

Dan sat in his desk chair, listening in silence.

"I can imagine her response to the discovery," John rambled on. "She'll feel betrayed. She'll feel I lied."

"Once you figured out who she was, why didn't you tell her then you were her boss?"

Dan's words interrupted John's soliloquy. He stopped and swung toward his brother with a dismissive wave. "I told you. That damn contract stipulation. Why did I let this go on so long?" Pacing across the room, John continued to process the situation out loud. "What's worse is she might believe my encouragement of her work was based on greed, and all I wanted was the financial gain her game might bring to our company."

He stood, staring out into the endless rain typical of a Seattle fall, searching for an answer in the patterns the raindrops made on the glass. But they only blurred his view and added to his frustration. He turned, raking a hand through his hair. "Dan, forget what I said yesterday. You need to do the meeting without me. Yeah, that might work." John paused momentarily and shook his head before he returned to pacing. "No, it won't work. Eventually, she needs to know the truth. I have to find the words to make this right."

Continuing to ignore Dan's presence, John tried different approaches to the conversation. "Hi, Melissa. Surprise. Bet you weren't planning on seeing me here.

Well, funny thing…. No, not so funny." He stopped and waved his hands as if erasing his words. "Try again. Maybe a more business-like approach." He stood taller and mimed reaching out his hand to shake. "Hi, Melissa. Let me formally introduce my brother Dan, my partner at Brothers at Play. We own and run the company together. It's a pleasure to finally meet the famous Rapunzel officially. Of course, I already know you as Melissa, and you know me as Howard's grandson. But it's nice to bring the relationship full circle to include our professional selves."

John groaned. "God, that sounds distant and cold, like she's someone I met at a Chamber of Commerce Meet and Greet. That's not going to work." Shoving his hands into his pockets, he picked up the speed of his pacing. "Okay, try again." He stopped and raised a hand in greeting. "Hi, Melissa. I know this is a surprise, but I can explain." He ran a hand through his hair. "Really? Can I? I doubt it. Not in a way that sounds even remotely forthcoming. Not now that she knows I deliberately omitted a key fact about myself. Think, John, think." He struck both sides of his head with his hands. "How can you convince her not to walk out, that she can trust you, and that you only want to help her?"

"And that you're falling in love with her."

John whipped around. "What?"

"You heard me. You're falling in love with her. It's as obvious as the look of anguish on your face, bro."

John sank into the chair in front of Dan's desk and buried his head in his hands. "I've blown it. I've waited too long to tell her the truth about me."

"Tell me, what worries you the most? That she walks away from the company as our artist, we won't be the ones to produce her game, or she walks away from *you*?"

He glanced up. "Pops asked the same question."

"And?"

"From me," John answered in a soft voice. "From me."

A knock on the door interrupted the conversation. Dan's admin poked her head in to announce Rapunzel was in the building and on her way to his office.

Dan stood. "I'll leave you."

****

Melissa checked out her outfit in the elevator door's reflection one more time after exiting on the fifth floor. She had changed four times and still wasn't completely satisfied. She couldn't decide what image she wanted to project. Did she want an artsy look with bright colors and the scarf her grandmother made her? Or should she go more corporate professional, with a navy dress and heels? Or super casual, like she guessed most people at Brothers at Play would be dressed—in jeans and one of the T-shirts from a fantasy game she worked on?

Nothing was perfect. She finally settled on a combination—black dress jeans, leather boots, a soft blue blouse, and Grams's scarf. If nothing else, wearing the scarf would give her courage. She wiped her sweaty hands on her jeans and gripped her tote bag tightly. *Now or never.*

She opened the office door and stepped into a beehive of activity. Everywhere, people hunched over computers, gathered in front of whiteboards, or dashed from one place to another. A cacophony of game sounds, cheers, groans, and chatter filled the air.

About twenty people filled the large open space, but an exact count was impossible. They all buzzed around singly and in small clusters.

Interspersed between the workspaces were a basketball net and a table tennis setup in the far corner. A few beanbag chairs clustered around an extra-large TV screen. Game controls were left propped in the chairs. The atmosphere was a combination kindergarten playroom and NASA control room. Approaching the front desk, Melissa realized she didn't even know the real name of the person she was meeting.

The young woman behind the reception desk was dressed very casually. She wore a T-shirt with characters from one of Brothers' games over tattered jeans. She turned away from a game in progress. "Good morning. How may I help you?"

"I know this sounds strange, but I have an appointment with one of the brothers who owns the company. I don't even know his real name. Sarah from graphics set up the meeting, and she just called him the wizard."

The young woman's face lit up. "Oh, you must be Rapunzel. We've been expecting you. I believe you're meeting with Dan. I'll give Sarah a quick call, and she'll come and take you to his office." Holding up a finger, she pressed a button on the phone console. "Sarah, Rapunzel is here." She swiveled back to face Melissa. "We're so excited to have you in the office. We all love the graphics you did for *Den of Dragons*. I especially love the gowns you gave the women for the ball. I desperately want one of those dresses."

Melissa grinned. "Thanks. I really appreciate hearing that." The name Dan niggled her brain. John's brother was named Dan. *Could this be John's company? No way. He would have told me. But it's just like what John described.*

"Here's Sarah. Sarah, this is Rapunzel."

Lost in thought, Melissa was startled.

A tall redhead approached with her hand out in greeting.

Sarah dressed casually in jeans, a black turtleneck sweater, and a fringed leather vest.

All she was missing was a black beret and she could have just stepped out of a poetry reading in a smoky coffee shop from the sixties.

"Hi, Rapunzel, so great to finally meet you in person. I feel like I already know you since we've been corresponding via email for so long now. Before I take you to the wizard, I want to swing by the graphics area and introduce you. We've all been dying to meet you and are thrilled you're here in person. Everyone loves your work. You're amazing and so creative. You make our characters really come alive." She paused to breathe. "Okay, enough babbling. Come with me."

Sarah guided her through the labyrinth of worktables and whiteboards to the center of the chaos. Many curious gazes followed her approach.

The area was filled with clusters of graphics taped to whiteboards. She was immediately reminded of her wall at home. She recognized several of her graphics from *Den of Dragons*.

Sarah called out, waving her hands to get everyone's attention. "Gang, this is Rapunzel. Rapunzel, this is the gang." With a sweep of her arm, she indicated the half dozen or so people at the nearby workstations.

Melissa was instantly surrounded by a group of people all clamoring to shake her hand and blurting out a torrent of questions.

"Do you really live in Seattle?"

"Are you going to be doing the graphics for the next version of *Dragons*?"

She never got to say a word before Sarah announced she had to take Rapunzel to meet the wizard. Cries of "Good luck" and "Come back and see us again soon" followed her to one of the few doors in the office area. Sarah knocked, and when told to enter, she opened the door. "Good luck. They're going to love you," she whispered.

Floor-to-ceiling windows overlooking the Space Needle and beyond to Lake Union dominated the room. She could still see a few boats dotting the lake despite the rain. A male voice spoke softly.

"Hi, Melissa. Or would you prefer I call you Rapunzel?"

She finally registered the man standing next to a large conference table. "John. What are you doing here?" She pressed a hand to her stomach as it did the familiar flip-flop. She stepped forward, then abruptly stopped. Suddenly, her world was spinning. Snatches of conversation rushed through her head. *My brother Dan… The office is controlled chaos… Whiteboards everywhere…*

She took a few steps backward, bumping into the closed door. "This…this is your office? Your company?" Her voice quivered, and both hands clenched the strap of her bag, pulling it tight across her chest.

John continued to stand silently, slowly nodding.

He reached out a hand.

Melissa immediately put out a hand to stop him. Her mind scrambled to sort through what she was seeing. Then the pieces fell into place. "You knew I was Rapunzel! You knew I worked for you! You knew, and you said nothing." Her voice was tight with emotion. She pressed one hand against her breastbone as her heart raced.

"Melissa, I wanted to tell you. Yes, I co-own Brothers at Play with my brother Dan. I…I can explain." He pulled out a chair and gestured for her to take a seat.

Melissa continued to stand and glare. "Explain? Explain what? That you deliberately lied to me for weeks." She closed her eyes briefly, reaching for the back of a nearby chair as her body swayed. "That you let me pour out my dreams. That you urged me to keep working on *SOS* so you could…could what?" She dropped her bag onto the chair and stepped closer with each accusation, punctuating her words with a finger aimed at his chest. Stopping, she exhaled heavily and continued in a low voice crackling with anger. "So, you could steal my game idea and profit from it."

John again approached and was stopped by a raised hand. He hunched his shoulders and lowered his head.

"No, no, never. I'd never steal your idea. I encouraged you because it's a great idea." He stood, silently opening and closing his mouth a few times. "I want to help you make it. I just didn't find the right time to tell you who I was."

Her fingernails bit into the palms of her clenched fists. Inside, her stomach twisted in knots. This was not the pleasant flip-flop she usually felt around John. This was a hard ball of anger. *I thought we were at least friends, if not becoming something more. I trusted him.* "How long have you known?" she asked in a low voice.

John stared at the floor for a moment. The muscles in his cheeks twitched. "Pretty much from the beginning." He paused, loosening his grip on the back of the chair. "I told you I recognized the game characters on your T-shirt. When you told me you were the artist who created them, I was shocked."

Melissa crossed her arms across her chest and glared through half-closed eyes. "You should have said something then."

John stared at the floor and shoved his hands into his pockets. "Yes…I should have. I don't know why I didn't." As he met her glare, he winced. "When I checked, I found out you were Rapunzel, and you required we only refer to you that way. I was torn. You were clear you had your reasons for using an alias." He pulled his hands from his pockets to reach out, then dropped them to his sides.

Melissa spun on her heel, strode briskly toward the window, and stared out at the drizzle, deliberately keeping her back to John. Without turning, she spoke in a whisper. "So, you decided to just keep that bit of information to yourself. You didn't value our friendship enough to tell me the truth." The hurt caused by his deceit continued to build. Her heart ached with the weight of his betrayal. She wanted his friendship. More so, she had hoped for his love. He only wanted her game. The ache turned to fury. Whipping around, she pointed her finger directly at his chest. "Sounds like your company was more important than our friendship. That all you cared about was profit."

Her pointed finger morphed into a raised palm.

John reached out but stopped. He backed away, raising both hands high. “No, that’s not it at all. I just… It was obvious your privacy was extremely important, and that’s why I hesitated. I didn’t want you to be uncomfortable blurring the lines between your personal and professional lives. You went to a great deal of effort to separate them.”

She stood rigid, arms folded across her chest. “Yes, it’s important to me to keep them separate.” Her voice shook with anger. “The fact that you are also technically my boss *is* uncomfortable. I thought you were my friend. I trusted you.”

John stared at his hands and slowly shook his head. “Melissa, please try to understand. I am your friend. That’s the most important thing. I wanted to be more than just a friend and hoped our relationship was headed that way.”

“How can it? You lied to me.” Melissa tapped her chest with a clenched fist.

“I didn’t really lie,” John replied softly.

“It was a lie by omission.” She spat out the words.

John nodded. “You’re right. It was a lie by omission. I did try several times. Remember the sudden rainstorm? And my request to have dinner? I planned to tell you tomorrow. Melissa, please believe me when I say I wanted to tell you.”

“Wanting to and actually doing it are two hugely different things. You had plenty of time to tell me the truth. You say you want to be more than friends, but your actions say something else.”

John stepped closer. His arms hung loosely at his side.

She didn't step back but clasped her arms more tightly across her chest and turned away.

"No, just the opposite. Our friendship means the world to me. So much so I was afraid to tell you who I was. I was afraid you'd react just like this and never want to see me again, and I didn't know how to tell you so you'd understand."

His voice sounded hoarse. She paced, with her back still to John. "It's simple." Her voice was tight, and she continued in a mocking tone. "You just say, you know, Melissa, that gaming company you're doing the graphics for, that's my company." She paused. Her voice dropped to a near whisper. "I can't trust you now."

"Please." He groaned. He stood, cupping his head as he stared at the floor.

Melissa snapped her head up and stared directly at John. "I hope you have enough of your grandfather's integrity not to steal my idea for the game. That's a risk I'll have to take, but it's the *only* risk I'm willing to take. I won't be accepting the contract for the graphics for the *Den of Dragons* sequel, either." She strode across the room, yanked up her bag, and flung the strap over her shoulder. Without a backward glance, she headed toward the door. She had to get out of here before she broke down. The pain clawed at her throat, and tears pricked at the back of her eyes. She refused to let him see her cry.

"Melissa, please, please just listen."

Swallowing hard, she whirled to face him. "Why? So, you can continue to lie? I've played this game, and I won't fall for it again. People have betrayed me before, but not now. For all I know, you only encouraged me so you could get your hands on my game." She stood with one foot tapping the floor. "You thought, oh poor, naïve Melissa, playing at developing a game, hiding behind an alias, so trusting because I'm Howard's grandson. I can outsmart her. I'll pretend to like her, and she'll come right to me with this idea, and I can make money from it." She flung the words out like she was throwing darts.

He moaned and slumped his shoulders. "No, Melissa, that's not true."

"I'm surprised you even bothered to show your cards now." Unmoved by his apparent misery, she railed on. "You could have let me meet with your brother and had him make the deal without me knowing any better. Or is there really a brother? Is he just part of your clever game?"

John straightened and took a step forward. "He's real, and so are my feelings for you." He stared her in the eyes. "I'd never do anything to hurt you. I encouraged you because your idea is great. It deserves to be made. I want you to have that success."

She shook her head. "No, you wanted the success. Well, you've lost this game." She grabbed her bag off the chair, flung it over her shoulder, then made a beeline for the door. One hand was pressed to her mouth to hold back the tears. Seeing Sarah approach, Melissa waved her off and rushed by. At the elevator, she pushed the down button several times. Once safely inside the empty elevator, she slumped against the back wall and let the tears flow. She was sure everyone in the office witnessed her anguish. *Fortunately, I will never have to set foot in that office again. Now, there's only one place I want to be.*

Chapter 11

An hour later, Melissa was on the road to Grams's house. She wanted nothing more than to spend the next few days sitting on the back porch, watching the water, drinking tea, and eating freshly baked muffins. When she got there, she was greeted with a comforting hug. Grams's gaze was filled with love.

"You don't have to say a word. Just be here and feel the love that surrounds you. Go sit on the back porch, and I'll be right out."

Grams emerged from the kitchen in a few minutes with a pot of freshly brewed tea and a plate of blueberry muffins. "The blueberries are from my garden. I had a good crop this summer. Now sit, relax, and breathe in. Sea air is a great purifier. It will help cleanse your pain. Later, we can talk. I'm going back inside and making something for us to eat. I'm sure you haven't eaten since you called me. You need food." Grams laid a gentle hand on her shoulder before she returned to the kitchen.

Melissa sat and gently rocked in the chair, listening to the symphony of sounds around her. The gentle lapping of the waves on the beach, seagulls squawking overhead, and the rhythmic *thump-thump-thump* of Grams's knife chopping vegetables supplied a soothing soundtrack to her rocking. The tea warmed her painful throat. Between sips, she rubbed her arms to keep from trembling. Gradually her muscles relaxed, and the knot in her chest loosened. Her heart still ached, but her head was clearing. Racing thoughts slowed down to a manageable pace. She took a deep breath and released it slowly.

Over dinner, Grams kept the conversation light, telling Melissa about the people on the reservation. Afterward, they sat in the living room in companionable silence.

Melissa curled up on the sofa, watching Grams work on her loom. Images and sound bites from earlier tumbled over and over in her head. At bedtime, Melissa drifted into a deep sleep, exhausted from the day's emotions.

Melissa sat on the back porch the next morning, sipping coffee with Grams. In a monotone, she told her the details of her relationship with John and how she discovered he had hidden his real identity.

Grams listened quietly.

At first, the words came in a rush, tumbling out as she stared at the water. Then, she slowed down and carefully described the encounter. She wrapped her arms tightly around her body. “What hurts so much is I was beginning to have feelings for him and hoped he was for me, too. I trusted him with my ideas and was starting to trust him with my heart. But I was wrong, again.” Her voice cracked with unspent tears. She refused to cry anymore.

“Again?” Grams asked.

She continued to stare out at the water and slowly let the memory come back. “Shortly after Mom and Dad died, Karen and Jan insisted I get out, and I finally relented. We went to our favorite place near our apartment. They thought the music and a few glasses of wine would cheer me up."

Grams nodded.

"We were having fun. Then, a friend from my first job after college spotted me and came over to our table. He acted happy to see me, and Karen invited him to join us. He did." She paused briefly, unwrapped her arms, and placed her clenched fists on her lap. "After the usual condolences, he asked what I was doing now. I said I was doing freelance work, and he talked about how he admired my courage, going out on my own. Said he still felt more secure working for a company with a steady paycheck. He wasn't at the same place anymore but was now on staff in the marketing department of a local company. We chatted about art, and he asked what I had done recently. He said he hadn't seen or heard my name in the graphic arena lately." Melissa paused again and absently smoothed out a wrinkle in her jeans. "I said I was using an alias now. He remembered Ms. Madeline's brutal put-down of my work, so he said he understood. But he kept pressing me about my alias. At first, it sounded harmless. It seemed like teasing, but I started to get uncomfortable."

Taking a deep breath, she laid her hands flat in her lap. "Karen and Jan noticed and suggested we leave. They made it sound casual, like we had always planned to go elsewhere. He took the hint and said goodbye. Walking out the door, Karen spotted him talking to a guy at the bar. She had a feeling she recognized the other guy but didn't remember from where until we got back to the apartment.

She paused to take a sip of her coffee. Finally, she

twisted in her chair to face Grams.

Grams nodded slowly, then set her cup on the table and reached over to touch Melissa's hand.

Melissa released a deep sigh. "Karen remembered seeing the man at Mom and Dad's funeral. He was one of the reporters hanging around, trying to get a story. He had been particularly interested in doing a story about me, comparing my work to Mom's. What he wanted was dirt of some kind for his article in a Seattle weekly. We realized my so-called old friend was trying to find out my alias to sell it to that horrid man. He was only talking to me for personal gain. I…I couldn't believe someone I knew could betray me like that."

Grams wiped a tear from her eye. "I'm so sorry. I never knew."

Melissa shook her head. "I never told you. Once it was over, I just wanted to put it behind me. But it taught me some people would willingly take advantage of a friendship for money."

"And you're afraid John was doing the same thing?"

Melissa set her coffee cup on the side table and leaned back with a heavy sigh. "I don't want to believe it. I trust Howard and find it hard to believe his grandson would be so conniving. But when he told me he knew I was Rapunzel and didn't say anything, it triggered the memory. My former co-worker's willingness to sell me out for money came flooding back. I got angry. I accused John of playing games and exploiting my idea for his personal gain." She crossed her arms, drawing her elbows close to her sides. "I wanted to trust him and was devastated at both the lie and what might have been his reason for it."

Grams sat silently for a moment, then reached out to take Melissa's hand in hers. "I know nothing I can say will take away the hurt. It's not like when you were a little girl, and I could put a colorful bandage on your scraped knee and kiss it to make it heal faster. A heart is much harder to mend, and it takes time. And time feels like an eternity right now." She gently squeezed Melissa's hand. "What I can say is to give yourself the gift of time and take care of yourself in the process. And don't throw away what you love out of fear. I know Howard is a special person in your life, and you care for him deeply. He was a comfort when you were grieving. He gave you somewhere safe to go so you didn't stay holed up in your house day in and day out. Don't let that go. It's important to go see him when he comes back to the snack stand."

Melissa blinked several times to keep back the tears.

"Don't let your fear of seeing John stop you from doing the things you love. That includes working on your *Save Our Salmon* game. Both are important to you, and the game is important to the world." Grams gave one more squeeze and stood to go back into the house.

Melissa stared out at the water for a long time. Her anger at John slowly morphed into determination. She wasn't about to let him or anyone else stand in the way of achieving her dream. *I don't need him or Brothers. Plenty of other companies will jump at the chance to produce SOS.* Pulling out her phone, she began to list the gaming companies she knew, starting with WizKids. Later, she'd research who to contact at each and start soliciting opportunities to make her pitch.

She'd give herself a few days to relax, but then she needed to get back to work. Decision made, Melissa stood and nodded toward the water as if it had acknowledged her resolve.

Grams sat in front of her loom, weaving colorful threads over and under as she softly hummed a familiar song. The pattern emerged as Grams's skilled hands danced across the vertical warp threads, switching colors of yarn. She used a shed stick to separate the warp threads, making it easier to pull the horizontal weft threads through. A comb helped her gently push the weft threads closely together to make a tight weave.

"How do you know when to change colors?" Melissa watched, fascinated by the process. "When I was a kid, I loved to sit and watch you weave. The way the images suddenly sprung to life was magic."

"The pattern is in my head. I can see the design before me, even before I pick up the next thread. So, I follow my head and my heart."

Melissa nodded. She understood what Grams had said, and she felt the same when she was in the flow with her art. "You told me before you want this tapestry to tell the story of the Lummis' commitment to the salmon and the environment. Is protecting the salmon why this project is so important?"

Grams paused, holding the shed stick in one hand. "In part. Yes, I feel it's important to educate others, and this tapestry is one way to do that. But more importantly, I believe I've been given this talent for a reason. I need to use it wisely. Our ancestors believed each of us has an obligation to leave this world better than we found it. That means preserving the land, the sea, and the creatures living in and on it. This piece isn't just about the salmon. It's about giving thanks for my gift by giving back to others in the best way possible."

Melissa leaned forward in the chair and propped her elbows on her knees. "I finally understand. I'm determined not to let my anger at John stop me. I'll find another company to work with. I see now I'm following a long tradition of the Lummi culture. Like yours and Mom's, my art also has the potential to teach and inspire."

Grams smiled and continued to weave. "You are finally starting to value your talent."

Melissa spent the next few days roaming the beach, watching Grams weave, and letting her mind wander. She needed to return to her life in Seattle soon to find another way to produce this game.

Tuesday morning, the solitude of her walk was interrupted by the ring of her cell phone. The number was unfamiliar, so she ignored it. It rang again almost immediately. *No voicemail? Could this be Karen calling from work? Did something happen to Jan and the baby? Whoever it was, it must be urgent.* She answered on the third ring. An unfamiliar male voice spoke with urgency.

"Hi, Melissa. This is Dan McDonald from Brothers at Play. Please don't hang up. I'm not calling about, or for, John. I want to talk to you about your *Save Our Salmon* game idea. If you remember, Sarah first set up a meeting between you and me to discuss it." His words came out in a rush without a pause for breath.

"I told John I wasn't interested in discussing it with Brothers at Play anymore." Her tone was sharp.

"Wait. Please give me a minute." Dan hurried on.

"I know. He told me, and I'm sorry about what happened. I'm still very interested in meeting with you and discussing the possibility of working together to produce your game. John did share more about it after you left, and I think it's an awesome idea. I'd very much like to help you get it made. John has nothing to do with this. He doesn't even know I'm talking to you."

Still holding the phone to her ear, she gazed out at the water, rolling a pebble she had picked up from the beach in her other hand. "I don't know. I'm thinking of showing it to some other companies to see if they'd be interested."

"Please, I'm begging you. Give me a chance. You know the quality of our work, so you know we'll do a great job. And I hope you still feel we've been fair with you in the past and will be with this deal, as well. You know Pops would skin us alive if he heard we were even a hair out of line in our dealings with you."

She paused, clutching the pebble in her fist. "I'm just not ready to see John or work with him yet, if ever."

"I understand. I told my brother he was an idiot not to have told you immediately who he was. But please don't punish the rest of us for his stupidity. You'll never have to see him. I promise. I can meet you anywhere to talk about this. You don't need to come into the office at all. Plus, John is still managing Pop's stand, so he won't be here for another two weeks. Please say you'll at least meet with me and explore the idea before you go elsewhere," Dan pleaded.

Getting the game produced is the priority. That is what is most important, and Dan is offering a way to make it happen. "I'm not in Seattle right now and won't be back until tomorrow. The soonest I could meet you is Thursday."

"That's perfect. There's a great little coffee shop around the corner from our office. I can meet you there any time."

She ended the call after agreeing to meet at ten on Thursday morning. She slowly paced the beach. *What was that old saying? Where there's a will, there's a way.* Dan had just handed her a way, and she was determined to use it. Bouncing the pebble up and down in her hand, she stopped and gazed out at the water. Then, with a gleeful laugh, she gave it a strong toss into the incoming waves.

Chapter 12

Thursday morning, Melissa drove downtown to meet with Dan. She sang along with the radio to quell her nerves. At a stoplight, she patted her tote bag on the passenger seat. *I can do this. I will make this happen.*

Entering the coffee shop, she paused just inside the door and looked around cautiously.

A tall, lean man in his late twenties with dark-blond hair and midnight-blue eyes waved from a nearby table.

"You must be Dan?" she asked, slowly approaching the table.

Jumping to his feet, Dan put out his right hand in greeting. "Yes, and you're Melissa or Rapunzel? Which should I call you?"

"Melissa is fine." She continued to glance around, clutching her tote bag nervously.

"He's not here," Dan stated. "He's at the snack stand at Green Lake all day. I promise I didn't tell him we were meeting. Let me get you a drink. What would you like—coffee, latte, cappuccino?"

"A cappuccino would be nice."

Dan left to place their orders at the counter.

She closed her eyes and took a calming breath. Opening her eyes again, she studied Dan while he chatted with the barista. Despite the difference in hair color, he clearly was John's brother. He was about the same height and had the same lean frame. He smiled much quicker than John, reminding her more of Howard. Like Howard, his eyes twinkled. John's were always more serious. Mentally, she stopped herself. *I'm not thinking about John. This is a business meeting. It's not meet-the-family day.*

Dan returned laden with coffee and two enormous chocolate-filled croissants. He grinned sheepishly. "I couldn't resist. The nice barista told me they were baked fresh just an hour ago." He sat back with a sigh. "I know. I'm an incurable romantic. Give me a pretty face, and I'll buy anything."

Melissa smiled. "I know where you got that trait from. You obviously learned well from your grandfather's example. He loves to flirt with every woman or girl who stops at his stand."

Dan grinned. "I can tell you know Pops very well. Have you seen him recently?"

"No, but I might go see him after our meeting." She reached for the back of her neck to twist a strand of hair.

"That would be great. I know he'd love to see you. And just so you know, he gave John a talking-to about honesty and how to treat a lady. He's on your side." Dan winked.

Melissa gasped at Dan's statement. She raised both hands in protest. "Oh no, I don't mean for anyone to take sides. This is between John and me."

Dan just grinned and shook his head. "Not to worry. Pops never holds a grudge for too long. But he can be very opinionated and isn't afraid to tell any of us where we went wrong. He says it's part of the grandfather oath." Dan paused to take a sip of his coffee. Putting down his cup, he gestured toward Melissa's tote bag. "But, enough about Pops and John. Would you show me your storyboard for the new game? I'm excited to see it. If your idea is half as good as I think it will be, I want to help you produce it. Let's talk about that."

Melissa settled more comfortably in her chair. "Yes, let's." She opened her tablet and angled it so Dan could see it with her. She pulled her hair back with one hand, so it fell down her back. "Okay, I'll walk you through it." She squared her shoulders. "First, let me tell you what prompted the idea."

Dan scuffed his chair closer to the table and leaned in to study the tablet. For the next forty-five minutes, he listened, taking occasional notes.

Melissa told him about her reaction to what she learned at the tribal meeting. She then took him through the screens she created, showing how the player could earn points for each positive action and lose points for not removing an obstacle or not completing a challenge in time. At each level, the tasks became more difficult. She answered the questions he posed and gave more details throughout the presentation.

Her last few slides showed her research on the game's viability. "I know Brothers has focused mostly on fantasy games. This would be a departure. When I did a market search for similar games, I found there weren't many. This is a new concept for gaming. But when I researched what topics teenagers and twenty-something-year-olds are concerned about, I learned the environment and mankind's impact on the planet is near the top. Climate change issues are usually in the top three of what's most important when this age group is polled. So, I am confident there is a market for this type of game."

Dan nodded. "Being a late twenty-something myself, I know how important this topic is to my generation." He sat back and faced her directly. "I want to do this with you. How can I convince you we'll do a great job of making *Save Our Salmon* come to life? With your vision and amazing graphics and our computer skills, I know this will be a huge hit."

Melissa studied Dan's face. What she saw was genuine interest in her game. "Brothers at Play was my first choice to partner with." She paused, glancing away briefly, and then faced Dan squarely. She put both palms down on the table and leaned forward slightly. "I don't want to ever see John or work with him. I'm also super embarrassed to walk back into your offices. I left in tears, and I'm sure everyone knows. I don't want their pity."

Dan shook his head. "They don't pity you. Rapunzel is too admired for that to happen. If they pity anyone at this point, it's John. They don't know what he said or did, but they're convinced he screwed up somehow. You don't have to come into the office. We'll find a neutral location if we need to meet in person. And I'm the only other person at Brothers outside of HR who knows your real name. We will continue to honor that part of our past agreement if it's what you want."

After a brief pause, Melissa nodded. "They know me as Rapunzel. Let's leave it that way."

Dan took a deep breath and let it out slowly. "Of course, we'll draw up a new contract for this joint venture. What do you say?"

Melissa squared her shoulders and looked Dan in the eye. “I say have your lawyer draw up the contract, and I’ll review it with my attorney. That’s all I can promise for now.”

“Deal.” Dan extended a hand across the table.

She hesitated for a moment, then nodded and shook hands.

They both stood and gathered their belongings.

“Are you parked nearby?” Dan asked.

“Yes, in the garage just around the corner.”

“Then I’ll say goodbye for now. I’m happy to meet you finally. I’m glad you’re open to working with me on this.”

“Dan, we haven’t talked about the sequel to *Den of Dragons*. I’m not sure I want to work on it, especially if it interferes with my ability to devote my time to *Save Our Salmon*. Am I putting you in a bind?” She brushed a lock of hair behind one ear.

Dan shook his head. “No worries. *Save Our Salmon* just became our top priority. So, it will make perfect sense to everyone that Rapunzel is working on it, instead. There’s no rush on the other game. The current version was just released and is selling very well. We have time.”

“Thank you.”

“Now, I’d better buy some more of those croissants, or I’ll get lynched when I get back to the office.”

She glanced over at the young woman behind the counter. “And, of course, you can’t pass up another opportunity to flirt with the pretty barista.” She headed out into the sunshine, feeling lighter. *SOS is going to become a reality. I just have to avoid John.*

****

The following week, Melissa received a contract in her work email. She read it carefully and sent it on to her attorney. He was the same person who handled the legal work for Mom's art projects and Dad's programming consulting. She trusted him completely to ensure she got a fair deal with no surprises. After a few minor adjustments, they agreed the contract was a good one, and she would receive a generous percentage of all future sales and merchandising. She signed the contract and sent it back to Dan.

He obviously had been waiting since he responded immediately and agreed to all her edits.

Dan suggested an online meeting with his team for early next week. He assured her they would still know her only as Rapunzel, and since they had already met her in the office, what was the harm in her appearing on camera?

Realizing he was right, she agreed to the first of many meetings to work with the team to create the new game. Excited to begin, Melissa committed to a meeting on Monday. At the appointed time, she clicked on the link to log into the meeting. Before turning on her video camera, she took a few deep breaths to calm the butterflies in her stomach.

The image on her screen showed a bright room with a long conference table. One wall was covered by a large whiteboard with the words *Save Our Salmon* in bold letters.

This is real. My game is about to be made. She rubbed her hands on her jeans to ease her tension.

Several people milled about, chatting as they settled into their seats. The atmosphere was lively. Pads of paper, colored pencils, coffee cups, and water bottles cluttered the conference table. The scene was remarkably similar to her own workspace. Taking a deep breath, she turned on her camera.

Dan waved and smiled. "Okay, gang. Let's get this show on the road."

The last few stragglers quickly sat in open chairs and directed their attention to Dan.

Dan kicked off the meeting. "I know everyone here knows each other, but Rapunzel doesn't know you. I want to review everyone's roles in this project. First, let me introduce Rapunzel. Not only is she our lead graphic designer on this project, she is also the creator of *Save Our Salmon*. She will be involved in every decision and have the final say on all designs and concepts. Now, let me tell Rapunzel what everyone does."

He had sent her the list of all the team members, but this was her chance to put names to faces. She leaned in to study each person.

Dan went around the table and pointed to each person as he gave their name and area of responsibility. "This is Davey. He is the head programmer. His team consists of Tim, Martha, Stew, and Joanne."

They all waved in turn.

"Next are the other members of the graphics team. Arabella and Anna Lee will handle the background. We call them the A-team. Drew and Dwight are the D-team and will handle the non-human characters. Rapunzel will, of course, be doing the human characters. Last but not least, here's Sabrina. She will help write the script for the actors who voice the characters."

Melissa smiled back at the team members. She had

seen many of them that day in the office, but now she could put names, faces, and roles together. The group was a range of styles from nerdy-funk to preppy-casual to Southern belle and a touch of subtle Goth. Each had their own unique look that reflected their artistic or computer programming prowess. Except for Davey and Sabrina, all looked like they were fresh out of college.

"Now, I'm going to turn this over to Rapunzel and let her walk you through her vision. I'll tell you, it's awesome. You're all going to love this."

Melissa shared her screen and took them through the storyboard. As with Dan, she started with the current situation affecting the salmon and the Lummis' commitment to protecting them and the environment. She shared her ideas for how the game would progress and how players would earn points. When she completed her presentation, the atmosphere was electric with ideas.

Davey jumped up, grabbed a marker, and began making notes on the whiteboard.

His team of programmers threw out ideas on how to code the game. They were already identifying where they could use existing code from other games and where they would need to write new code.

The A-team and D-team sketched ideas for the backgrounds and animals and held them up to the camera for her to see.

An hour sped by as the group bounced around ideas, sometimes as a whole group and other times in smaller clusters.

The programmers mostly huddled around the whiteboard, drawing lines, *x's*, and *o's* like an elaborate tic-tac-toe game.

Annabelle opened her tablet and shared images from previous works that might work for *SOS,* at least as a starting point for inspiration.

Dan continued to sit at the head of the table, grinning from ear to ear. Occasionally, he'd catch her eye and give her a wink.

In the final minutes of the meeting, everyone agreed on the next steps and dashed off to work on their assignments.

Dan asked her to stay. "How do you think it went?"

"Is every team meeting like this? It's like being caught in a whirlwind. I'm dizzy from all the energy and activity." Melissa pressed her hands on either side of her head.

"Yep, that's pretty much the norm. They're a great team, and they'll work their butts off to make your game a success. In part because they love the idea, but mainly because they respect you and want to do justice to your vision."

Melissa put a hand to her heart and smiled back. "This was amazing. Once I got over my nerves, I loved every second of it. Thank you, Dan. This is everything I hoped for."

"Awesome. So glad you're happy with the team." He glanced down at his notepad. "I suggest we meet three times a week for now. That way, everyone will have time to complete assignments between meetings. And of course, the other graphic teams will send you drafts in between." He continued to check the items he had captured during the meeting. "The key thing for you, at this point, is to continue to flesh out the levels for the game. Don't worry about how. You just tell us what you want the player to do in each level. It's

Davey's team's responsibility to work out the logistics." With that, he saluted and signed off.

Melissa twirled around in her chair. "Yay." She threw her hands into the air as she spun. When the chair came to a stop, she leaned back and stared at the painting on the wall. "Okay, Mom, I'm doing it. It's just a start, but I hope you're proud of me."

****

Sunday, Melissa met Karen and Jan at the Mad Hatter Tea Shop for afternoon tea.

Jan gazed at the whimsical décor "oohing" and "aahing." "I just love this place. It always reminds me of *Alice in Wonderland.* I half expect the White Rabbit to hop out and serve us tea." She wiggled in her chair. "This belly of mine makes it hard to get close to the table now."

Melissa grinned. "You've definitely grown since we last got together. How are you doing?"

Jan's eyes glowed as she gently stroked the baby bump. "So much better now that my morning sickness is gone. I didn't dare eat breakfast before school for fear I'd need to dash to the teacher's lounge bathroom. That could be a little traumatic for third graders to see their teacher suddenly clap a hand over her mouth and run out. Now, I could eat a horse every day."

Karen gestured to the menu. "I don't see any horses on the menu, but I do see lots of yummy tea sandwiches and scones. I think you'll survive to eat another day." Once their order was placed, Karen turned to Melissa. "Okay, time to spill. What's happening with John and your game idea?" She propped her chin in her hands and stared at Melissa with her eyes wide open.

"Well, um..." Melissa stalled, picking up her teacup to examine the pattern of English roses. "I guess I haven't talked to either of you in the last few weeks."

"We noticed." Karen rolled her eyes. "Please, go on."

Melissa carefully set her empty teacup on the table and straightened it. *Best to get it all out at once.* "Well...I'm not seeing John anymore."

Karen and Jan both gasped.

Jan leaned forward to clutch Melissa's hand. "What happened? What did he do?"

Melissa gave Jan a half smile. "It's more what he didn't do." She paused.

Their server placed their individual teapots on the table and turned over the timer, instructing them to wait to pour until the sand had run out.

Both Karen and Jan swung back to Melissa.

"It's a complicated story, but I'll try to give you the short version." She told them about her decision to pitch her game to the owners at Brothers. When she got there, she found John in the office.

Karen set down her teapot with a thud. "What? What was he doing there?"

Melissa bit back a chuckle at Karen's reaction. "I asked him the same question."

"And?" Karen leaned forward.

"And he explained he and his brother were the owners of Brothers." Melissa sat back, watching their shocked expressions.

Jan blinked rapidly. "Wait. And you had no idea?"

Melissa just shook her head.

Jan gestured wildly. "He never said where he worked?"

Again, Melissa shook her head. "I knew he did computer programming, but I assumed he was a contractor like my dad. He talked about how my dad was his ideal, so I just guessed he did the same thing."

Karen shook her head. "But you've done work for Brothers for over a year now. Didn't he know who you were?"

"Oh, he knew all right. He just neglected to tell me." Melissa crossed her arms tightly across her chest. Her voice had a hard edge.

"What happened?" Jan asked softly.

Melissa uncrossed her arms and leaned forward. "I stormed out. After telling him I would never let him touch my game, and I wouldn't accept any further work from them, either." She paused for a moment. "Then, I ran to Grams and cried my eyes out until I decided he wasn't worth the tears."

Jan took Melissa's hand and stroked it. "You poor baby. I'm so sorry."

Melissa smiled at her comforting gesture and patted Jan's hand.

Karen's lips puckered. "You're absolutely right. He doesn't deserve a second thought, let alone a single tear. But wait…now what are you going to do about your game? Can you talk to another gaming company?"

Melissa fiddled with the tea sandwich she put on her plate from the three-tiered platter. "No…I actually signed with Brothers to have them develop the game."

Both Karen and Jan almost leaped out of their seats. "What? Why? How?"

Melissa waved a hand to reassure them. "It's all right." She told them about Dan's call and meeting him at a coffee shop.

Jan blinked several times. "But what about John? Won't you see him in the office?"

Melissa shook her head. "I made it very clear I wasn't ever setting foot in that office again. I'll work remotely with the team."

Karen leaned back and crossed her arms. "Are you sure you can trust this Dan? Are you confident they will do right by you and your game?"

Melissa shrugged. "I have to believe they will. Dan seems very sincere. And they're Howard's grandsons. I trust that Howard wouldn't have encouraged me to work with them if they weren't."

Jan took a sip of her tea, her eyebrows wrinkled. "I don't mean to be critical, but how did you not know John was the co-owner of Brother's? Didn't you check them out before you initially signed?'

Melissa sighed. "That's a good question and one I've asked myself. I did, or at least I had my lawyer do so. He assured me they were a good company with a great reputation. I did go to their website, but only to look at some of their current games to study their graphic style."

Karen squinted and pursed her lips. "You never looked up the company?"

"Yes, but their website is a marketing site that only promotes their games."

"There's more places to search online other than a company website." Karen shook her head. "There's a whole world wide web out there."

"I do computer graphics, not espionage," Melissa retorted. "Besides, you did a search for him online and didn't find anything, remember."

Karen stared down at her fingernails for a moment.

"You're right. I did try."

"So, super sleuth, how was I supposed to do any better?" Melissa teased.

All three of them burst out laughing. The tension from the conversation evaporated.

"But what are you going to do about John?" Jan asked.

Melissa shook her head. "Nothing. It's over. I can't trust him anymore. I'm going to use his company to produce my game and forget about him." She switched the subject to ask about their lives while they enjoyed the luscious sandwiches and pastries. What she didn't share was her concern that it might prove to be difficult once John returned full time to the company. But it was a risk she'd take to have *SOS* produced. If she stayed in the safety of her home, then everything would be okay.

Chapter 13

The SOS team met several times a week for the next two months. They exchanged hundreds of emails and devoted what seemed like every waking moment to bringing *Save Our Salmon* to life. They batted around ideas as the game grew, adding more challenges and new opportunities to create safe spaces for the salmon to spawn. Thanksgiving had come and gone with Melissa ordering a turkey sub to commemorate the day. Christmas was fast approaching.

In mid-December, Dan made an announcement. "Hey, gang, we've been doing excellent work, and I'm proud to say we are slightly ahead of schedule. So, starting this Wednesday, the nineteenth, we're closing Brothers at Play until January second. I want everyone to *completely* disconnect and enjoy the holidays. That means lots of fun, friends, family, food, and drinks for two whole weeks. If anyone feels tech withdrawal and tries to text or email me with any new ideas, you won't get a response. I won't even read them. If you happen to have some sort of epiphany, find an old-fashioned pen, and paper, and write it down, put it in a drawer, and see me January second."

The comments began to fly.

"Yay. I can go home for a real meal for a change."

"I might actually get to do some shopping this year and not just hand out gift cards I bought at the drugstore at the last minute."

"I might have to re-introduce myself to my kids, but it will be *great* to spend some time with them."

Melissa continued to sketch ideas on paper, barely listening to Dan.

"Rapunzel, do you have plans for the holidays?"

"Huh, me?" She jerked her head back to the computer screen. "Yeah, sort of. My grandmother asked me to spend some time with her for Christmas. So now that we're not working, I will head up there. It will be good to be with her, and who knows, I might get some more ideas for the game while there."

"You don't sound super enthused." Dan frowned.

Melissa hesitated. Last Christmas, they were still grieving, and she wasn't looking forward to this year. Too many memories. She'd rather work. "Oh, I am to spend time with Grams. I can still work over the holiday. I agree everyone else needs a break."

Dan immediately shook his head and pointed his finger, like a modern version of the World War Two poster of Uncle Sam.

"Oh no, you don't. You've put in more hours than any of us, and we all need to step back for a while. We'll come back with lots more energy afterward than if we try to push through now. We've got a few months before we premier *SOS* at the big video game exposition, E-Three, in March. We've got time. We should be able to begin beta testing in late January." He leaned back with a slow grin. "Trust me, we're good."

She had to laugh at the sternness in Dan's voice. "Okay, I trust you. But my pizza delivery guy is going to be upset. He's gotten used to delivering at ten o'clock most nights," she joked.

"I know what you mean, man. I might experience more pizza and wings withdrawal than tech withdrawal," quipped Davey.

At the meeting's end, Dan indicated he wanted Melissa to stay for a moment. Once the room cleared, he leaned closer to the screen. "I wanted to let you know John is back in the office full-time. Pops has gone back to the stand for at least half days. I know he'd like to see you."

Melissa's chest tightened at the mention of Howard. She wanted to see him but didn't want to talk about John. She took a deep breath before replying. "Thanks for the update. I'll…I'll see about stopping by to see Howard."

That evening, Grams called to say she had a last-minute meeting at the art museum in two days. So, she would be coming to Seattle. She suggested they change plans and spend Christmas together there, instead of Melissa coming to the reservation.

After agreeing, Melissa glanced around at the mess surrounding her. She had been so absorbed with *Save Our Salmon* that she had neglected most of the housework. The house wasn't dirty, just cluttered with sketches everywhere. The cupboards were bare since she had survived on pizza and other take-out food for weeks. And she hadn't put up a single decoration. She didn't even have a tree. She had less than twenty-four hours to make the house presentable and buy some basics so they could at least cook dinner tomorrow. The tree and decorations could wait until Grams arrived. They could do it together.

The next afternoon, the sound of a car pulling into her driveway meant Grams had arrived. Melissa quickly put down the knife she used to chop vegetables and hurried out the back door. "Grams, let me get that." She grabbed the suitcase after giving her grandmother a quick hug. "Let's get inside out of this rain. I'm making chili for dinner."

Pausing inside the door, Grams unwrapped her scarf and hung up her damp coat. She walked over to the stove, lifted the lid on the pot, and inhaled. "Oh, perfect. I love the aroma of sautéing onions and peppers. I have just the thing to go with it. I made a batch of corn muffins."

Melissa set one of Grams's bags on the counter and peered inside. "Yeah, you just happened to do some baking before you came. Let me see. Judging from the size of this bag, you must have made enough corn muffins to feed half of Seattle."

Grams gave a little shrug and smiled. "Well, I might have made a few other things, too. I know how busy you've been and figured you've been living on pizza, so I assumed some good homemade cooking wouldn't go to waste."

Melissa laughed at the accuracy of Grams's comment and started to remove the various containers from the bag and line them up on the counter. "I knew I didn't need to go to the grocery store. I did, anyway, so we can stuff ourselves like little pigs for the next several days."

The sound of happy chatter and the enticing smells of onions, peppers, tomatoes, ground beef, and spices simmering on the stove soon filled the room. While they cooked together, Melissa talked about the team's progress on the game. "The group of people Dan assembled is awesome. They keep coming up with new ideas and changes, making *SOS* even better. It's been a long time since I've been part of a group of creative people."

Grams smiled at Melissa and gestured for her to go on.

"I want to show you some of the graphics the other artists have done. They're working on the background and the animals while I do the people. Reminds me of your tapestries. One of the artists told me they've studied your work so they could replicate the colors and designs used in traditional Lummi art. They don't know you're my grandmother. Dan was the one who recommended they look at your work for inspiration."

"Do you think they'd like to see what I'm working on now?"

"Really? They would be ecstatic." Melissa stopped to hug Grams.

"Good. I brought some sketches and photos to show the people at the art museum tomorrow, and I'd be happy to show them to your team members, too."

"That would be great. Everyone is on a holiday break now, but I can make copies and share them when we all get back together on the second." She paused for a moment, her finger on her chin. "I'll need to figure out what to say about how I got them, but I'll think about that later," she concluded with a happy shrug.

"So, you're still working as Rapunzel?"

Melissa knew that tone. She didn't hear it often, but when she did, Grams was concerned. She ignored Grams's gaze, focusing on stirring the chili. "Yes, that was part of the deal when I signed the contract. I want to remain anonymous."

Grams stepped behind Melissa to hug her and then

returned to setting the two places at the kitchen table.

Melissa ignored the sound of Grams opening the cupboards and rattling silverware and continued to stare into the bubbling chili. *Hiding behind Rapunzel is weak. I know it, but I'm not ready to give it up just yet.* After dinner, Melissa carried two steaming cups of tea to Grams in the living room.

Grams stood in front of the large painting above the fireplace. "I love this piece. Your mom didn't keep many of her pieces, but this was one of the few paintings she refused to sell. I remember when she exhibited it once in a showing at a gallery downtown. She had many offers then, but she brought it home and hung it here."

Melissa set the tea on the coffee table and went to stand next to Grams. She put one arm around her shoulder. "I love it, too. Whenever I need to connect with her, I sit here and study the scene."

The painting showed a rocky beach scattered with weathered driftwood. The sky was the blue-gray so typical of the Pacific Northwest. The kind of day that couldn't decide between sunny or overcast. Choppy water reflected the same shades of blue-gray, blending the water and sky into a muted backdrop, separated by the darker gray outline of the Olympic Mountain range on the horizon.

The only spot of color was the red jacket on the little girl who ran along the beach with her arms stretched out to welcome the incoming waves. The wind blew her long dark hair around her head like a halo, obscuring her face. Although her expression couldn't be seen, the image conveyed joy and wonder. She appeared to be dancing along the shore and hopping away from the sea foam where it rolled in. The image of the little girl invited the viewer to share in her delight, see the water, feel the wind, and experience the raw beauty of nature.

As they sat together on the couch facing the artwork, Melissa let her mind drift back to that day at the beach with Mom, remembering her excitement at the sight of the waves. In a dreamy tone, she shared the memory with Grams. "I can feel her presence when I look at this. She was behind me, taking photos while I played with the waves. The rough water was frightening, but Mom was there, and I knew she would keep me safe. After we returned home, she and I sat wrapped in a blanket, drinking hot chocolate by the fire. When Dad emerged from his home office, he joined us on the couch while I told him about my adventure. 'The Three Musketeers,' Mom said. 'All for one and one for all.' "

"That's a beautiful memory." Grams wrapped her arms around her.

"I believed it would be the three of us against the world forever." Melissa gazed wistfully at the painting.

"You know you're not alone. You'll *never* be alone." Grams's voice was soft and gentle. "Your parents are right here with you every moment." She gently pressed her hand over Melissa's heart. "And you have me, always. You still have your best friends, even though you abandoned them for a while. You have your new teammates from Brothers at Play and Howard." She paused. "Have you seen him recently?"

Melissa felt her shoulders stiffen, and she shifted her gaze to her hands resting in her lap. "No, I've avoided going to the stand. I've been super busy, but really, I'm afraid to see him. I worry he'll want to talk about John."

Grams turned, so she faced Melissa. Her expression was grim. "Melissa, listen to me." Her tone was sharp. "You need to stop hiding from life and from people. You're surrounded by people who love you and want to be a part of your life, but you push us away. You need to step out of the lonely tower you've built and open yourself up to the joys of being with others. You've become Rapunzel in more ways than just as an alias for your work. You're the one who locked yourself away. You also have the power to escape."

"If you let people in…" Melissa glanced away, avoiding Grams's piercing look. "Then they have the power to hurt you."

"There's always a risk with love."

Melissa glanced back to see Grams slowly shake her head.

"Yes, some people won't live up to your expectations. Some will leave or be taken from you. You think you're saving yourself from further pain, but instead, the pain you feel now will never leave unless you replace it with happiness. And that happiness comes from being with people who care for you. Right now, all you have in your life is me. As much as I love you, I, too, will have to leave you one day."

Melissa clutched Grams's arm. Her throat constricted. "Grams, what are you not telling me?"

Grams smiled and patted Melissa's hand where it clung to her arm. "Nothing. I'm fine. But that's the reality of life. I'm in my late seventies. You will have many, many years to live after I'm gone. It breaks my heart to think you'll be alone."

The idea of Grams dying someday was unbearable. She clasped Grams's hand, squeezing it tight.

Grams gently stroked Melissa's hand. "Our fishermen have a tradition to always fish in a group. Several boats go out together, with a group of men in each boat. They know they need to be able to count on each other to help bring home a harvest. One person cannot do it alone. This is especially true in tough times—when it takes many hands to fight the rough sea. In calm waters, the load is lighter when sharing the work. Back on shore, there's great joy in enjoying the bounty together. It's the same with life. We all need others to be in the boat to share the burdens. We also need others to share in the moments of joy."

Melissa sat staring into space.

Grams stood and took the now cold tea into the kitchen.

Can I give up the safety of Rapunzel? Am I ready or able to take the risk? What if…?

Chapter 14

Howard leaned back in his chair and studied the flames in his fireplace while he waited for John to make his next move.

John glanced up from the chessboard when Dan strolled into Howard's den.

Dan poured himself a glass of whiskey from the bar and slumped into a nearby overstuffed armchair.

Howard smiled smugly, seeing John focus back on the game. He had taken advantage of the distraction to remove John's last pawn, setting up the classic two-pawn checkmate move. "Checkmate." He scooped up John's king and laid it on the board before turning to Dan. "Dan, I see you've helped yourself to my good whiskey. The least you could do is pour your old Pops a wee drop. And pour one for your brother, too. He needs it now that I've just whipped him for the second game in a row."

Dan did as asked and handed each man a glass with their whiskey neat.

"Now switch places with John. He's no challenge. He's too depressed to think straight," Howard demanded.

John just grunted and stood to relinquish his seat.

Howard winked at Dan and nodded toward John. "He's got a heart condition," he teased.

Dan glanced at his brother.

John slumped in the comfortable leather chair and stared remorsefully into his glass.

"Melissa?"

"Yes, Melissa." Howard swirled the amber liquid around in his glass before taking a sip.

"You two can stop talking about me as if I'm not here. I can hear you," John grumbled from his corner of the room.

Howard set down his glass and turned to face John. He assumed his "cross-examining a hostile witness" voice. "Good. Then listen to me. It's about time you stopped moping and started courting. It's been over two months, and all you've done is get increasingly sullen by the day. You won't feel better until you talk to her and beg for her forgiveness."

"She made it clear she doesn't ever want to see me again. She was emphatic with Dan that Brothers would only get the production rights to her game if I stayed away from the project…and from her." John stared at his glass.

"So, you're saying the rights to the game are what's most important?" Howard challenged.

John jerked his head up. "You know that's not true. The game was never what I wanted. But the game's important to her, and I want her to have her success. I won't get in the way."

Howard slumped back in his chair, muttering into his glass. "You've developed too many medieval-type games." Then he raised his voice. "That kind of chivalry is for the knights of the Round Table, not love. You know the saying, 'All's fair in love and war'? If you care for her, you have to prove it and fight for your relationship. You need to find a way to tell her how you feel and hope she feels remotely the same." He raised his glass in a mock salute. "My guess is she does, or she wouldn't be trying so hard to avoid you."

"You young bucks have no idea how to romance a woman." On a roll now, Howard leaned forward and made strong eye contact with both men. "When courting your grandmother, I gave her flowers every chance I could. Her favorites were pink and white roses. Sometimes, I could only afford to buy one, but I'd pick the prettiest one at the shop. As I started to make money, I could afford to buy her a dozen, but what she still treasured most were the times I came home with just one perfect bud. Find a way to touch her heart."

John stopped playing with his drink and sat up. "I'll give it some thought. Thanks, Pops. You're right. Time to stop moping."

Satisfied he had made his point, Howard shifted his attention back to the chessboard and watched Dan ponder his next move. "Excellent. Now let's wrap this game up and go make some dinner." With a quick move, he captured Dan's bishop and positioned his queen to checkmate Dan's king.

The three men headed for the kitchen.

Howard put his arm around Dan, holding him back a little. He leaned in so John wouldn't hear him. "Help your brother find a way to talk to Melissa again. There must be something you can do to get them together."

"I'll think about it. The most obvious would be if we needed his help with the game, but everything's going along smoothly."

"What if it wasn't?" Howard winked.

"What? You mean make up a problem only John

can solve?"

Dan opened his eyes wide and spun around to stare at his grandfather.

"You're wicked. I hope you never used those tactics in the courtroom. I think it's malpractice, or maleficence, or whatever you lawyers call it when you cheat."

Howard just grinned and slapped Dan on the back. "All's fair in love and war."

"What's taking you two so long?" John yelled out from the kitchen. "This meal won't make itself, and I'm not Cinderella. So, you bums better get in here and help if you want to eat."

"Hold on, Cinderella. Help is on the way."

Dan laughed as he hurried to the kitchen.

Howard hung back for a moment, grinning. He was confident he had just put an idea in Dan's head. Now, he just needed to get John to take some action, and all would be well again.

Chapter 15

"Grams, how would you feel about inviting a few of my friends to Christmas Eve dinner?"

Grams stopped wiping the counter and turned to face Melissa. "I like that idea. What prompted it?"

"As if the concern you expressed last night wasn't enough?" Melissa laughed. She added the soap to the dishwasher and pressed start. "To add fuel to the fire you started last night, Karen just texted to say Merry Christmas and asked if I was up for getting together over the holiday. She's not going to her parents since they'll be in Baltimore to spend the holiday with her older sister and her new baby. So, she's just hanging around. She mentioned Jan and Derrick were also around. Jan's over seven months pregnant and unable to travel, so we could invite them, too."

"I think it's an excellent idea. Invite your friends, and I'll start a batch of Christmas cookies. Then let's figure out what to make and get shopping."

Melissa noted Grams's smile before she headed toward the pantry.

Later that day, a package arrived for Melissa. She carried it into the kitchen, where Grams was baking. Setting it on the counter, she searched but didn't find a return address other than the company's name. Puzzled, she carefully opened it to reveal a box of golden pears nestled in red tissue paper. She picked one up to admire its perfect shape and color. It would be at its best in just a day or two.

Grams took the latest batch of cookies from the oven and crossed over to the kitchen island to stand next to Melissa. “Who sent you the pears?”

“I don’t know. Oh, here’s a note.”

I couldn’t find a partridge or a pear tree, so I hope this suffices. I wanted to let you know I’m happy for you that Save Our Salmon *is going so well. Dan says it will be a hit.*

Merry Christmas, John

Melissa’s back stiffened. She crumpled the note and picked up the package, heading toward the trash can.

“Oh no, you don’t.” Grams took the box from her hands and set it on the kitchen counter. “These will make a perfect dessert for Christmas Eve dinner. I know just what to make with them.” Then she took a pad of paper and pen and began planning the rest of the menu.

Melissa stood, staring at the box of pears. She still held the crumpled note in her hand. “How did he get my address? I never told him where I live.”

Grams glanced up from her menu planning and chuckled. “That’s easy. He could have asked Howard, or he could have gotten it at work. I’m sure it’s on your contract. Besides, don’t you tell me you can find anything on the Internet now?”

“Maybe, but it’s invasive,” Melissa grumbled.

“Or something else.” Grams smiled and returned to planning the menu.

Placing the card on the counter, she slowly smoothed it out and stared at it, arms tightly crossed against her chest. What was John up to? She wouldn't fall for whatever his game was. A couple of perfect pears wouldn't convince her John was sincere in his feelings. She left the card on the counter and stalked out.

Another delivery brought a small aquarium with two miniature turtles the next day.

Doves are a bit messy and don't make the best companions, but hopefully, these two turtles will give you someone to talk to when you're alone.

Merry Christmas, John

"He's got a good sense of humor," commented Grams.

"Humph." Melissa placed the aquarium on the hutch this time and tucked the card under the edge. She picked up the container of turtle food that accompanied the turtles and sprinkled some into the aquarium.

The two turtles paddled over to the edge to enjoy their treat.

She smiled when one looked as she tapped on the glass. The smile quickly disappeared when she reminded herself that it was a futile attempt on John's part to regain her favor. She still didn't trust him.

Day three was Christmas Eve. This time, the package contained three bottles of French wine.

Thought I'd take a little liberty and substitute wine for the hens.

Enjoy. John

"This will be perfect for dinner." Grams picked up one of the bottles to read the label. "Yes, the Bordeaux will go well with the roast for tonight." She arranged the three bottles on the hutch, next to the pears and the aquarium, displaying the note prominently.

Melissa stood, studying the collection of gifts, arms crossed, tapping her foot. “How long do you think this is going to last? You don’t think he’s going to send twelve gifts?”

“Why not?”

“But why?” The hairs on the nape of her neck bristled.

Grams continued seasoning the roast for dinner later. “I believe it’s called courting—an old-fashioned tradition, but an effective one.”

“Courting?” Melissa frowned at Grams. A jittering sensation occurred in her stomach, and she pressed a hand to quell it.

Grams chuckled. “Yes. Think Romeo and Juliet. Romeo stood under her balcony, serenading her. In Victorian times, a man might show his affection by writing letters or poems, singing romantic songs, or sending gifts.”

“Not going to work.” Melissa attacked a potato with the peeler.

“Careful. You want to leave enough of the potato to cook.”

Melissa slowed down, careful to remove only the peel, and chopped it into quarters. Putting them on to boil, she stomped out of the kitchen to tackle the dining room.

Grams’s light chuckle followed her.

She took out her frustration regarding John’s motives for the next hour by putting away her computer and monitors, removing the sketches, and hiding her usual clutter. Her mind cleared as she focused on preparing the room for the holiday feast. The table was soon covered in a bright-red tablecloth and Mom’s

Christmas-tree-design plates. An arrangement of greenery with two white candles occupied the center. The table was set for five. She stood there, staring at the gaily decorated table, happy to see Mom's cherished dishes shine again.

Grams came up behind her and wrapped her arms around her. Together, they silently shared the memory of last Christmas. With an extra squeeze, Grams released her and hurried back into the kitchen.

Melissa quickly wiped the tears from her cheeks while slowly surveying the rest of the area. In the past two days, she and Grams had bought and decorated a tree for the living room. The white lights created the perfect backdrop for the red and silver ornaments. Scattered amongst them were family favorites like the miniature snow globe she had chosen when she was ten. Every year, she and Mom would search for the perfect new ornament to add to the tree. They searched all year, not just at Christmas time. Many came from places they visited, such as Florence and even Hawaii. Each held a special memory.

The house smelled of evergreen and roast beef. With the roast in the oven and the table set, she and Grams dashed upstairs to change into their Christmas finery. Pausing momentarily in front of the mirror, she ran her hands down to smooth the gold miniskirt she paired with a black-and-gold-striped sweater. She pulled her dark hair back into a low ponytail festooned with a gold bow.

The doorbell rang, and Melissa hurried down the stairs. She opened the front door to greet Karen. Once Karen entered, they gave each other a warm hug. "I'm so happy you asked me for dinner tonight. I'd be home alone watching *It's a Wonderful Life* and eating a bologna sandwich while wishing I was eating my mom's awesome pork roast with mashed potatoes."

"You're so bad. Someday, you're going to have to learn to cook." Melissa hooked arms with Karen and led her into the living room.

Karen grimaced and shook her head. "No way. I'm going to marry a famous French chef, and he'll make me luscious meals every night, complete with champagne."

"Dream on. We don't have a pork roast tonight, but we have mashed potatoes, so you should survive."

Soon, the doorbell rang again, announcing the arrival of Jan and Derrick. The three came together in a loose hug, working around Jan's seven-month pregnant belly. Shedding her coat, Jan headed immediately for the cozy chair and ottoman near the fireplace. "I hope you don't mind, but they become overstuffed burritos in minutes unless I get my feet up."

"Burritos? That's a funny choice of words. My sister used to say hers looked like she had elephantiasis." Karen laughed.

Shifting her weight to find a comfortable position, Jan released a low moan. "I can't help it. I constantly crave Mexican food, so everything reminds me of something to eat."

"And she's starving all the time." Derrick groaned. "She sends me out for tacos in the middle of the night. I finally started buying a bag on my way home from the hospital, so I didn't have to go back out an hour later."

Grams returned, carrying a tray of appetizers. Setting it down, she leaned over to hug Jan. "Don't stand." Grams placed a gentle hand on Jan's shoulder.

"I can hug just as easily from here. How are you feeling, dear?"

"Like a Thanksgiving Day parade balloon. Huge and past my time."

"When are you due?" Grams inquired.

Jan smoothed her red jersey top over her expanding stomach, gently patting the baby inside. "Actually, I have seven weeks, three days, and eight hours to go. But who's counting? My last outing will be my baby shower in early January. Melissa and Karen, you're both invited and must come."

"We'll be there," they both replied.

Karen turned to Melissa. "We need to go shopping immediately."

"Do you know if you're having a boy or a girl yet?" asked Melissa.

"A girl." Jan gently stroked her stomach with a contented smile.

"Yay, that means lots of pink and ruffles. This will be fun. Girls' clothes are way cuter than sweatpants and T-shirts for little boys." Karen clapped her hands quietly and grinned at Jan.

"Wait a minute." Derrick raised his hands in a T-formation. "I plan to teach her to play basketball and other sports."

"Okay, we'll find her some pink sneakers." Melissa rolled her eyes.

"Don't get too carried away," pleaded Derrick.

"Maybe we'd better go a little lighter on the froufrou stuff." Melissa smiled at Derrick. "Remember, we weren't exactly girly girls in college. I seem to recall a lot of ripped jeans and plaid flannel."

"Speak for yourselves. I was always a princess,"

retorted Jan.

"Yeah, you and your fairy-tale princesses." Karen pantomimed a curtsy.

A three broke out in laughter.

"Now, we'd better feed Her Highness before she sends poor Derrick out for tacos again." Melissa laughed as she stood and reached out to help Jan get up from her chair.

For the next few hours, the group ate, talked, and laughed. Everyone complimented Grams on the perfect medium-rare roast beef.

Melissa said she had made the mashed potatoes and green beans, to which her friends expressed disbelief.

"I've only known you to order pizza or microwave something." Karen laughed. "In all the years we roomed together, I don't think we ever turned on the oven or stove. All our pots and pans were still brand new."

Her friends departed later that night with the promise they'd get together soon and see each other at Jan's baby shower bearing gifts.

"I don't need gifts," Jan whispered, hugging Melissa. "I'm just so happy to see my friend back."

Grams stood at the door with Melissa to watch her friends depart.

With a deep sigh, Melissa closed the door. "It was good to see Jan and Karen. It's been too long. I'm not letting that happen again." She caught Grams's not-too-subtle smile as they linked arms to return to the kitchen to clean up.

Chapter 16

Christmas morning brought sunshine and another delivery. When Melissa opened the door, no one was there. On the porch was a medium-sized box. She looked around for a delivery truck but didn't see one. She carried the box into the kitchen and set it gently on the counter.

"Another package. This is day four. That's four calling birds. I wonder what John sent you this time?" Grams paused after moving the pancakes on the griddle onto a plate and into the oven to keep warm.

"This is getting ridiculous," Melissa grumbled. Still muttering, she picked up a pair of scissors to slit the box open.

"But I see you're still going to open the box." Grams wiped her hands on her apron and joined her at the counter.

"I might as well see what he sent." She shrugged. The box was marked fragile, so she opened it slowly and carefully removed the item cushioned in bubble wrap.

Once unwrapped, she held up a small figurine of four birds sitting on a tree branch, their mouths open in song. She rotated the ceramic figurine around in her hand. The sun coming in through the window illuminated the deep-pink heads of the birds. "Grams, do you know what birds these are?" She held the figurine out to show her.

"Yes, they're purple finches. They're the prettiest of the finches."

Melissa continued to turn the figurine in her hands. "The art is so delicate. Do you recognize the artist?"

Taking the figurine, Grams gently inspected the piece. "No, I don't. It's hand-painted, not mass-produced. The signature on the bottom just has the initials *CR*, not a name. Such a lovely piece." She handed the figurine back to Melissa.

Setting down the finches, Melissa checked the box and fished out the card.

Today is four calling birds. I thought, as an artist, you'd appreciate the delicate hand-painting of this piece. I hope it fills a spot in your home with joy.

Merry Christmas, John

Melissa stood momentarily, tapping the card against the palm of her left hand. "Hmm, interesting. I like it." She set the birds on a shelf in the hutch alongside the box with one pear, the two turtles, and the two empty wine bottles. The third was still to be enjoyed. Melissa stood, studying the gifts. "I don't know why I'm keeping the empty bottles and the pear box. I'll throw them out later." She caught Grams's raised eyebrow. "Grams?"

"I didn't say anything."

"I know, but you're thinking something." She wagged her finger at Grams.

Grams just smiled and turned back to the oven to get the pancakes. "Breakfast is ready, so let's sit," she announced over her shoulder.

After a last glance at the gifts, Melissa removed plates from the cupboard and set the table.

The rest of the day passed quietly. They exchanged a few gifts and enjoyed leftovers from last night's feast. The conversation returned to Grams's plans for her tapestry and what to get for Jan's baby shower.

They spent the day after Christmas at the Garden and Glass Museum, admiring the vivid colors and elaborate structures of blown glass. The exhibit also included a display of Native American pottery and tapestries.

Over lunch in the greenhouse area, Melissa talked about the different tapestries on display. "Grams, why aren't any of your tapestries here?"

"The museum curator and I spoke during the planning of this exhibit, and we decided it should feature newer, up-and-coming artists instead of old has-beens like me."

Melissa paused and gestured with her fork. "You're hardly a has-been."

"I like to think I still have much to contribute, but I also know it's time to introduce new talent to the art world." Grams gestured with an open hand in the direction of the exhibit. "I was pleased he used several pieces by students from my classes."

They arrived home late in the afternoon to find another package at the front door. Melissa picked it up. A faint ringing sound came from the box as she walked. She set it on the counter in the kitchen and carefully opened the box. She paused once the box was open, her hands hovered over the tissue paper. "I'm a little nervous about this one. Today would be five gold rings."

Instead of rings, the box contained five golden handbells ranging in size from three to seven inches, each with a bright-red bow. The note read:

When I think of rings, I think of the ringing of bells. Enjoy these golden handbells. They remind me of the ones used by carolers at Christmastime. I hope they add music to your life,

John

Melissa picked up each in turn and gave it a shake to hear the delicate sounds. From the smallest to the largest, the tone deepened into rich vibrations that echoed throughout the kitchen. They reminded her of the bell ringers who stood outside the stores this time of year, seeking donations for many local charities. She placed the five bells on the hutch alongside the lone pear, two turtles, three wine bottles, and four finches. Stepping back, she studied the assorted gifts, one hand resting lightly over her heart. A warm sensation spread across her cheeks. She quickly shook herself and shoved her hand into her pocket. *What will tomorrow bring?*

On day six, Melissa and Grams returned from lunch at the market along the waterfront downtown to find a large box next to the door. The box was light for its size. Inside was a cozy goose-down throw in vivid blues and greens. The swirling design reminded her of Monet's water lilies. Removing the card, she read the words out loud.

"Goose eggs might not make it unbroken, so I chose goose down instead. This will keep you cozy on chilly winter evenings. Thinking of you warmly,

John"

When she looked up, she saw Grams smiling.

Melissa didn't say a word. She just took the throw to the living room and draped it over the back of her favorite chair. She stood stroking the soft throw, pondering the message implied by the gift. It spoke of comfort. She could envision cold nights bundled in its warmth in front of the fire.

That evening, she and Grams sat admiring the Christmas tree and flickering fire in the fireplace.

"I've been here seven days now, and my fingers are itching to return to my weaving. I think I'll leave the day after tomorrow."

Melissa shifted to face her. "Grams, I'm going to miss you. I could help you move your loom here, and you could stay longer."

Grams smiled and reached out to pat Melissa's hand. "I love that you like having me here, but I have other commitments at home. My classes will start again in just a few weeks, and I need to prepare for them."

Melissa started to protest.

Grams held up her hand. "Besides, it's time for you to reach out more to your friends and get back into life. I hope you will follow up on Karen's suggestion to get together to go shopping for Jan's baby gifts."

Melissa hesitated briefly. "I will…after you leave. As long as you're here, I want to spend my time with you. What would you like to do tomorrow?"

"I'm glad you asked." Grams gazed at the tree for a moment with a small smile. "I do have an idea. How about a nice walk around the lake tomorrow afternoon? I saw in the paper the park is decorated for the holidays with luminaries along the path and lights in the tree. It would be fun to see the lights in the late afternoon. We could get a bite to eat while there."

"Sure, it should be nice weather. Wait…exactly where are you suggesting we eat?"

With a mischievous smile, Grams shrugged. "Some little place near here."

"Grams, I'm not ready to see Howard. He's too connected to John. And what if John is there, too?"

"You'll have me with you." Grams reached over to pat Melissa's knee. "You need to reconnect with Howard. It's not fair to him to lose your friendship over this. And it's not good for you to lose a good friend."

Melissa mulled it over for a moment. *Grams has a point*. "All right, but if John's there, we're not eating, just stopping to wish Howard an early Happy New Year."

"Fair enough. I think tomorrow morning I'll bake him some cookies. Do you think he'd like chocolate chip or oatmeal and raisin best?"

The next day, around four in the afternoon, Melissa and Grams headed to the lake. The air was crisp, but plenty of people enjoyed being outside. Kids rode their new bikes or whizzed by on the rollerblades they found under the Christmas tree. A few runners were trying to jog off the extra cookies and other goodies consumed over the last few days. Small groups of moms pushed strollers while infants slept cuddled in fuzzy blankets.

"Come spring, Karen, Jan, and I will be strolling around the lake while Jan's baby happily explores her new world."

They walked arm in arm and marveled at the lights everywhere. The trees looked like stars had fallen from the sky, settling comfortably in the barren branches. Colorful elves, snowmen, and miniature Christmas trees were interspersed with the white luminaries. In the distance, a band played holiday songs at the bandstand.

A cluster of food trucks circled the area. The scent

of spicy tacos and barbequed pork competed with the aroma of hot dogs and popcorn from Howard's stand.

Nearing the snack stand, Melissa saw Howard surrounded by a cluster of kids, begging their moms for ice cream despite the chill.

Howard pretended to guess what flavor they wanted by making up outlandish combinations of mud, twigs, grass, and bugs.

The kids were all giggling so hard they could barely say what they really wanted.

When Howard spotted them, he grinned from ear to ear. He quickly filled the orders, wished the moms "Happy Holidays," and flipped his sign to *Closed*. After putting three hot dogs on the grill, he stepped out from behind the counter to hug them both.

"Girlie, you are a sight for sore eyes. I wasn't sure I'd ever see you again. I was ready to disown my foolish grandson to get you back. Elaine, I haven't seen you since…well, in a long time. Come sit, both of you. I've got the dogs going. My treat."

Howard added condiments to the three perfectly grilled hot dogs and put them in a small box to carry to the table.

Melissa noted the slight limp from his recent hip surgery was still evident. She jumped up to help him carry the hot dogs and bottles of water back to the table. "I see you have competition."

Howard glanced over at the various food trucks parked near the bandstand. "Yes, the organizers of the event invited several trucks to come. It's a good thing. The crowds are large enough that I couldn't feed everyone even if I tried. Plus, I shut down around five, and the music lasts until ten. They can have all the folks who come later."

Grams smiled at Howard when he sat. "I, for one, know your hot dogs surpass anything they're offering."

Howard grinned, passing around the hot dogs. "Here we go, my ladies. Three of the best hot dogs in Seattle with all the fixings and bottles of my finest water. How was your Christmas? What have the two of you been doing?"

Grams gave an overview of their activities. "But the most fun has been waiting for John's gifts to arrive each day."

"*John's* gifts? What do you mean?" Howard stared, wide-eyed.

His voice had a slight hitch.

"Didn't he tell you he's been sending Melissa a daily gift based on the 'Twelve Days of Christmas'? Today is day seven, so I'm curious what he'll think of for seven swans a-swimming. I'm surprised it hasn't arrived yet. They've been coming mid-afternoon for the most part."

"I hope he's not filling your yard with a bunch of birds," Howard exclaimed.

"No, no. They've all been clever adaptations of the song's theme." Grams quickly assured Howard. She gave him a quick accounting of the six gifts so far.

"Howard, you didn't have anything to do with this, did you?" Melissa narrowed her eyes. She was sure he had been behind the idea.

"No, this is the first I've heard about it." He shook his head.

When they finished eating, Melissa carried the trash to the bin. Heading back, she saw Grams and Howard leaning toward each other talking quietly.

"What are you two whispering about?"

Their quick attempt to straighten and start talking about the weather was suspicious.

"Nothing, dear. Should we head back home?"

Melissa hugged Howard. "I'll be back very soon."

"I'm taking that as a promise." He returned the hug, giving her an extra squeeze.

She and Grams headed toward home. Her thoughts lingered on the scene of the two of them huddled together. *What could they be conspiring about?*

****

That evening, Howard anxiously awaited John's visit. Howard greeted him with a hearty slap on the back when John walked into the room and immediately offered to pour him an Irish whiskey.

John took the drink and narrowed his eyes.

Howard posed at the fireplace like the lord of the manor, slowly sipping his whiskey while silently staring at John. "You'll never guess who visited me at the snack stand today."

John slumped deep into the overstuffed leather chair, staring into his drink in hand. He glanced up. "Okay, I'll bite. Who was it?"

"A lovely young lady named Melissa and her equally lovely grandmother, Elaine." Howard continued to sip his drink, slowly awaiting his grandson's reaction.

"Melissa? My…umm, well, your friend Melissa?" John lurched forward in his chair and nearly choked on his drink.

John's reaction didn't disappoint.

"Yes, my friend Melissa. She looks very well. Seems to be having a nice holiday with her grandmother," he added casually.

"So, she looks good. I mean, I'm glad. Did she mention anything special about her holidays? Any surprises?"

Howard laughed, shaking his head as he noticed John struggle to sip his drink without choking.

"You can stop beating around the bush. I heard from Elaine that you've been sending her daily gifts. I'm proud of you, boy. I said you needed to court her, and you really stepped up. 'Twelve Days of Christmas.' I love that idea. Couldn't have done better myself."

"How is she reacting? Does she seem to like them?" All pretense of muted interest disappeared. John set his drink aside and sat upright.

"Elaine said at first she was going to throw them away once she realized they came from you."

John groaned.

"But don't panic. Elaine stopped her. And it seems now she is starting to look forward to them."

Relief visibly washed over John. His gaze shifted heavenward, and he sat back, his shoulders slumped.

Howard toasted John silently with his glass. "Elaine brought me up-to-date with what you've sent so far. I like how you're using the theme but not taking it literally, like the two turtles instead of turtle doves and French wine for the three French hens. What else do you have planned?"

John paused for a moment. "I know what I'm sending tomorrow, but I'm still working on what to do for the others."

Howard took the chair opposite John and set his drink on the side table. "Okay, let's strategize. Let me think for a moment." After a brief pause, Howard began thinking out loud. "I think it's time to be bolder. Send some things that are a bit more romantic. Something uniquely Melissa."

John shook his head. "I think it's too soon. I don't want to scare her off."

Howard leaned forward and waved his hand in the air. "Pooh, every good courtship needs a dash of romance. Besides, you want her to know you're interested in more than just being friends. So, you need to show her. You have her attention, so you need to build momentum and get her thinking about you, not just the gifts."

John sat back, staring at the fire.

Howard blustered. "That's the point, right? You want to prove she means something special *to you*, and you want a real relationship." He studied John, trying to gauge his reaction to his ideas.

John finally hunched forward, resting his elbows on his knees. "I have an idea that might fit the bill."

"Great, let's hear it. I might be able to help."

John shook his head. "No thanks, Pops. I need to do this on my own. But I hear you about adding more romance. I can take it from here."

Howard shrugged off his disappointment about not having the chance to influence John's plan more closely. *The boy has done well so far*.

"Okay, how about a game of chess instead?"

For the next hour, Howard easily tromped John. John's mind was clearly not on the game.

After a final drink together, John left.

Howard gazed into the fire, savoring the last of his drink. He was convinced John's plan was exactly what was needed to get him and Melissa back together again.

Howard was already envisioning the beautiful great-grandbabies they would give him. Satisfied that his plot was working perfectly, he leaned back and enjoyed his whiskey.

Chapter 17

On day seven, as expected, another box arrived at Melissa's front door. This time, it was a pink pastry box tied with twine. Once opened, the box revealed seven delicate puff-pastry swans. A luscious vanilla cream filled the *pâte à choux* bodies. Graceful pastry S-shaped necks completed the effect of seven swans swimming on a bed of blue icing.

On day seven, I send you seven graceful swans to sweeten your day.

Happy Holidays, John

"I'm liking this John more and more each day." Grams peered into the box, admiring the delicate swans.

"Sure, that's fine for you. He didn't lie to you." Melissa's expression quickly changed from an amused smile to a frown.

"No, and he didn't really lie to you, either. He left out an important fact about himself and then attempted to correct it." Grams spoke gently.

Melissa set the box of pastries on the counter with a thud, jiggling the delicate swans. "Are you taking his side in this now?" She stood with her hands on her hips.

"I'm always on your side. I'm just pointing out he seems to be trying very hard to make amends." Grams continued in a calming voice. "Obviously, your relationship is special enough to him to make the effort to try and fix it."

"Maybe." Melissa's stomach did a quick flutter.

Grams softly touched Melissa's shoulder. "Talk to me. There's more here."

Melissa stared at the pastries, her hands in her pockets. Swallowing hard, she turned and leaned against the counter. "I…I thought we were becoming more than just friends. I convinced myself he felt the same way. Now, I feel foolish because I guess I was the only one feeling that way."

"How can you be sure he doesn't also want a deeper relationship?" Grams gently probed. "Right now, you're still too blinded by your hurt to see what he's trying to do with his gifts."

Melissa stared out the window briefly, then walked slowly to sit at the table. She buried her face in her hands.

Grams took the chair opposite her, gently pulling Melissa's hands away from her face and holding them tightly.

Tears pricked at the back of Melissa's eyes. "I don't want to be in a relationship where I feel I'm the only one being completely open and honest. I want what Mom and Dad had. They were true partners. They didn't have secrets. I want that kind of love."

Grams nodded, silently listening.

Melissa stared at her hands in Grams's for a moment. "I admired how he stepped in to care for Howard's stand, even though he had his own business to run, just because he loved him." She continued in a hushed voice. "I hoped he was helping me with the game because he was starting to have similar feelings for me. But people who care about each other are honest with each other."

Grams paused. She lowered Melissa's hands to the table, releasing them with a soft pat. "But you didn't tell him you were Rapunzel. Weren't you also hiding a part of yourself?"

"But that's different. I...I—" She stopped when Grams squeezed her hands. Melissa pulled back and lowered her hands to her lap. She forced herself to really think if she had been completely honest with John. She wrestled with the idea they both had held back pieces of themselves. "I planned to tell him but didn't get the chance."

"And why is that? What's stopping you from letting John and the world see you for all you are?"

"Because...I'm afraid." Melissa's words came out haltingly.

"Afraid? Talk to me, Melissa. This is deeper than feeling hurt because John didn't tell you about his connection to Brothers, isn't it?"

Melissa nodded. Putting her hands back on the table, she straightened her chair. For a moment, the only sound in the room was the soft patter of rain on the window. The gray sky and persistent drizzle separated them from the outside world, making the kitchen feel secluded. The aroma of the vegetable soup on the stove and fresh-baked biscuits warmed the air.

She took a deep breath and released it slowly. "When people learn who I am, that I'm the daughter and granddaughter of Celeste and Elaine Whitestar, they expect I've also accomplished big things. I can see the disappointment when they discover I don't have works of art hanging in museums worldwide. That I do graphic design for computer games, instead."

Grams looked away briefly.

Melissa could see the tears glistening when Grams looked back.

"Melissa, I am so sorry you felt being Celeste's daughter or my granddaughter was a burden you had to endure."

Grams quickly wiped away the few tears that had fallen.

"You are enough just being you. You will always be more than enough in my eyes."

Melissa stared at the ceiling for a moment. Emotions roiled inside her. Times her art was ridiculed or dismissed flashed like lightning bolts in her brain. Each illuminating scene after scene, accompanied by the roaring thunder of criticism from her first professor, Mad Maddie, and wannabe art critiques who emerged from the crowd to unfavorably compare her work to Mom's after the funeral. Taking another deep breath, she thrust the storm away until it *rumbled* in the background, still present but distant.

Shifting her glance back to Grams, she smiled tentatively. "Grams, I am so proud of what you and Mom have done and what you continue to do. I don't regret being your granddaughter. I love you and love it when people talk about the joy your work brings them." She paused briefly, staring at her hands. "I've come to see my art does have value. *Save Our Salmon* is allowing me to use my art to inspire people and help them see the world in a new way, just like you do. This is my way to continue the family legacy."

"Yes, I'm glad you can see you are carrying on the family legacy. The medium isn't what matters. I'm delighted *Save Our Salmon* is allowing you to realize your creativity can do something bigger than the art itself."

Melissa let Grams's words soak in, shoving the storm farther away. Sighing, she released the last of the tension in her shoulders and sat back. "I do know that now. I do believe *SOS* is bigger than just a game."

Grams nodded and then peered intently at Melissa. "How does all this connect to John?"

She straightened her back and shook her head slightly. "It shouldn't, but I panicked. At the moment, all I could think was I had made a terrible mistake in sharing my heart, and I needed to go hide again to protect my heart and myself."

"So, you came home and erected more walls. You closed yourself off even more." Grams spoke softly. "Honey, it's time for those walls to come down. They aren't protecting you. They keep you from the joys of life, from your friends, and from discovering your full potential as an artist. What you're doing with your gift is brilliant. The world needs to know who you are."

Melissa raised her head, focusing on Grams. The storm had passed. The time had come to tear down the walls and let go of the need to hide behind an alias. Letting go of Rapunzel was still scary, but it was what she needed to do. "I know you're right. I've been too scared, but it's time to make changes and be proud of who I am."

Grams reached across the table. She squeezed Melissa's hands. "Remember, you aren't alone. And you've already started. You have a team of creative people helping you bring your game to life. They need to know the real you, not the storybook character you invented. Your friends Karen and Jan already love you. They know the whole you and love you for it. Howard has seen all the puzzle pieces of your life and is still your good friend. Knowing more about you won't force people away. It will bring them closer." Grams squeezed her hands again and looked Melissa in the eye. "Now, do you still care for John?"

Melissa hesitated. She blinked several times. "I…I think I do."

"Then you're going to have to find a way to be strong and forgive him. Take a risk and keep sharing your inner self. Trust yourself. Trust in your value and trust your heart. Be who you are. You will always be enough." Grams stood and filled the teapot with water. "Now, let's enjoy a cup of tea and those delightful pastry swans."

Melissa continued to sit, staring out the window. *Can I trust my heart? Can I trust John again? I have to try. It's time.*

****

Melissa sat on the bed the following day while Grams packed her small suitcase. "Do you have to go?"

"Yes, my dear. I need to get back to my work. But we still have some time. I'm not going until I see what John sends you today."

"Today's day eight. That's eight maids-a-milking. I can't imagine what it could be. Eight cartons of milk?" Melissa shook her head with a laugh.

Grams wagged her finger. "He's been more imaginative than that so far, so it should be interesting. In the meantime, let's head to the kitchen. You have some nice leftovers that will make a delicious lunch."

The sound of chopping and Christmas carols filled the air. Both women sang along with enthusiasm, if not perfect pitch.

"Good thing we're artists, not singers. No one would come to our concerts." Grams chuckled.

When the doorbell rang, Melissa wiped her hands on the kitchen towel and hurried to answer it. She returned with a small square white box tied with a red ribbon. Removing the card, she read the message out loud.

"When I think of maids-a-milking, I think of milk chocolate. As a kid, I believed brown cows gave us chocolate milk. Now I know the best chocolate comes from the Chocolate Emporium in downtown Seattle. I hope you enjoy them.

Happy Holidays, John"

Inside the box were eight pieces of milk chocolate in the shape of milk buckets. Melissa laughed and picked one up to hand to Grams. "You're right. He is much more imaginative than I expected. He must have had these specially made. I've never seen them before, and I've been to the shop many times."

After agreeing to enjoy the chocolates after lunch, she placed them with the other treats and gifts on the hutch. The collection now took up most of the space. Both yesterday's swans and today's chocolate told her John had been listening during their times together. She had mentioned her addiction to chocolate at least once. She couldn't remember the context but often joked about needing a chocolate fix occasionally, and her favorites were from the Chocolate Emporium. She was beginning to see he had paid more attention than she had given him credit for. *Could there be something more personal in his feelings? Grams may be right. He is trying hard to win me back and not for the game.*

After a warm bowl of stew and more of Grams's

delicious corn muffins, Melissa carried Grams's suitcase to her car.

Grams wrapped Melissa in her arms for a farewell hug. "I loved this time we had together. Together, we made this Christmas special again."

Melissa hugged her back, not wanting the hug to end. "I promise to come for another weekend with you soon."

Grams placed both hands on her shoulders, peering deep into Melissa's eyes. "In the meantime, I hope you follow up on Karen's and Jan's requests to stay in touch and get together with them again."

Melissa nodded solemnly. "I promise I will. I told Karen I'd call her to pick a time to shop for Jan's baby shower."

Grams carefully backed out of the driveway, blowing kisses out the window.

Melissa stood, waving until Grams merged with traffic and disappeared from sight. Back in the house, Melissa put her computer back on the dining room table, thinking out loud about what to do next. "I promised Dan I wouldn't work on the game over the holiday break, so I need another project."

After a few minutes, an idea popped into her head. Grams said she needed to share herself, her real self, with others. The perfect start would be to use her talents to create a series of pictures to decorate Jan's baby girl's nursery. Jan loved fairy tales, especially the classic princesses. Even as an adult, she delighted in all the movie versions of *Sleeping Beauty*, *Cinderella*, and *The Little Mermaid*. Whenever a new movie came out, she'd drag Karen and her to see it the first weekend. They'd sit in a dark theater surrounded by giggling eight-year-old girls, munching popcorn, mesmerized by the animation and music. A series of princess pictures would be the ideal way to give Jan something personal.

She spun her magic on the computer screen for the next several hours. She opted for the classic Cinderella and Snow White. They were Jan's favorites. She added Rapunzel as the third in the series for a touch of personal humor. She wanted to give Jan's daughter the sense that princesses could be both heroic and adventurous. She depicted each princess in a setting that highlighted her bravery and ingenuity.

Cinderella, who bore a slight resemblance to Jan, stood behind a counter laden with vegetables and spices. In the background was a sign that read *Cinderella's Catering*. The mice carried in fresh vegetables and fruit for her to use while two bluebirds held a recipe up for her to read.

Snow White, with Karen's signature dark curls, sat behind a desk piled high with ledgers while the seven dwarfs rolled out maps of the mines. On the wall were charts showing the business's rapid growth.

Even Rapunzel got an upgrade, swinging out of her tower window on a braided rope made of her dark locks. Her new, shorter haircut flew around her face. She clenched a paintbrush in her teeth and a sketchbook under one arm. Melissa sat back and smiled. *Still, lots of details to fill in, but it's a great start.*

She sat back with a satisfied sigh. These pictures would come from her as Melissa, not Rapunzel. *My first step in shedding the safety of Rapunzel. The next step will be harder, but I'm determined I'm not turning back now.*

Chapter 18

The next day, Melissa woke to the usual late December sky of gray clouds threatening rain. She lit a fire in the fireplace and sat to continue working on the pictures for Jan's baby gift. Grams had reminded her she had plenty of leftovers to eat when she called last night to say she was safely home, so she had no need to venture out. Grams had spent her last two days stocking her freezer with enough casseroles, stews, and soups to last half a lifetime.

About mid-morning, her doorbell rang.

A young man in a delivery uniform held out a white envelope with her name and wished her an early "Happy New Year" before he dashed back to his van.

Melissa stood, tapping the envelope against her chin. *Nine ladies dancing?*

The envelope contained two orchestra-level tickets to George Balanchine's *The Nutcracker*. It also had two passes to the Nutcracker Suite for refreshments, pre-ballet and during intermission. The note read:

I never counted them, but I'm confident the ballet will have at least nine ladies dancing. I hope you can call a friend and enjoy New Year's Eve at the ballet.

John

She clutched the tickets to her chest and smiled. She loved ballet, especially the *Nutcracker*. For years, while growing up, Mom made it a mother-and-daughter holiday tradition. They would wear their fanciest red and green dresses and go to a matinee performance.

Dad would meet them afterward for a special high tea at one of the downtown hotels. Later, they would drive home through the streets past houses glittering with Christmas lights, continuing the illusion of a fantasy land.

Melissa always fell asleep dreaming of sugarplums and graceful ballerinas.

After a brief hesitation, she pulled out her cell phone. When Karen answered, she got right to the point. "How would you like to come with me tomorrow night to a performance of the *Nutcracker*?"

"Are you serious? Yes, yes. I love that ballet and haven't seen it in ages."

Melissa laughed at Karen's excitement. She could envision her jumping up and down. Melissa couldn't help her excitement bubbling over in her tone of voice. "Same here. I hear they have completely redone the staging and have created a fantasyland."

"How did you get such fabulous tickets?"

"It's a long story. I'll tell you tomorrow night. Just come here by five, and we'll go together. Plan to stay overnight to watch the countdown at midnight and talk all night like we used to."

"I'll bring the bubbly and my pajamas."

"See you then."

Did John somehow know the ballet held a special memory for me, or did he assume that, like most women, I'd welcome the idea of a night out at a glittering gala event? She propped the tickets within view before turning back to her computer screen.

The next day, sunshine peeked through the few

wisps of white dotting the sky. Melissa planned to go for a run and visit Howard later. In the meantime, she went back to work on her princess pictures. She envisioned Jan's reaction when she unwrapped them at the upcoming shower. As Melissa now expected, the doorbell rang mid-morning.

This time, the delivery person held a large flat box about four feet by three feet.

Taking it, she realized the box wasn't heavy, just bulky. She placed it carefully on the kitchen counter and peeled back the brown paper wrapping. What appeared was the ballroom scene from the recent version of *Den of Dragons*. The intricate drawing showed several characters waltzing across the stone floor. The ladies' gowns swirled in a rainbow of colors. The gentlemen were all dressed in their finest attire. Some wore colorful military uniforms complete with sashes and medals. Others wore classic gray and black morning suits with cummerbunds coordinated with their dance partners. In its elegant oak frame, the result resembled a piece in a museum or art exhibit. Intrigued, Melissa read the card.

When I thought of ten lords-a-leaping, I remembered this scene you created a few months ago. You perfectly captured the elegance of the gala and the feel of romance in the air. I could almost hear the music and see the couples waltz across the screen. Art of this quality and beauty deserves to be shown in a way that honors the artist's talent. I hope you hang this with pride so others can see the magnificent worlds you create.

With admiration, John

She stepped back to take in the whole image. The

pleasant flip-flop feeling in her stomach had returned. She once told John that Mom's and Grams's works hung in museums. Melissa picked up the artwork gingerly and carried it into the dining room. She set it against the wall and stood back, one finger tapping her chin. She did a slow circle, studying all the walls in the dining room. With a decisive nod, she moved the piece to the wall opposite her computer and left to get a hammer and nail. Once hung, she gently stroked the wooden frame while she straightened the picture. Sitting back at her computer, she sighed with delight.

Despite her best intentions, the day flew by, and now she had to prepare for her evening out. She made a promise to herself to see Howard tomorrow.

The doorbell rang promptly at five. Karen waltzed in, clearly already in the party mood.

She handed Melissa a bottle of champagne. "For later," she declared. But first, I'm dressed to impress and anxious to get our evening started." She twirled, slipping off her coat to reveal the quintessential little black dress, rhinestone chandelier earrings, and silver heels.

Melissa stood back to take in the whole image. "Can you actually walk in those heels? They have to be at least three inches high."

"I'm not planning on going very far. I mostly plan on posing while we sip champagne and nibble canapes with the upper crust in the Nutcracker Suite. Then I'm sitting for the ballet." Karen struck a pose, one hand on her hip. She strutted her stuff across the living room like she was on a runway in Paris, New York, or Milan. She even adopted the classic model attitude of a pouty face and blank stare.

"Well, two can play at this game." Melissa sauntered down the imaginary catwalk, swinging her hips to show off her sleeveless red cocktail dress with a hint of a black lace underskirt peeking out well above her knees and matching red heels.

Karen clapped as Melissa vamped her way across the room. "We will steal the show. People will be like 'Ballet, what ballet?' But did you see those two fabulous creatures during intermission?"

Laughing, Melissa swung Karen toward the kitchen, placing her hands on Karen's shoulders to guide her. "Come into the kitchen. I didn't want us drinking champagne on an empty stomach, so I prepared some sandwiches to tide us over until the canapés."

Sipping tea and munching on sandwiches, the two shared stories about how they spent Christmas Day. Karen had pictures of her baby nephew on her phone, which her mother had sent from Baltimore. "I kind of wish I was with them. I'd love to be cuddling this cutie. But I'm also glad I'm here with you."

Melissa told Karen about the excursions to the art galleries with Grams. "I loved having Grams here, but I'm also happy to spend New Year's Eve with you. We haven't had a real late night, just talking and eating since I moved out."

The ballet was everything she remembered from childhood. The dancing was exquisite, and the new set design was a fantasy land. They spent intermission hobnobbing with Seattle's rich and famous in the Nutcracker Suite. Their ribs would ache tomorrow from poking each other so many times to point out someone famous or an incredible dress or jewels.

Back home, they quickly changed into comfortable pajamas and slippers and curled up on the couch in front of the fireplace. The TV was on mute so they could see the fireworks from the Space Needle when they began at midnight.

Karen moaned and rubbed her aching feet. "Who knew glamour came at the cost of such pain? These shoes are going back into my closet to be admired like art but not worn again any time soon."

Melissa stretched out her feet and wiggled her toes to loosen the cramps. "I agree, but playing Cinderella at the ball for the evening was fun. Speaking of Cinderella, let me show you what I'm making for Jan's baby." She picked up her tablet off the coffee table, opened it to the graphics she created with the fairy-tale princesses, and handed it to Karen.

Karen slowly flipped through each of the pictures in silence.

Melissa watched her, twisting a strand of her long dark hair and biting her lip. "You're killing me. Say something."

"I can't. These are so beautiful," whispered Karen.

"They're not finished yet. I still have more to add, but you can see my direction with these."

"Absolutely, I do." Karen continued to switch back and forth between the three screens. "I love all the little details, like the bluebirds holding the recipe. And you made each princess look like one of us. Jan is going to *love* these."

Melissa slumped back against the arm of the couch and exhaled. "I'm going to print them out and put them in pretty pink frames."

"You need to sign these. I've always known you're

talented, but these are beyond anything I've seen of yours."

Melissa let go of the strand of hair she had been twisting, smoothing it back in place. "They're computer graphics, but I'm learning to be proud of my talent."

"You should be. These are *adorable*. But even more than that, they tell a powerful story about female potential. The idea of Jan hanging these in her little girl's room to inspire her to dream big and make those dreams come true is amazing. You took the concept of the fairy-tale princesses and made them unique with your innovations."

"You really like them?"

"It's beyond *like*. I covet them. I want my own set, but I know these are one of a kind you created just for Jan's baby. I'm jealous of a little girl who isn't even here yet."

Karen continued to flip through the images, stopping at the one inspired by *Cinderella*. She laughed as she held it up for Melissa to see. "I remember Jan dragged us to a theater filled with moms and their little girls whenever a musical version came out. I was glad it was dark so they couldn't see we didn't have a child with us. And this Rapunzel is you, isn't it? We used to call you that in college. I assumed that is how you choose it as your alias for your art."

"Yes, it's kind of my coming-out piece. Grams talked to me while here about opening myself up and sharing who I am with others. So, I'm starting with these. I intend to put my own name on these, not Rapunzel."

Karen exuberantly high-fived Melissa. "Yay. It's about time you took full credit for your work. I know you decided to use an alias after that disaster with 'she who shall not be named' at your first job. It made sense then. I understood how hurt you were by her comments. But I never really understood why you continued to hide."

Melissa fidgeted with her champagne glass, stalling. She searched for the words to help Karen understand. "It's hard to explain. Well…not hard so much as embarrassing." She took a sip. "I was afraid of what people would expect if they knew who my mom and grandmother were. Mad Maddie wasn't the first person to make the comparison and find me lacking. That honor belongs to my first art teacher in college."

Karen nodded. "You told me about him."

"Then there were a few nasty references to my art in comparison to Mom's in some of the articles printed after Mom and Dad's funeral."

Karen leaned forward to touch Melissa's hand. "Those people were despicable. But, Melissa, you're incredibly talented. I hope you know I think you're as talented as your mom and grandmother. And you know I love their work."

She smiled at Karen's admittedly biased loyalty. "Thanks, it means a lot. I believe it now, too. I'm also planning on telling the team at Brothers at Play my real name. I will ask them to call me Melissa, instead of Rapunzel."

Karen picked up the champagne bottle and poured more into their glasses. "Here's to the release of Rapunzel from her tower. Goodbye, Rapunzel, you served your purpose, but now it's time to go. And hello to Melissa. Welcome to the world. We've been waiting." She clinked glasses and sipped. "Okay, now it's story time. Why do I think this somehow ties to tonight's ballet tickets?" Karen settled back, her arms wrapped around her knees.

Melissa straightened. After taking another sip of her champagne, she began her story. "All right. Well, the tickets are from John."

Karen jolted upright. "John? You mean *the* John you told me about who was running Howard's snack stand while he recovers from his hip surgery? The one who turned out to be the co-owner of Brothers and did not tell you? *That* John?"

Melissa nodded slowly. "Yes, *that* John."

Karen leaned forward and set her champagne glass aside. "Okay. So, how does that ancient melodrama connect to two tickets to the ballet?"

Melissa also set her champagne glass on the coffee table and took a deep breath. "Ten days ago, John started sending me daily gifts. He has been following the theme of 'The Twelve Days of Christmas.' "

Karen twisted around, scanning the room. "What did he send you? Do you have turtle doves, swans, and geese in your backyard?"

She laughed at Karen, looking around as if a stray goose would waddle in. "No, he was far more creative. Come into the kitchen, and I'll show you."

Once in the kitchen, Melissa pointed to the array of items on the hutch. "First was a box of pears for a partridge in a pear tree. Grams used some in the dessert she made for Christmas Eve. Day two was these two little turtles. He said turtle doves were messy, so he decided on the turtles. On day three, I got three bottles of French wine, instead of French hens. We drank two of them at dinner on Christmas Eve."

Karen picked up the remaining bottle of wine. "Hmm, it was a nice wine." She set it back. "You never said anything then. I just assumed you had bought the pears and wine."

Melissa shuffled her feet and stared at the floor for a moment. "I know. I wasn't so sure I was happy about the gifts."

Karen cocked her head to one side. "And now?"

"I'm thinking."

Karen picked up the figurine with four singing finches. "I assume this is day four."

"Right, day five was these five handbells—bells ringing, get it?"

Karen picked up the bells one at a time to listen to each sound. "Yeah, brilliant. I like this. Keep going."

Melissa gestured toward the living room. "Day six was the cozy goose-down throw you've been curled up under on the couch. Day seven was seven cream puff swans. I saved the last two for us to eat tonight. Day eight was eight chocolate milk buckets. I saved two of those, too. Day nine was the tickets to the ballet for nine ladies dancing."

Karen glanced around the kitchen. "Okay, today was day ten. Where's today's gift?"

"It's in the dining room. Ten lords-a-leaping reminded him of a scene I created for *Den of Dragons*, so he enlarged it and had it framed."

Karen followed Melissa to the dining room and stared. "Wow, it's amazing. This is the perfect gift." She stood there, studying the artwork for a moment, then turned to Melissa with a serious expression. "Okay, time for the truth. You said, at first, you weren't sure how you felt about the gifts."

Melissa fidgeted, twisting the sash on her robe, and stared at the floor. "I still felt betrayed. And when Grams said the gifts were his way of courting me, I was upset. I didn't want to be courted."

Karen frowned. "Melissa, it's been months. Maybe it's time to let go of the hurt and see what he's trying to do with these gifts."

Melissa gently ran a finger along the framing. "I know. This one touched me. I think I might be ready to come out of my tower and talk to him again. Not right now, but soon."

Karen reached over to hug her. "You've had so much to deal with in the past year. But I admire your strength. You'll find the right ending to your story. Now, let's finish the bottle of bubbly, and I could use more of those sandwiches we had earlier. I'm hungry. Plus, you said something about cream puffs and chocolate."

The fireworks over the Space Needle signaled the start of a new year. Melissa relaxed as she and Karen drank the rest of the champagne, nibbled on the last goodies, and discussed plans for the coming year.

Later in bed, Melissa lay staring at the ceiling. Today was a new year and an opportunity to start anew. *I told Karen I would tell the team at Brothers I'm Melissa. It's time to live my own life. How will they react? Will they understand why I've hidden for so long? Is this how John felt when he knew he had to tell me the truth about himself?*

****

Karen and Melissa slowly emerged from their bedrooms, wrapped in warm robes and fuzzy slippers to greet the New Year. They sat at the kitchen table to drink coffee and eat some of Grams's apple muffins warmed in the microwave.

"What time do your daily gifts arrive?" asked Karen.

"Usually mid-morning,"

"Great, I'm staying until today's gift arrives. I'm dying to see what he comes up with for eleven pipers-piping."

"Me, too. I have no idea what he'll do. Eleven of anything is a bit much."

At mid-morning, the doorbell rang.

Both Melissa and Karen rushed to answer it. The rectangular package on the front porch was slightly larger than a shoe box. Taking the box to the kitchen to open, she and Karen tried to guess what was inside.

Curiosity won out, and Melissa hurriedly slit open the tape holding the box closed. Tucked into a bed of tissue was an old book. The cover showed signs of much use over the years, but it was still in excellent condition. It was obviously well-loved and treasured for several generations. The embossed leather cover revealed the title in faded gold letters—*Brothers Grimm and Other Stories*. Melissa gingerly lifted the book out of the box and laid it on the counter. Then, she opened the envelope and read the message out loud.

"Eleven pipers piping was a challenge. I decided not to send you the flute section of the Seattle Symphony, so I searched for some other way to think about pipers. Then I remembered the tale about the Pied Piper. You'll find an original version of the tale inside. I hope this story, and the many others in this book, sparks your imagination and feeds your creativity.

Sincerely, John"

She stood there, hugging the book to her chest. “How could he have known Dad read me fairy tales at bedtime when I was little?”

Karen laughed. “Not to burst your bubble, many parents did the same thing. But seriously, I think the connection between the two of you is greater than you’ve admitted. All his gifts have been the perfect blend of sentimentality and humor that appeals to you.”

Melissa set the book back on the counter, gently rubbing her finger over the embossed lettering on the cover. “True, it’s getting harder and harder to convince myself to ignore him.”

Karen shook her finger at Melissa. “I think that’s the point. One more day, and then I think it will be your move. What are you going to do?”

“I think we need to talk,” she whispered, her gaze focused on the note.

Karen grinned. “Good.”

Melissa decided to visit Howard once Karen went home. She hoped he had opened his stand today. The weather app on her phone said the temperature was chilly, so she zipped her jacket and tugged a knit hat down over her ears. A light jog kept her warm. She could see Howard behind the counter at the stand, bundled against the cold. No customers were in sight.

“I wasn’t sure you’d be here today. It’s cold out here,” she called out as she neared.

“Hey, my favorite customer. I was just thinking about shutting down. I don’t think I’ll have too many customers today. Between nursing hangovers from a night of merriment and the chilly weather, people will stay home where they’re warm and cozy. Why aren’t you doing the same?”

"I don't have a hangover. I wanted to wish you Happy New Year, if you were here."

"What do you say I lock up here and treat you to a hot cappuccino at the coffee shop nearby?"

Melissa dropped into an exaggerated curtsy. "I say, lead on, fair sir."

The two chatted while Howard closed, and they strolled to the coffee shop on the corner.

Melissa warmed her hands on the hot cup and lowered her head to study Howard over the steam. "Has John talked to you about the gifts he's been sending?"

Howard shook his head. "I promise, I've had nothing to do with it. Why? Is there something wrong with them?"

She stirred her coffee for a moment and then leaned back, peering at Howard over the rim of her cup. "No. They've been very nice, and the last few have had special meaning."

"So?" Howard's one eyebrow shot up.

"So, I wondered if he had gotten any of his ideas from you. He seems to know more about what I like than I thought." She leaned forward, resting her elbows on the table, and slowly sipped her coffee. She suspected Howard might have had a hand in this. *If not, could it mean John was sincere in his attempts to apologize? That he really did care?*

Howard sat back with a smug smile. "I did talk to him about the gifts after you and your grandmother visited me, but he was mum about his plans. I was going to make a few suggestions. You know, to help him out, but he said he was determined to do this on his own."

Melissa sat silently, absorbing Howard's words.

"Thanks, Howard. He's done a good job on his own."

"What day is he on now?"

Melissa smiled. "Tomorrow is day twelve."

"And then what?"

Melissa paused. "The next move is mine."

Howard cocked one eyebrow and sat silently.

She stared out the window briefly, watching the falling snow. Then she continued, mostly to herself, "I haven't decided exactly how, but we need to talk…soon."

Melissa and Howard said goodbye after consuming their hot drinks and promised to see each other again soon at the stand. She hurried home, hands in her jacket pocket to stay warm. She planned to finish the graphics for Jan today because they would be back to work on her game tomorrow. Then, she needed to decide about John.

Chapter 19

Early the following day, Melissa sat at her computer with her fingers wrapped around a hot cup of coffee. She began checking emails for any updates and announcements from Dan. She was pleased to see a meeting invite for later that morning.

The team meeting began promptly at eleven. They spent the first several minutes regaling each other with tales of holiday adventures and funny stories. Everyone had spent lots of time with friends and family during the two-week break. The fact that many had spent time outdoors skiing and snowmobiling was evident from their sunburned faces.

"Rapunzel, how about you?"

"My grandmother came to spend the holiday with me. We went to art exhibits and did a lot of baking and cooking together. It was a quiet but nice time."

"Okay, we should get down to business," Dan announced.

"Dan, if you don't mind, I'd like to share something with the team before discussing the game."

Dan nodded.

"When I heard the A-team was studying some of Elaine Whitestar's tapestries as inspiration for the backgrounds, I was thrilled. Your choice was far more appropriate than you could've imagined. I got copies of her sketches and photos for her latest work and have her permission to share them. I'll put them on the screen now while I explain the meaning behind her design." She clicked slowly through the scanned images and told them about Grams's vision for this tapestry. "I shared with you earlier that the Lummis are called the Salmon People and take their responsibility for the earth very seriously. They believe this is their role in life, and Elaine wants her art to inspire people to see and appreciate the beauty of nature and feel the need to protect it. I told you when we started this project my inspiration for *Save Our Salmon* came from hearing about the present-day danger to the salmon from the proposed dock for the oil company in Bellingham. What I didn't share was why I was at the tribal council in the first place."

At this point, Melissa stopped her screen share and came back on the screen. She wanted to see their faces and for them to see hers when she told them the rest. "I haven't been completely open about my connection to the Lummi Nation or who I am behind the alias of Rapunzel. I've decided to stop hiding and let you know the real me." She took a deep breath. "Elaine Whitestar is my grandmother. Celeste Whitestar was my mother. Through their blood, I am also a member of the Lummi Nation. My dad was Michael Anderson, so my legal name is Melissa Anderson."

The group stared in silence.

"First, this is so totally awesome," Arabella spoke. "They are *only* two of the most incredible artists of modern times. That explains why your designs blow my mind. You certainly got your share of the family talent."

Davey raised his hand. "You said Michael

Anderson? Does that mean your dad was *Dr*. Michael Anderson?"

Melissa nodded.

"You sure you don't understand computer programming more than you say? He was a freaking genius. I met him in grad school and didn't wash my right hand for days after shaking hands. I was convinced some of his programming magic would rub off."

The comments spilled forth. Everyone expressed their delight in knowing who she was.

"You're like local royalty," gushed Arabella.

She looked around the group, waiting for the one question she expected was on everyone's mind.

"Why have you been hiding behind Rapunzel?"

"That's not a fair question. I'm sure she had her reasons," Dan quickly interjected.

She waved a hand to stop him. "It's a fair question, and I will answer it. To be brutally honest, I was afraid."

Melissa noted everyone's perplexed expressions. As she related the challenges of growing up in the shadow of two famous artists, she watched their expressions change to understanding. "My college roommates used to call me Rapunzel because I was happy being alone in my dorm room doing graphics. Solitude became a habit. But it's time to change. You have shown me the strength and joy that comes from being a part of a team. I feel like you've accepted me as me, so I want to be real and truthful with you, too."

"I think I can honestly speak for all of us when I say we love working with you," Arabella spoke up again. "You're the queen of graphics in my eyes. Your creativity and ability to make scenes come to life is what every other graphic artist dreams of doing. I'm honored you've chosen us to be your teammates. I know Dan picked us, but you've been our leader since day one."

The whole team exploded into applause, several standing and cheering.

Melissa smiled, *really smiled,* at her new friends. "I have a request. I would like this to be our last online meeting."

The group gasped.

"As of tomorrow, I'd like to come into the office and work with you face-to-face." She spoke quickly before they could object. "I'll still do work from home, but I would like our meetings to be in person. All of us. Can we do that, Dan?"

Dan grinned and nodded. "Yes. Tomorrow, one o'clock, conference room."

"Pizza for all of us tomorrow," yelled one of the programmers. When Dan gave him a questioning look, he countered. "If Melissa is coming into the office for the first time, then we have to celebrate. I say pizza. By the way, I can call you Melissa, can't I? Or do you still want to be Rapunzel?"

"Rapunzel is gone. I'm Melissa." A wave of relief rushed through her body, and she sat back with a sigh.

****

Since John's gifts usually showed up mid-morning, Melissa was surprised when she glanced up from her computer around three and realized nothing had come so far. Determined not to think about it, she returned to work on the game's graphics.

When her doorbell rang about thirty minutes later,

she opened the door to find a young man dressed in a band uniform holding out an envelope.

He made a crisp turn on his heel and marched down the steps. Then he pulled out a whistle and blew it.

From her driveway marched a parade of drummers dressed in sharp red and gold uniforms. They lined up in front of her, beating their drums in a steady rhythm.

She found herself silently counting—twelve drummers drumming.

They all stopped at the sound of another sharp whistle, arms raised and drumsticks poised above their drums. "Three, two, one." The new piece began, and the drummers marched in perfect synchronization, forming merging lines that kept dissolving and re-forming into new patterns.

The melody was familiar, and she struggled to find the words behind the strong percussion. Slowly, the lyrics came to mind. They were playing "Call Me Maybe" by Carly Rae Jepsen. Curious, she opened the envelope and took out the note. It simply read:

Melissa, here is my phone number. I hope you'll "Call Me Maybe," so we can talk.

Sincerely, John

She smiled at the significance of the song and John's request. The ball was most definitely in her court now.

A small crowd gathered on the sidewalk in front of her house. She noticed the people driving by had slowed and lowered their windows to listen.

As the band finished, the crowd applauded, and several cars honked their delight at the show.

The drummers all bowed, and the leader saluted

Melissa. He blew his whistle one more time. They all marched back to the vans parked in her driveway.

Approaching the vans, she debated whether she should tip the band.

The band director accompanying the young players noticed her expression and quickly reassured her nothing was needed. “Don’t worry. They have been well compensated for this performance. The person who requested it made a very generous donation to the school’s music program and arranged for a pizza party for all at one of the parents’ houses afterward. Besides, they had a blast doing this.”

One of the adults accompanying the drummers approached Melissa smiling, one hand over her heart. “Whoever he is, he is clearly over the moon in love to arrange this. I envy you. I’m lucky if my husband remembers to buy me flowers on Valentine’s Day.”

The song’s refrain echoed through her head even after the drumline left. She found herself humming the tune over and over and thinking about what the woman had said. *Over the moon in love. Could it be true? If so, how do I feel? Am I ready to admit I’ve fallen in love with him?*

Chapter 20

The following day, Melissa stood in front of her closet, pondering what to wear for her first in-person team meeting. She wanted to look nice but not overly dressed up. She had noticed in their online meetings, almost everyone on the team wore jeans and very casual tops, ranging from button-down shirts to ragged T-shirts to colorful prints.

Arabella tended toward retro sixties with tie-dye and paisley. Anna Lee wore ruffled blouses and her hair in a jaunty ponytail with colored ribbons. Sabrina had a more sophisticated appearance. She dressed primarily in black, punctuated by scarves in bold autumn colors like burnt orange, forest green, and goldenrod. The programmers, Tim, Martha, Stew, and Joanne, dressed like one would expect for computer nerds—baggy T-shirts or sweatshirts covered with funky sayings or crazy math equations. Stew's favorite shirt was an Einstein portrait with the saying, *In the presence of genius*. Joanne leaned a little more toward Goth but not over the top.

Considering all this, Melissa opted for her favorite black jeans, a belted white shirt in a man's style, and one of her grandmother's woven scarves. Walking into the office for the second time in her life, she hesitated just inside the door. The last time she had been here, it had ended badly. *Does anyone remember?*

Dan was at the front desk to greet her. "John's not here right now." He leaned in as he guided her to the conference room.

She let out the breath she hadn't realized she had been holding. Once she was in the conference room with the team, all her anxieties melted away. Everyone was thrilled to see her, coming up to shake her hand or, in the case of Arabella and Anna Lee, a warm hug.

The pizza arrived.

While eating, each group gave updates on the status of their work. Everything was progressing as hoped. They had encountered a few minor technical issues, but Davey assured everybody the tech team had them well in hand and was working on the fixes. Nothing should slow them down. After the updates, the team broke up into smaller groups.

Melissa showed the other graphic artists what she was working on so they could coordinate the backgrounds and creatures with her vision. Time passed quickly. When they wrapped up, she hurried through the office with her head down. She got into the elevator, pressed the lobby button, and leaned against the back wall with a sigh of relief.

The next three days passed smoothly. She hadn't seen John yet, and that was fine. She still wasn't sure what to say or how to start the conversation.

When the meeting started on Monday, Melissa sat at one end with the other graphic artists, discussing a few new ideas.

Suddenly, Davey loudly cleared his throat. He stared at his hands and glanced sideways at Dan. The rest of the tech team also stared at their hands, avoiding eye contact with the group. "We've been pulling our hair out for a few days now, and I have to admit we're stuck. Something is causing the program to crash every time a player reaches level four. We've gone through every code and can't see the problem. Right now, I'm not sure how to fix this." He placed both hands on the table and lowered his head.

Melissa glanced at Dan, trying to judge his reaction. *Is this a bad problem? Or just a glitch that could be resolved quickly*? Dan had assured them all they were well on track to demo the game at E-Three, but could this set them back enough to miss the exposition? Worry began to gnaw at her brain.

"Okay, guys, this type of thing happens." Dan leaned forward and directed his response to the tech team. "You know that. It's not the first, and it won't be the last time we run into a glitch. That's the nature of programming. I'm sure you've been burning the midnight oil working on this. I'm guessing about now you're exhausted and not thinking clearly. Maybe a fresh pair of eyes will help. I can work with you this afternoon, if you want."

Davey squirmed in his chair.

She noted he didn't fully meet Dan's eyes. "Oh gee, umm…thanks, Dan. I'm sure you'd add value. But no offense, I think we need the coder-in-chief on this one. I know you said he wasn't working on this project." He stalled briefly, glancing over at Melissa. "But I, for one, would really like his brain on this problem."

Melissa's back stiffened. *Davey is asking for John's help.*

"I'll…well…I can see if he has some time to help." Dan glanced at Melissa, rubbing the back of his neck.

Melissa could feel everyone's gaze on her. She stared at her hands for a moment. Squaring her shoulders and swallowing the lump in her throat, she answered Dan's unspoken request. "If John is the best person, then we need to get him to help us."

Dan stood with a barely suppressed grin and a wink at the tech team and left to find John.

In the few minutes it took for Dan to return with John, the team continued to work on other aspects of the game.

Melissa remained deep in conversation with the other graphic artists and didn't look up when John entered the room, though she was aware of him. Glancing up, she observed John's movements.

He gave his full attention to Davey.

Davey gave a concise but very technical explanation.

Melissa surreptitiously studied John, careful to look away at any hint he might glance in her direction. The tech talk was completely over her head, so she blocked it out, focusing instead on her emotions. At the sound of John's voice, she felt her stomach do that flip-flop it used to whenever she saw him. She leaned in closer to study Arabella's screen, pretending to be intensely focused on the graphics. The heat continued rising on the back of her neck, and she could feel it coloring her cheeks. *It's your move*.

After listening for a few minutes, John suggested Davey and the tech team adjourn to his office to work on the glitch together using his larger monitor.

Melissa stayed in the conference room with the graphics team to review progress and discuss the next steps. An hour or so later, she closed her tablet and packed up her supplies. Stepping out of the elevator in the lobby, she stopped when a familiar voice called out her name.

John strode across the lobby floor. "Melissa, I hoped I would catch you before you left." Once he was standing in front of her, he hesitated. "I, um, just wanted to see how you are doing. I know you didn't want me to be a part of this project. Are you okay the tech team called me in?"

Melissa readjusted her bag on her shoulder and silently studied him.

John shoved his hands in his pockets, slowly shifting from one foot to the other as he stared at the floor.

She gave her stomach a moment to stop tumbling before replying, "Yes, when they said they needed your help, I agreed we should call you in. I'm glad you're helping. I've been meaning to call you and thank you for all the wonderful gifts you sent for the Twelve Days of Christmas." She smiled to let him know her gratitude was genuine.

John let out a long sigh. "I'm glad you liked them. Any chance you have time to grab a cup of coffee and talk?"

Melissa noted the plea in his voice. "Yes, I think we need to talk."

Together, they walked to the nearby coffee shop in silence.

Melissa glanced at John several times, trying to judge his feelings. He was stoic and showed little emotion.

John held open the door at the coffee shop, gesturing for her to go ahead.

This was the same one where she had met Dan a few months ago. Entering, she nervously ran a hand through her hair, smoothing it back from being blown by the wind. The same barista she had seen before was behind the counter. They placed their order and found a table. Once seated at one of the small round tables, "I see Dan's favorite barista is still here," Melissa commented, deliberately stalling the needed conversation.

John glanced back at the counter and nodded. "Yeah, Dan has become a real coffee addict. He comes by at least twice a day for his fix. And I don't mean the caffeine."

Melissa shook her head in disbelief. "He hasn't asked her out yet?"

"No, I've told him a hundred times to stop stalling and just ask her. I might set up a blind date for them to end the agony."

She peered at John over her coffee cup. "Hmm, a setup. Kind of like the setup this morning with the programming glitch in *Save Our Salmon*?"

John snickered. "Oh, you caught that one, too. Once I studied the program, I realized there was no reason the team couldn't have figured it out on their own. They're our best programmers."

"I caught on with how the whole tech team stared at their hands and refused to make eye contact. Dan also didn't do a good job of hiding his wink at Davey or his triumphant grin when he left to go get you."

John chuckled. "Yes, I think we were set up. And I have a fairly good idea who instigated it. I saw Dan and Pops conspiring together over the holidays."

Melissa opened her eyes wide. She set down her

coffee cup with a small thud. "Howard? You really think he had a hand in this?"

John nodded. "He's been on this kick of needing great-grandbabies to play with now that all of us grandkids are older. I think he decided since I'm the oldest, I'm first."

Melissa raised a hand to her mouth. "Seriously? You really think he's been pushing you toward finding someone to marry so you would have babies?"

"He's been none too subtle about it, either." John sat back with his arms across his chest. His grin spread.

"Oh." The heat flamed on her cheeks. "You can't think…You think he means me and you?" She gestured back and forth to each of them.

John uncrossed his arms and picked up his coffee cup. "Yep, that's exactly what I think. I was suspicious when he insisted I take over the stand for him alone. I planned to share the responsibility with Dan and some of our cousins, but Pops was adamant it had to be me. Claimed it would do Dan good to get out from under my wing. So yes, I'm guessing he's had his hand in this from the very beginning."

As the information sank in, Melissa arched her eyebrows. "He must not have been too happy when I got mad and stormed out of your office."

"Technically, Dan's office, but no, he called me several names when he found out. Some were in Gaelic, so I don't really know what they mean, but they didn't sound very flattering. I think one was something about a blind, three-legged sheep or something like that."

Melissa burst out laughing. All the tension of seeing John again melted away.

John quickly set his coffee cup down. "Are you

okay?"

Nodding, she wiped both eyes with her napkin. Through her laughter, she told John how she now saw this as a game where she and John were unwitting players. Howard had played them both. "Now, thinking back, I don't believe he was interested in the game but decided it was a way for us to continue to meet. You're right, and he wasn't very secretive about his desire for us to get together."

John started laughing with her. "Pops and his games of chess. I guess he got bored with the cooperative pawns on the board, so he decided to try playing with live ones instead. We just happened to be his first victims. Sorry to be mixing metaphors." He shook his head. "I need to warn my cousins. I'm afraid now that he's gotten a taste of being the ultimate chess master, he's far from done."

Melissa finally got control of her emotions. She glanced around the room to see if everyone was staring.

Dan's favorite barista smiled.

Sighing, she turned back to John. "I've heard of old-fashioned matchmakers, but I always envisioned them as little old ladies in paisley prints and lacy shawls, muttering something about dowries. But Howard? Now, that's a surprise."

"I didn't see it, either. But in hindsight, it's starting to make sense."

Melissa nodded, picked up her coffee cup, and slowly sipped. "Now, what do we do?"

John paused. "How about we try starting over on our terms?"

Melissa sat for a moment, noting John's sincere expression. "Sure." She held out her hand. "Hi, I'm

Melissa, the artist formerly known as Rapunzel. I do freelance graphics and am currently working with a gaming company called Brothers at Play."

John took her hand and shook it. "Hi, Melissa. I know your work as Rapunzel. You're a fantastic artist. In fact, I liked your work so much I convinced my brother we needed to hire you. The funny thing is, I own Brothers at Play with my brother Dan."

She feigned surprise, raising her hands to her mouth. "Seriously? That's so cool. Hey, I know you mostly produce those fantasy games, but I have an idea for a new game called *Save Our Salmon*. Would you be open to a pitch? This friend helped me put together a great presentation I'd like to show you."

John wiggled his eyebrows. "I'd love that. Let's set a date to talk more."

Both collapsed again into laughter.

The coffee shop door opened, and Dan hurried over to the table. "From outside, I couldn't tell if you were laughing or crying. You're both laughing, right?"

"Yes, we're both laughing, little bro. You can call Pops and let him know his scheme worked. We're talking to each other again."

"Scheme, what scheme?" Dan shoved his hands into his pockets, rocked back on his heels, and stared at the ceiling.

John just continued to laugh. "You've got a lousy poker face. No wonder Pops beats your tail off in chess. Now order your coffee, flirt with your barista, and ask her out already. Then go back to the office and leave us alone. We've got a lot to talk about."

Her head spun. *Where do I want our relationship to go now? Can I go back to the place where I trusted him?*

****

Later, Melissa met Karen at a restaurant in a well-frequented shopping area of the city. The restaurant was very popular with the young after-work crowd, so they had to wait a while for a table. Once seated, they both ordered a glass of wine.

As soon as the server walked away, Karen leaned across the table. “So, tell me. What did John send you for day twelve? I’ve been dying to know.”

Melissa described the drumline from a local high school and the note asking her to ‘Call Me Maybe.’ ”

Karen’s eyes lit up. “Did you call him?”

Melissa shook her head. “No, but I have seen him. We talked.”

Karen practically leaped across the table. “Keep talking. What did he say? What did you say? How did it happen?”

Melissa explained they had been meeting in person at the office since she had told the team who she was. She continued with the story of the programming glitch they claimed only John could solve which resulted in him coming to today’s meeting. Afterward, he asked her to go for coffee to talk. “We talked for over an hour.”

“I’m assuming all his digits are still intact, or you didn’t slip some poison into his coffee. How did it end? Are you going to see each other again?”

Melissa nodded, trying to hide her grin. “Yes, we agreed to start over and see where this goes. I’m seeing him tomorrow night for dinner. Plus, I assume I’ll run into him in the office now and then.”

Karen leaned back against the booth, grinning from

ear to ear. "This is *awesome*. Your fairy tale is ending happily ever after, after all."

Melissa waved her hand, dismissing Karen's comment. "Whoa, let's not get too carried away just yet. We've agreed to be friends and see what happens."

Karen raised an eyebrow. "Just friends?"

Melissa gave Karen a stern glare. "For now. We'll see where it goes."

"Sure, we'll see where it goes. No problem. Seriously, how do you feel?"

Melissa paused, looking around the restaurant before focusing again on Karen. "I'm excited, I'm nervous, and I feel all jumbled up inside."

"I think that's called love." Karen began humming the "Wedding March."

Melissa tossed her napkin at Karen. "Stop it. You're as bad as Howard."

Karen stopped humming. "Howard? How does he fit in, other than being John's grandfather?"

Melissa shared what she and John had surmised was Howard's role in their meeting and then encouraged her friendship.

Karen chuckled. "All for great-grandbabies. Got to admire that kind of planning. Hmm, Jan might soon have company."

Melissa gave Karen a wicked grin. "Don't get ahead of the story. We'll see what happens. You better behave. I haven't decided on bridesmaids yet."

Karen tossed the napkin back. "Oh, pooh. You know you couldn't possibly get married without me. I'll be right next to you in Tyrian purple—my new favorite color."

"You're impossible. It's a good thing I happen to

like purple, too. Now, speaking of colors, we need to think pink. What are we going to get Jan for her baby shower? That's why we're out tonight. We need to get something for Sunday."

The two friends got down to the serious subject of baby gifts. "Don't forget we want to get something special for Jan, too—something unrelated to babies," Karen added.

Several hours later, the friends parted ways, loaded down with bags of shopping success. They had bought several tiny outfits and toys for the baby, a pretty nightgown and robe set for Jan, and a few odds and ends for themselves. The after-Christmas sales were just too tempting.

Back home, Melissa carried her purchases to her room to put away before getting ready for bed. She let her mind wander back to Karen's insistence her happily ever after was coming true. Despite Karen's enthusiasm, Melissa told herself it was too early to think about it. But the gentle flip-flop in her stomach said otherwise. *Time will tell.*

Chapter 21

When John passed Melissa in the hallway the next day, he said he'd pick her up for dinner at six.

Although John said "casual," she still changed her outfit three times before she settled on a black tweed miniskirt with a fuchsia cowl neck sweater and black knee-high boots. She left her hair down and straight. She was ready when the bell rang promptly at six.

Stepping into her house, John handed Melissa an arrangement of snow-white hydrangeas, red roses, and wintry silver brunia.

"Thank you. These are beautiful. I'll put them in water."

In the dining room, he stopped before the framed graphic hanging on the wall. "Your art looks good here." John spun in a slow circle to examine the rest of the room. "I take it you don't entertain with fancy dinners too often." He grinned and gestured to the cluttered tabletop.

"Takeout is more my style." With a laugh, she continued into the kitchen. The kitchen was a different world. Everything was neatly tucked away or occupied corners of the countertop, leaving lots of open space for creating culinary masterpieces. The room appeared ready for a photographer to take pictures for a culinary magazine.

John gestured toward the professional-level

appliances. "You cook?"

She shook her head, laughing. "The kitchen was my mom's domain. I loved to sit at the breakfast bar and watch her cook. She learned when she was studying art at the Sorbonne in Paris. She started with French cooking, then expanded to other cuisines once she came back home. Gifts for Christmas and her birthdays were always easy. Just buy her the latest best-selling cookbook, and we'd lose her for hours. Unfortunately, I didn't inherit her culinary skills. The mess in the dining room—that's all me." She put the flowers in a vase and placed it on the counter. Turning, she gave John a silly grin. "Now, you know I can't cook, and I'm an untidy worker. Are you sure you still want to go out with me?"

"I'll take my chances. Besides, as you said, there's always takeout." John chuckled.

John chose a locally owned, family-style Italian restaurant for dinner.

The host greeted John by name and ushered them to a small booth in the corner.

The table was covered with a classic red-and-white-checkered cloth and a Chianti bottle coated with the drippings of past candles. The current white taper cast shadows on the wall behind it.

They were no sooner seated when a young man in a long white apron came over with a basket of bread and a small bowl of olive oil and herbs. He gave them a shy smile and placed the items in the center of the table.

He was followed by an older man with a salt-and-pepper mustache, carrying a bottle of Chianti and two glasses. "*Mio amico*, welcome to my humble restaurant. Ah, who is this *bella signora*? You must introduce me."

John gestured toward Melissa. "Mario, this is my

friend Melissa."

Taking her hand when she offered it, Mario raised it to his lips, gently kissing the back of her hand. "If my lovely wife weren't in the kitchen, I'd steal you away from John and teach you the romance of Italy. But alas, you come to me forty years too late, so I will entice you instead with my *pasta deliziosa.*" He shooed away the approaching server. "I, personally, will cook for you tonight. I'll start with an antipasto with the finest Italian cheeses, salamis, and olives." With a wink to John, Mario disappeared behind the swinging door leading to the kitchen.

"How do you know Mario?" Melissa asked, surprised at the obvious friendship.

"He's friends with Pops. They've known each other for years. Pops had just started his law practice when Mario walked in, saying he wanted to buy a restaurant and needed a lawyer to help with the paperwork. He was only twenty-three years old, fresh off the boat from Naples, but dreamed of owning a restaurant here in America." John picked up his wine glass and sipped. "Pops was invited to the opening night. Since then, he's eaten here at least once a week. He and Mario play chess at the back table whenever there's a lull in the crowd. Mario's son, daughter, and grandchildren mostly run the restaurant now, but Mario is never too far away."

"I should have guessed Howard was the source of the friendship. I forget he was a lawyer."

"When Pops retired from his law practice, leaving it in my dad's hands, he still wanted something to do. He says he likes the stand because his customers are always happy to see him, unlike some of the people who came into the law office. Not everyone who needs a lawyer needs them for a happy reason, as Mario did. So, Pops traded in his suit and tie for an apron and pair of barbeque tongs." He smiled and tapped his wine glass against Melissa's. "But enough about Pops. Tell me more about how you chose graphic art."

They talked about their past for the next two hours, sharing stories from their childhood and college years. Melissa was in awe of John's closeness to his family. She couldn't imagine having so many aunts, uncles, and cousins. All she had was Grams, but John was devoted to all of them. They also discussed John's plans to grow Brothers and her desire to expand her idea into more environmentally focused games once *SOS* was on the market.

Mario and his grandson delivered dish after delicious dish to their table.

Following the antipasto was a plate of carbonara, still sizzling hot from the pan. Then came a veal scallopini that melted in her mouth, with a side salad of arugula and sliced beets. Dessert was a small dish of spumoni with a delicate *pizzelle* dusted with powdered sugar and demitasse cups of expresso.

The last dishes were cleared away.

Mario brought out two stemmed aperitif glasses with Sambuca and three coffee beans in each. "In Italy, three beans mean you must come back," he explained.

Melissa took a sip of the licorice liqueur. "Perfect ending to the best food I've ever tasted. Thank you, Mario, for the wonderful dinner. I will definitely be back."

"You will never eat pasta as good as mine, which means I have won your heart, and you will return soon." He turned to John. "Tell your Papa *ciao*. Remind him he owes me another chess game. He beat me the last time, and I need to get my revenge."

Stepping out into the chilled night air, Melissa glanced up the street. "I'm so full I need to walk off some of Mario's pasta. Do you mind if we wander for a little bit?"

John patted his stomach. "No, I need to work off some of the meal, too. I might also need to add a few extra miles to my run tomorrow."

The two wandered past the lighted shop windows in comfortable silence. They passed other couples strolling hand in hand and a few clusters of people window-shopping at the various unique shops. Everyone was enjoying the crisp winter air. The night was clear, creating a canopy of stars overhead.

"We haven't talked about why you were so angry at me. Why did you run away?" John's voice was soft. "Can you talk about it?"

Melissa stopped. "I panicked."

John turned and arched one eyebrow. "Panicked? I don't understand."

"I've been hiding behind an alias to protect myself." Looping her hand over John's arm, she continued to walk slowly. "I'll spare you the gory details. Rapunzel became my shield. When I realized you knew my secret, I feared the worst."

John was silent for a moment. "The worst? How?"

When she reached the car, she leaned against the door, hands in her pockets, "After Mom's and Dad's deaths, I had a few instances where someone, reporters mostly, tried to take advantage of me for monetary gain. I became leery of new people, always assuming there was a reason to distrust them." She pulled her hands out and clasped them briefly in front of her chest. "I know I was irrational. Now, I can see the bind you were in. But I wasn't reacting rationally. I was hurt and uncertain of your motives, so I chose to do what I've always chosen—to run away."

John took both of her hands in his. "Melissa…" He started to pull her into his arms but stopped and held her hands gently. "Melissa, I'm so sorry. My world fell apart when you walked away. I was lost. Pops called me an idiot when he found out what happened. That was mild compared to the names I called myself."

She gently pulled her hands away and gazed down the street at the cars slowly driving by. "I couldn't understand how someone who seemed so honest and caring wasn't honest with me. I wanted so much to trust you, to believe you cared for *me*, not the game or what you might gain from it—just me."

John stood silent, looking past her. He shifted his gaze to her face, took a deep breath, and let it out. "Melissa, I failed you. You were completely open and honest with me. I was the one with the secret. How can I prove to you I'm the good guy? Do you think you could ever fully trust me again?"

She took one of John's hands in hers. "I want to. I really want to. I feel like with our new beginning we're both getting a fresh start. To be fair, I wasn't completely honest with you, either. I didn't tell you I was Rapunzel."

John shrugged. "True, but you didn't know I had any connection to Brothers, so there was no need for you to tell me. So, you worked under an alias. That was your personal decision. The team at Brothers all use gaming names on our website. It's a common practice. I was the one who knew we were connected professionally, so it was my responsibility to say something. I'm the one who failed." He briefly closed his eyes and took a deep breath.

She laid her other hand on top of his and smiled. "Let's just say we both missed a few opportunities to be open with each other. But this is a good start. Just talking about how we feel and being honest with each other now."

John smiled. "Pops said I needed to court you to win you back."

Removing her hands from his, she leaned back against the car again. Crossing her arms across her chest, she gave him a feigned frown. "Now, about those gifts. As much as I loved them, I don't need more drumlines or ballet tickets. I'm still consuming the goodies from your twelve days."

John grinned. "Okay, no more surprise gifts. Well…maybe the occasional flowers. From now on, I'm going to court you face-to-face. Be prepared to be wined, dined, and adored."

Melissa laughed lightly at John's earnest tone. "I can handle that. But what I really want is *this*, being together and talking, sharing our thoughts. But you can add chocolates to those flowers every once in a while." She winked.

John pulled her into his arms.

With a sigh, she allowed herself to melt into his warm embrace and opened herself to the possibility that, just maybe, they could be more than friends.

Chapter 22

When she came into the office for the team meetings, she frequently saw John. They went out for coffee again later in the week and made plans to get together on Saturday.

Saturday, Melissa woke to a cloudless sky promising a glorious day on the slopes near Seattle. John had asked if she skied, and she admitted she had, but not in many years.

As they drove, John told her about the ski area, and they chatted about the status of *Save Our Salmon.*

They had started the beta testing, and she was anxious to hear comments from their test gamers.

Once they were out of the city, they marveled at the change in scenery. Fresh snow blanketed the mountains. "It must have been a day like today when they decided what to call this area." Melissa gazed at the scene, delighted with the mounds of snow by the roadside. Back in the city, no hint of the wintry wonderland existed, just a short drive away. "The snow sparkles like thousands of perfect crystals. It's beautiful."

The line at the ticket window moved quickly, so they didn't take long to purchase their passes and put on their gear. Heading to the chair lift, she wobbled a little as she propelled herself forward. "Remember, I haven't skied for a while."

"No worries, we'll start gently and ease into the more challenging slopes when you're ready," he reassured.

Their first few runs were on the easier slopes, and she was beginning to regain her confidence.

"You're doing great." John congratulated her at the bottom of the run. "Want to take a break for some hot chocolate? Then we can tackle something a little more technical."

"Sure, lead on. I'm ready to sit for a while." She pushed herself with her poles toward the lodge. Inside the warm lodge, she found a table near the windows while John got the hot chocolate.

He soon returned with two mugs brimming with whipped cream.

She took a careful sip, testing to ensure the liquid chocolate did not burn her tongue. Then, she took a bigger swallow, letting the creamy chocolate warm her throat and stomach.

Laughing, John leaned over to wipe the smudge of whipped cream off her nose. "How are you feeling? You look like it's all coming back quickly."

She held the mug, warming her hands from the cold outside. The steam rose to create a small cloud over the mug. "I feel good. I can't believe I let so much time go by since I last skied. It feels great to be outside, feeling the sun and wind."

"We can do this more often. There's another ski place up north at Mount Baker that's fun, too. Maybe we can go next weekend, if the weather cooperates."

She smiled at his suggestion of another date. The warm feeling in her chest came from more than just the hot chocolate. "If not, I'm sure we can find something else to do. I love museums and art galleries. I could show you my favorites."

"Sounds like a plan." He gave a thumbs-up. "Let's get in a few more runs before lunch."

They finished the last of their hot chocolate and gathered their gear.

This time, John increased the difficulty level a little.

She found she could keep up easily. Her confidence grew with each downhill run.

After the third run, John led the way toward the gondola.

Once she realized where he was headed, she stopped. "Wait, I'm not sure I'm ready for the Black Diamond runs yet."

John turned with a grin. "I didn't mean to scare you. I made lunch reservations for the restaurant at the top. The gondola's the only way to get there. We'll take it back down again, instead of skiing this section of the mountain. It's considerably steeper."

"Whew. You had me worried for a minute." Relieved, she followed him to the line for the gondola.

The gondola glided up the mountainside as skiers floated down the mountain like colorful moving dots, zigzagging their way down a massive sea of white. The closer they got to the top, the snow-burdened trees gave way to steep slopes of virgin snow. Once the gondola stopped at the restaurant, they stepped out onto the platform. After depositing their skis in the rack outside the door, they entered. The host crossed John's name off the list and escorted them outside to a table next to a portable heater.

"I hope you don't mind sitting outside?" John

asked as they sat.

"No, I'm glad we're out here. I'm toasty warm with the heater, and I wouldn't give up this view for anything. This is spectacular." Melissa gestured with wide arms, taking in the entire vista.

"Most of the mountain climbing happens on the other side." John pointed out the treacherous glaciers and deep crevasses that endangered those who dared to climb to the summit of Mount Rainier. "On a summer day, teams of roped-off, intrepid climbers pick their way across the ice to reach the peak."

"Have you ever climbed it?" She leaned forward, resting her elbows on the table, and cupped her chin as she gazed at the clouds circling the mountaintop.

John shook his head. "No, I've never gone all the way to the summit. I have friends who have, and they say it's an awesome experience." He leaned back and crossed his arms loosely over his chest. "I've hiked to Camp Muir on day hikes, but that's as far as I've gone. It's a challenging hike, but hundreds of people do it on a nice summer day. Beyond there, you need to know what you're doing and have the right equipment to reach the top."

As the wait staff set down her steaming hot soup, she nodded. "Thanks." She waited until John had his sandwich. "How is Howard? I haven't had time to see him recently."

John shook his head and rolled his eyes. "The old rascal is gloating now that we're seeing each other. He's acting like he's pulled off the victory of the century."

"I'm sure he's proud of himself. Little does he know how close he got to the opposite result." Melissa grinned at the thought of Howard wallowing in his victory.

"I know. That's why he's so satisfied with this. He thinks we never would have gotten back together if he hadn't meddled." John set his sandwich on his plate and leaned forward. "You know, now that he's had this win, he'll be convinced he can arrange everyone else's love life. I've already seen him looking at my brother with a certain interest."

Melissa held her napkin to her mouth to stifle her laughter. "Yikes, we might have created a monster."

"My thought exactly. I've been trying to think of a way to take him down a peg, but so far, I don't have a clue how." With a shrug, he picked up his sandwich and took a bite.

Sitting back, she squinted at John while she pondered his statement. "Hmmm. I like the idea. Let me think about it for a while, too. Maybe we can come up with something."

John raised his glass of cider in a toast. "To us, bringing down the old man."

She clicked glasses and joined in his laughter.

After lunch, they skied a few more runs before heading home.

She was tired but thrilled with an enjoyable day on the mountain. Much to her embarrassment, she fell asleep about halfway home.

John laughed off her apologies and helped her unload her gear.

Melissa gave him a self-conscious smile. "I'd ask you to stay for a while, but I'm sure I'll just fall asleep again. I need a warm shower and early to bed."

"I'll take a rain check." John gave her a quick kiss

on her cheek.

She headed upstairs for the shower, singing. *Being back with John was even better than before. I hadn't noticed the tension in our relationship until it was gone.*

****

Sunday morning, Melissa gathered the large gift bag filled with packages wrapped in pink floral paper and tied with pink bows. She and Karen had gone a little overboard with the gifts, but Jan was the first of their threesome to have a baby, and they wanted to make it special. Excited and a little nervous about the framed pictures she made, she placed them carefully in the overflowing gift bag. *Will Jan love them? Of course, she will. They are fairy-tale princesses, after all.* Bag in hand, she headed to her car to pick up Karen for the shower.

The ladies played several silly baby shower games and laughed at each other's fumbling mistakes. They raced to diaper and dress a baby doll in record time, failed to name a variety of baby paraphernalia correctly, and guessed which parent would be the best at various parenting tasks like diapering, burping, feeding, etc.

Now, gift time had arrived. Jan sat in the place of honor, surrounded by a mound of gifts wrapped in various pastel paper. She opened gift after gift of adorable tiny dresses, sweaters, and teddy bears. The more experienced mothers were the ones who bought the essentials like mobiles to entertain the baby and clothes in larger sizes for later. When Jan got to Melissa and Karen's bag, she first opened the fun gifts. She held up a cute rattle shaped like a kitty, a set of bibs, and a couple of little sleepers everyone swore were perfect for a newborn. As she opened the box with the lacy nightgown and matching robe, Jan blushed. "You seriously think I can wear this anytime soon?"

"Maybe not immediately, but the day or night will come when it will be perfect." Karen winked.

"Wear that, and there will soon be another little one coming," quipped another guest.

Lastly, Jan took out the three pictures. The first one she unwrapped was Cinderella. "Ooh, you made this?" She clutched the framed picture to her chest. "Melissa, this is adorable. You made this for my baby?"

Melissa nodded, delighted and relieved to see Jan's happy reaction to the unique gifts.

Jan held the framed picture in her hand and studied the details. "I love it. Oh, I love that she's an independent woman with her own business. That's such a great image for my daughter."

"There are two more," Melissa prompted Jan.

Jan handed the first picture to the woman beside her and quickly unwrapped the next one. "Snow White. She's one of my favorites. The seven dwarves are so cute. Oh, this is wonderful."

Passing it on, she opened the third picture. She ran her finger over the image of Rapunzel and glanced at Melissa. "The last one. Rapunzel. It's you. You're swinging out of your tower." She reached over to hug Melissa. "These are incredible. I can't wait to hang them in the baby's room."

The pictures were passed around, and the other guests "oohed" and "aahed." Later, one of the women approached Melissa to ask if she could make a similar set of pictures. She explained her daughter-in-law was expecting her third child, who was finally a girl. She would happily pay whatever Melissa charged for her work.

Melissa told Karen about the request on their way home.

"I'm not surprised. Jan kept picking up and admiring the pictures for the rest of the party." Karen gave Melissa a gentle punch on the arm. "I've been telling you you're terrific. Maybe now you'll believe it."

Melissa smiled at the comment. "She told me over and over how much they mean to her. This was the first time I realized my art could have an emotional impact." She stretched up a little taller. "People have told me my art for the fantasy games is good, but I've never actually seen anyone react in person."

"It's exactly like how you've said your mom's and grandmother's art makes people feel. Now, you haven't told me anything about John. Have you seen him again?"

She filled Karen in on their dinner at the Italian restaurant and yesterday's skiing adventure. "We also discussed finding a way to discourage Howard from meddling with other potential romances. Since he feels he might have succeeded with us, John thinks he'll move on to his other adult grandkids."

"So, now you and John are trying to find a way to turn the tables on him?" Karen asked.

"Yes, we figure turn-about is fair play. The trouble is, neither of us has any idea how to do it yet."

"You will, and when you do, you need to tell me. You have such an exciting life."

She glanced over at Karen to see her grinning. She just laughed at the comment. That was not how she would have described her life just a few months ago.

But things had changed a lot recently and all for the better. Her stomach had returned to flip-flopping every time she was with John. *Could I be…?* She shook her head and gripped the steering wheel tighter. *Time. Give it time.*

Chapter 23

Melissa and John continued to spend time together over the next several weeks. They took advantage of her trips to the office to meet for coffee or a quick lunch. They also enjoyed another skiing adventure and a weekend touring her favorite small art galleries. Mario's restaurant continued to be a favorite, although they explored the wide variety of cuisines offered by the numerous restaurants throughout Seattle. Each time they got together, they'd brainstorm how to teach Howard a lesson about meddling in everyone's love life, but nothing was exactly right so far.

Gradually, Melissa began to think of John as more than a friend. In the past weeks, she learned a lot more about him. She loved how he would listen to her ideas about *SOS* and life in general. But she still wasn't willing to acknowledge she was falling in love, let alone tell him. Despite the good times together, she held back. She didn't want to get hurt again if he wasn't feeling the same way about her.

In early February, Melissa headed to the stand to see Howard again after a long session at her computer. The air was still crisp, but she could see the promise of spring in the buds on the trees.

Howard stood alone at the stand, staring out at the lake.

Catching his eye, she mimed she was looking for a

hot dog.

He had it on the grill by the time she reached the stand.

"How's my favorite artist?" He stepped around the counter to hug her before returning to his grill,

"Doing great. The day's too nice to stay inside, so I decided to visit one of my favorite chefs."

"What? One of? Do I have competition? Who?" Howard waved his tongs in the air. "Are you meeting some other incredibly handsome chef?"

"Mario is a pretty tough contender for my affection. He does make an amazing fettuccine."

Howard waved his hand in front of his face and shook his head.

"That old has-been? Ha. So, he can boil some noodles. No biggie. I've got the best sausages in Seattle, grilled to charred perfection and topped with only the finest condiments. There's no competition."

"It's a good thing you aren't the competitive type." Melissa laughed at Howard's exaggerated rebuff of Mario's cooking prowess.

"I gather John took you to Mario's for dinner?"

Melissa had to bite the inside of her cheek to keep from laughing out loud at his obvious attempt to ask about her and John. "Yes, we've been a couple of times." She kept her tone casual. "Every time was incredible. Mario insists on no menu. He goes into the kitchen, and out comes these delightful Italian dishes." She wagged a finger. "By the way, have you been there recently? He says you owe him a rematch."

"No, but I should go see him soon. He hates to lose, so every time I beat him, he wants an instant rematch. If he wins, he's content to savor his victory for a while. But enough about Mario. How are things with you and John?" Howard gestured her toward one of the picnic tables.

"Isn't that a bit personal?" She gave him a feigned look of dismay.

"Of course not," he answered, talking over his shoulder. "I helped to bring you two together, and I have a vested interest in ensuring he doesn't screw it up again."

She allowed herself a silent chuckle. "Oh, I see. So, you arranged this relationship?"

Howard approached the table with her hot dog in one hand and two bottles of water in the other. He handed her the hot dog and sat. "Of course. You wouldn't have met if I hadn't made sure John took over my stand while I recovered. So, I'm responsible for both of you now."

Melissa narrowed her gaze, squinting at Howard. "Are you telling me you deliberately fell off your ladder just so you could set up a meeting between John and me?"

Howard hesitated briefly. "Well…no, not the fall. That wasn't planned. But when I saw an opportunity, I took it." He slapped his hand on the table in a dramatic gesture.

"Aha, but it backfired." She pointed with her hot dog and gave him her best stern expression.

He shook his head slowly. "Yes, that was a mistake. I told John he needed to be completely honest, but he didn't listen. So, once I learned he messed up, I had to help him find a way to fix it."

She cocked her head to one side, studying him. "You told me you had nothing to do with the 'Twelve

Days of Christmas' gifts?"

"I didn't. But I did nudge him a little to find a way to court you. He'd better not mess up again." He arched his eyebrows and glared.

"He's doing just fine." She pretended to wipe her mouth with her napkin to hide her grin at Howard's obvious concern.

"Good, now you two need to move this relationship along a little faster. I'm not getting any younger, and I need to be able to dance at your wedding."

This time, Melissa's gasp was real. "Well, don't start polishing your dancing shoes just yet. We're a long way from that kind of commitment. Right now, I'm focused on getting *Save Our Salmon* ready for the launch at E-Three next month."

"I assume you're going to the convention?"

"Yes, Dan, a few members of the team and I are going together." Her tone shifted from bemused to more serious. "I'm anxious to hear feedback from the distributors and the fans attending. The feedback from the beta testing has been very positive. The testers love the idea of learning how to help the environment." She gazed off for a moment. "There's been the usual assortment of glitches and bugs, but so far, nothing has stumped the programmers. We're all excited to present it at the expo."

"Just don't let any of those tech guys in San Francisco get any ideas and convince you to come work for them."

"What?" Melissa stopped wiping her mouth and stared at Howard. "Why would I go somewhere else? *Save Our Salmon* isn't even on the market yet, so I'm not getting too far ahead of myself here." She caught

Howard's quick look of relief.

"Good to hear. Just stay focused on your game here."

Howard leaned back, looking like he had just convinced a jury of his client's innocence. Melissa raised an eyebrow. "Speaking of my game, I'd better get back to it. I have a few more touches to make on the graphics before I'm done for the day."

"Okay, but I'm holding you to the promise that you'll spend more time with John once the conference is over."

"I never promised anything." She gave him a wink as she stood to leave. Once she was a distance from the stand, she grinned. *Oh Howard, you crafty old coot, you've given me an idea for the perfect payback.*

****

The next day, Melissa popped her head into John's office. "Got a minute?"

He glanced up from his computer with a grin. "For you? Always. What's up?"

She perched in the chair on the opposite side of the desk and slid forward to prop her elbows on the surface. "I spent time with Howard yesterday afternoon. He openly bragged he's the mastermind behind our relationship."

John sat back in his chair and grimaced. "Yeah, he's pretty smug about his cleverness."

"Well, he was a little too clever yesterday and gave me the perfect idea for teaching him a lesson about meddling."

John sat up. He clasped his hands together as he leaned forward. "I'm listening…"

She laid out her idea.

John's smile grew wider and wider. "Brilliant. Simply brilliant. Do you think we can pull this off?"

"Absolutely. We might have to let a few people in on the joke, but we can do this."

****

Time passed in a blur of events. The first excitement happened when Derrick called at six in the morning to say Jan had delivered the baby. Despite barely comprehending his semi-delirious rambling, Melissa understood that Mom and daughter were doing great, and Derrick was over the moon in love with both. She promised him she'd call Karen and tell her the news. She waited for a more civilized hour to catch her before she left for work. She relayed that Derrick wanted them to come to the hospital immediately to see the baby, but they both agreed to wait until they heard from Jan. About an hour later, Melissa opened a text from Jan with a photo of her holding a pink bundle.

—One of us is actually a mother. Things are changing fast—fortunately all good news.—

Jan begged her two friends to visit them at the hospital today. After exchanging texts with Karen, she agreed to go together later.

Karen arrived at six to pick her up. "Can you believe one of us is a mother? I keep thinking we just got out of college, and now Jan is doing the full adult thing and starting a family."

"I know. I had to remind myself we graduated eight years ago, and we're all adults." Walking through the hospital's main doors, Melissa paused for a second, a hand on her heart. She flashed back to the panic she felt after her parents' accident.

Karen turned and put a hand on Melissa's arm.

"Are you okay?"

She suppressed the momentary shudder that ran through her body. Taking a deep breath, she nodded to Karen with a determined smile. "Yes, just a momentary rush of emotions. I'm fine now."

They stopped at the desk as they entered the maternity area to check if Jan could have visitors. The woman behind the desk assured them Jan was eagerly awaiting their arrival and gave them her room number.

Once in Jan's room, all the gray shadows of sadness faded at the sight of her good friend sitting in bed holding her daughter. The overhead lights were off, and the nightlight behind the bed enveloped them in a soft glow. Melissa's fingers itched for a sketch pad and pencil to capture the moment. She paused to store the image in her head to re-create it later. The words *Madonna and Child* came to mind.

Derrick jumped up at the sight of the two friends, gesturing for them to come closer.

Both Derrick and Jan appeared exhausted and ridiculously happy.

Jan shifted the baby slightly, gently lowering the blanket to expose her face. "Meet Katie," she announced with a sappy grin. "Katie, this is your Auntie Melissa and Auntie Karen."

Hearing her mother's voice, baby Katie opened her eyes and stared at Melissa and Karen with the bluest eyes Melissa had ever seen. Seemingly content that they adored her on sight, Katie closed her eyes again and returned to sleep. "She's beautiful," whispered Melissa.

"So amazingly beautiful," agreed Karen.

"Do you want to hold her?" asked Jan.

"Me? No. Umm, maybe later." Melissa took half a step back, putting her hands behind her back.

"Like when she's five and doesn't break so easily," added Karen.

Jan just laughed. "She won't break. Babies are durable. If you could see what it takes to be born, you wouldn't be so nervous about hurting her."

Melissa had seen birth scenes in movies, and they didn't make it look like much fun. "We'll take your word for it. She looks so peaceful right now we'll admire her from here."

"How are you feeling?" Karen perched on the edge of one of the chairs in the room.

"Tired but happy. I think I might be too exhausted to realize how tired I really am. But now, I feel good. And hungry. Derrick, sweetie, you said earlier you wanted to show Katie off to your colleagues here at the hospital. She's resting comfortably, so now might be a great time to take her visiting. On your way back, you can get me a snack from the kitchen area near the nurses' station."

Derrick gently cradled Katie in his arms and headed out with a huge smile.

"I see the need to eat constantly didn't go away with giving birth," joked Karen.

Jan adjusted the sheets on the bed. "Oh, I'm not really hungry, but I wanted to send Derrick away so we could have a good girl talk." She turned to Melissa. "I want all the latest on you and John. Derrick will most likely get talking with the other doctors and nurses he works with, so he'll be a while. So, what's new?"

Melissa filled Jan in on the latest information about Howard.

"That sweet old man? He looks so innocent."

Melissa shook her head. "Don't forget he was a successful lawyer before he retired and bought the snack stand. I bet that innocent look helped him fool many a jury in his time. John and I have been trying to devise a way to teach him meddling can backfire. John's afraid now that Howard thinks he's had one success, he'll start in on the rest of his grandkids, beginning with John's brother Dan."

"So, have you come up with anything?" Jan leaned forward and tilted her head to one side.

"Yes." Melissa grinned triumphantly. "He said something the other day that triggered an idea. I shared it with John, and we both think it might work."

"I loved it. So devious, but that's what makes it such a great idea." Karen wiggled her fingers in front of her chin and gave Jan an evil grin.

"Wait. You know? Why don't I know? I want to be a part of it, too." Jan's gaze snapped back and forth between Karen and Melissa.

Melissa quickly reassured Jan. "You will be. You've just been a little busy lately."

"Oh…yeah. I guess that's true." Jan leaned back against the pillow and ran a hand over her somewhat flat stomach.

Melissa shared her idea with Jan, and the three of them happily brainstormed how each could play a part in the scheme.

Suddenly, the quiet calm of the hospital was broken by the wails of a demanding infant. Derrick hurried into the room, holding out a howling Katie.

Jan immediately soothed her by putting her to her breast to feed.

Derrick's look of panic disappeared. He spun on his heels, muttering he had forgotten to get Jan's snack, and dashed out of the room.

Jan grinned at the sound of her friends' laughter.

"Poor daddy," Jan cooed to baby Katie. "You certainly know how to get him rattled, little lady. You should have seen him in the delivery room. He was more nervous than I was about the birth. You'd think with all the time he spends in an operating room piecing bones back together, he would've been more at ease. But no. He was doing as much deep breathing as I was. Maybe more."

After a few more minutes admiring baby Katie, Melissa and Karen got up to go, promising to visit soon after Jan and Katie were home.

"And remember, I want any updates on Operation Takedown Howard," Jan reminded them.

"No worries. I'll need my two besties to pull this off." Melissa grinned and linked arms with Karen as they departed.

****

Two more weeks passed, and the team worked hard to prepare *Save Our Salmon* for the expo. The tech team addressed last-minute coding changes to ensure the game ran smoothly. Sabrina had the actors record additional dialogue spoken by the human characters. Melissa and the graphic team did final touch-ups to some of the scenes.

Melissa and John spent time together despite the crunch of work. In the evenings, when Melissa had to work late or was too tired to go out, they exchanged text messages before bed.

John was always attentive, asked about her day,

and indicated through his actions he cared. Anytime they crossed paths in the office, his face would light up, and he'd stop to give her a hug or a gentle hand on her shoulder. Their relationship had grown into something deeper than friendship. But still, the word *love* hadn't been mentioned.

On Valentine's Day, which would have been a perfect opportunity for him to express deeper feelings, he kept the date simple by going to Mario's and bringing her the requisite roses and a box of her favorite chocolates.

Of course, Mario gushed and talked about love, but John didn't.

The day before Melissa left for San Francisco in late February, she and John agreed to meet for dinner. *SOS* was as ready as it was going to be, so she eagerly agreed. They chose a new French bistro, which they both wanted to try. The atmosphere was classic French, with white linen tablecloths, tapered candles, wait staff in long white aprons, and soft, romantic music. *Maybe tonight is the night John will say more about his feelings.*

John reached across the table and took her hand.

Melissa's stomach immediately did the expected flip-flop.

"You'll be gone for the next several days. I'm going to miss not seeing you in the office." He caressed her hand as he spoke.

Melissa smiled wistfully. "I'll miss you, too." She waited for him to say more. She sat back with a sigh when he released her hand,

"How do you feel about the expo? Are you nervous?"

Melissa picked up her fork and set it back down on the table. She smoothed out her napkin before responding. “I am. At least a little. It’s hard to believe I will present *Save Our Salmon* at one of the largest tech conferences in the country. It seems like just yesterday when I went to the tribal council meeting with Grams and came up with the idea. Now, it’s real.”

John reached over and retook her hand. “I’m confident it will be a huge success. You’ll be the queen of the expo. Just don’t let any of those other guys try to steal my girl away. I’m counting on you to come home.”

“You’re starting to sound like Howard.” Melissa laughed lightly. “You know I’m coming home. I wouldn’t want it any other way.”

“Maybe once you return, we can spend even more time together. I want to meet your grandmother, and you should get to know more of my family than just Pops and Dan.”

Melissa gazed at her wine glass for a moment to savor the moment. “I’d like that. Yes, I’d love for you to meet Grams. I’d also love to meet your parents.” Throughout the rest of the evening, she waited for him to say more about their future, but the conversation remained focused on the conference. They drove back to her house in companionable silence.

John walked her to her door, and they lingered, saying goodbye. He pulled her into an embrace and tilted her chin up. He slowly lowered his head to kiss her. The kiss started gently but quickly grew in fervor.

She slipped her hands around John’s neck to pull him closer. Her heart beat faster, and her breath quickened.

They stepped back, both gasping a bit for air.

They had kissed before, but not like this. Melissa placed both hands on John's chest to steady herself as she gazed into his eyes.

His gaze held hers as he bent to kiss her again softly. "I'm going to miss you more than you can imagine. Go save the world with your game, and then come home to me," he whispered.

Once inside, Melissa leaned against the wall, slowly unbuttoning her coat. After removing her gloves, she brushed her lips with her fingertips. She dropped her hands to her somersaulting stomach. Humming softly, she headed upstairs and got ready for bed. Lying there, she gazed at the ceiling, replaying John's words over and over. *Go save the world and then come home to me…to me.* She hugged her pillow and drifted off into blissful sleep.

Melissa went by the stand the following day to tell Howard she'd see him again in a week.

"Now, remember what I told you. You need to come back here and marry John." Howard shook his finger in her direction.

"I told *you*, no promises." She hugged him and left to finish packing. Once she was a distance from the stand and out of Howard's sight, she texted John.

—The trap has been laid.—

Chapter 24

A few nights later, John stopped by Pops's house for a chess game.

After making his move, Pops leaned back casually. "Have you talked to Melissa since she's been gone?"

John studied the board briefly, ignoring Pops's question, and shifted his bishop to block Pop's last move. "I talked to her last night. *Save Our Salmon* is a big hit. She's been getting lots of offers to produce her next game. She's talking about creating new games to feature other animals endangered due to environmental issues."

Pops paused briefly to look at John. His hand hovered over the chessboard. "Why would she talk to anyone else about the next game? Why wouldn't she continue working with you?"

"She might, and Dan and I will do all we can to make it happen." John struggled to stay casual with his reply, picking up his bishop and setting it back before finally moving a pawn. "But these companies have far more resources than we do and can reach a much larger market. If her goal is to educate as many people as possible, then going with someone else might be the best way."

Pops's hand stopped in midair. "But what…? Would it mean she'd have to move away?"

Now, Pops sounded nervous. John coughed into his

hand to cover up the laugh threatening to explode. He focused on the game, only sneaking a look to see Pops's reaction. Pops stared off into space, seemingly oblivious to the game.

"Hmm, possibly. She could do some remotely, but there's a point where you need to be hands on with the rest of the team to ensure it all comes together as envisioned."

"Well, you just have to ensure she doesn't go anywhere. You can make her an offer she can't refuse." Pops picked up his glass of Irish whiskey and waved it around so dramatically that the liquid splashed over his hand.

This time, John laughed out loud. "You don't need to go all Don Corleone on me. I'll do my best, but ultimately, it's her decision."

Pops sipped and stared at John intently.

John could see the wheels spinning. He imagined this was what Pops must have looked like in the courtroom as he considered what approach to take with a reluctant witness.

"What if you make her a different kind of offer?"

"Like what?" He had no idea where Pops was going with this suggestion.

Pops leaned forward. His gaze drilled into John. "You know what I mean. Don't you think it's time to get serious and propose?"

John sat back with a sharp intake of breath. "Propose? No…not now. I'm not going to complicate her choices." Catching Pops's look of dismay, he decided he could taunt him a little more. "Maybe if she decides to move, then I'll go with her."

Pops glared.

If looks could kill.

Pops thumped his fist on the arm of his chair. "What? No. You can't. Your business is here. If you move, I'll never see my great-grandchildren."

John quickly suppressed his smile. *Now, we're getting to the truth of the issue. This is all about great-grandbabies.* "Whoa there, Pops. Aren't you getting a little ahead of the situation? We haven't discussed marriage, let alone children. Just give us time to see where our lives are going before you start planning our future."

"After all the work you did with the twelve gifts, you're just going to let her walk away without a fight. What's wrong with you, boy?" Pops muttered a few words under his breath.

John sat back, noting Pops's pinched expression. The tips of his ears had turned bright red. It was time to cool the conversation down and think about what he wanted. He leaned forward, elbows on his knees. "I want her to be happy, and if that means she needs to work with someone else, then I'll let her go. Then we'll see about the personal side. If it's meant to be, it will be." He returned his attention to the game, searching for a way to defeat Pops now that he had him off his game with the discussion about Melissa.

"That's what's the matter with you youngsters," Pops grumbled. "No fight. Sometimes, you need to make it happen, not sit back and wait. No wonder I beat you at chess so easily. You need to be thinking three moves ahead all the time. Now, pour me another whiskey and watch me checkmate you in just three moves." Pops sat there, scowling.

Later, John sent Melissa a text.

—The trap is fully baited. All you need to do now is spring it on him on your return.—

****

Melissa arrived home from the convention on a high. *Save Our Salmon* was the talk of the week. They'd had lines of people every day wanting to play the game and find out when it would be available. Several distributors wanted to place orders on the spot. Dan would manage the follow-up with the distributors with the date for release. By mid-summer at the latest, the game would be on shelves nationwide and available online. Just thinking this was becoming a reality was a little surreal. She had done it.

Melissa also had a couple of generous offers to work with other gaming companies on the next game. Hopefully, *SOS* and any new ones she'd design would awaken people to the many crises affecting the planet. *Grams is right. I can make a difference with my art. My medium can also touch people's emotions and help them see the world in a new way.*

****

Melissa and John drove north to spend the day with Grams on the Saturday after the expo. Melissa was eager to update her grandmother on recent events and have her finally meet John.

Pulling into the driveway, she saw Grams step onto her porch, wiping her hands on the apron tied around her waist. Once out of the car, Grams wrapped her in a welcoming hug.

John approached, handing Grams the flowers he brought.

She reached out to hug him, too. Grams took Melissa's hand and started toward the house. "Your timing is perfect. I just put the casserole in the oven. We'll sit out back and enjoy some tea while it bakes."

Melissa sat, soaking in the scents and sounds of the water. The tops of the waves sparkled in the sunlight. Despite the chill in the air, she was comfortable, snug in a heavy sweater. Sandpipers hopped along the sand, pecking at the debris carried in by the waves. Melissa shared how successful the game was at E-Three. "My dream is the lessons learned in *SOS*, and the new games I create will translate into action in the real world. Gamers will become activists for the environment. Even small changes can and will make a difference."

"I'm so proud of you. And your mother would be delighted, as well." Grams reached over to pat Melissa's hand.

When the kitchen timer beeped, Melissa stood to go inside to take the casserole out of the oven and set the table. She encouraged Grams and John to stay outside. Listening to the happy-sounding conversation filled her heart with joy. Her two most cherished people were getting to know each other. She laid out the plates and silverware, humming to herself. Placing the casserole in the center of the table, she stood back for a moment to breathe in the mixture of chicken, mushrooms, rice, and salty sea air.

She paused silently at the door to the back porch to watch Grams and John together. Grams had her hand on John's arm while she leaned in to listen. John was telling her about his family. She knocked gently on the door frame and announced lunch was ready.

They both turned and smiled.

Her stomach did that flip-flop thing again when John extended his hand to Grams to escort her into the house.

After lunch, Melissa announced she wanted to walk on the beach to search for more shells. She hoped to find another abalone to add to her collection.

John asked if she'd mind if he stayed back so he could have a closer look at Grams's tapestry.

The request seemed odd, but Melissa agreed and started toward the water's edge. She strolled along, enjoying the warmth of the sun and the chatter of the seagulls who flew above. Up ahead, she spotted a young woman with a toddler picking up seashells. Moving closer, she was delighted to see Jessica and Donnie.

Jessica hurried over to hug her, tugging little Donnie with her. She filled Melissa in on the latest update on the proposed pier. The tribe's community actions and presentation to the city council had done the trick. The pier was voted down just this morning by a margin of eight to two. The two members who voted to approve the pier were connected somehow to the oil company that made the initial request. She said her grandfather was present for the vote and would call a tribal meeting later today to announce the decision. But like most news in tight-knit communities, the information was spreading fast.

When Melissa returned to the house, she saw John sitting at the kitchen table, chatting while Grams boxed up to-go packages of the leftover casserole and other goodies. When she entered, she noted they both stopped talking.

Grams hid her smile behind her hand.

John quickly glanced away.

Something's up. They both look like the cat who

swallowed the canary, complete with feathers sticking out of their mouths. Melissa raised an eyebrow.

Grams stacked the food containers on the counter. "As usual, I made too much for just me, so you two must take some home for another day. I had time this morning, so I made a batch of blueberry muffins with the berries I froze last summer and a few dozen chocolate chip cookies."

Melissa glanced at John as he squirmed in his chair.

"I'm glad I got to see your Grams's tapestry. I can see why the team used it for inspiration for *SOS*." He busied himself, closing the lids on the containers Grams handed him.

She folded her arms across her chest and narrowed her eyes. "What's up? You two look like you're hiding something."

Grams wiped her hands on her apron. "No, no. We're just chatting. I was telling John about some of the Lummi folklore."

"Yeah, great stories." John continued to stack the containers. "You should incorporate some into the game."

Melissa dropped her arms and stared. "I did."

"Oh, yeah. Well, that's great." He shrugged and quickly looked away.

Giving up on getting anything out of either of them, Melissa laughed at the stack of containers. Grams was packing enough food to last at least a week. "Of course, you just happened to make a few extra things you need us to take off your hands. I love you, Grams."

"I love you, too, baby. Now, you and John better get on the road and back to Seattle while there's still some daylight. I'll see you soon at your going-away party."

Grams gave Melissa a long hug. Then she also wrapped John in one of her comfortable hugs.

Melissa studied them again. *Something is definitely up.*

Chapter 25

The next day, Melissa put on a light jacket and headed out to jog around the lake to Howard's stand. She kept rehearsing what she'd say. *I hope I can pull this off.*

Howard held up his tongs.

She waved off his offer of a hot dog. "I spent yesterday with Grams, and as usual, she loaded me up with food. I'll be busy eating her casserole and other goodies for a few more days. I just wanted to see you to tell you about the convention. Do you have time to talk?"

"Sure, let me flip my sign, then I'll sit with you. John told me your game was a major hit."

Remembering the positive buzz at the expo, she grinned and sat at the nearby picnic table. "It sure was. I'm still pinching myself. People lined up every day to see it. Dan came home with a stack of business cards from distributors who want to place orders as soon as the game is ready. And the best news is I've had several strong offers to produce the next in my series of environmentally focused games."

Howard stumbled, catching himself. "Why would you be interested in other offers? Won't Brothers do the next game?" He sat opposite her, arms crossed loosely.

She lowered her head, avoiding direct eye contact. "Maybe. I haven't decided yet. But I am seriously considering a few of the other companies."

"Doesn't Brothers have the rights to the game as part of your deal?"

His voice had taken on an excusing tone. She struggled not to burst out laughing at the transformation in Howard's voice. He had assumed his lawyer's voice—the one that reminded the opposing council they were on shaky legal ground. He must have been a formidable opponent in the courtroom. She wasn't sure she'd ever want to go up against him. She paused, as if giving his statement some consideration. "They do have the rights to *this* game. No one else can produce *Save Our Salmon*. But I have sole rights to the concept. So, if I decide to do another environmentally themed educational game, I can go anywhere."

"But why would you want to? Did Dan or John not treat you right? Do I need to talk to the boys?" Howard lightly pounded a fist on the table.

"No, they've been wonderful and extremely generous." She shook her head, smiling. "I've talked to them about this, and they agree if my goal is to educate as many people as possible through the games, a larger company with a greater market share would be the smarter choice. As great as the team at Brothers is, it's still a relatively small company compared to others."

"I can understand that, but even if you go with another company for the next game, you won't have to move, will you? You've been working remotely all this time, so why change?"

She noted the desperate tone. He kept glancing around, as if searching for the flaw in her logic. She could see he was deep into defending attorney mode. "One of the things I've learned in the past few months is how much I was isolating myself." She faked a sigh and let her gaze drift off to the lake. "The team at Brothers has shown me how wonderful it is to work closely with others. Together, we're far more creative than I was on my own. I don't want to go backward and lock myself up in my tower again." She straightened and placed both hands, palms down, on the table. "The days of Rapunzel are gone. I want to be Melissa in *all* aspects of my life—personal and professional. So, if I accept one of the offers, I'll move to wherever their offices are."

Howard slumped forward, letting his hands drop to the tabletop. His gaze drifted to his loosely folded hands. "But…what about John? You two were *finally* coming together. I had plans," he blurted.

Melissa ignored his comment about plans and went on as if she was thinking this through as she spoke. "I know, and that's what's making this decision so difficult. I do like John a lot, but I don't know if I'm ready to take our relationship to the next level. He'll always be a great friend."

"Friend? I don't get great-grandbabies from friends." Howard shook his head and muttered under his breath.

"What was that? I missed what you said." She faked a puzzled expression.

Howard dismissed her question with a wave of his hand. "Nothing. Just thinking how much I'll miss you."

She reached out to take his hand. "I'll miss you, too, Howard, but this might be my time to really fly. Besides, it might be good to get out of the house. It holds a lot of memories."

"So…you're serious about going someplace else?"

Howard dropped his voice to barely above a whisper.

"Yes, I think so. I haven't decided which offer to take, but the more I think about it, I can't ignore such an opportunity. I'll always be grateful to John and Dan for believing in me and helping to create *Save Our Salmon*, but now might be the time to go bigger."

"Is there anything I can say to change your mind?" he pleaded.

She almost broke. He sounded so defeated. But she and John were determined to play this through and hopefully stop Howard from future meddling. "Not really. Howard, you've been a dear friend to me and helped me so much in the past year. I'll miss you, but I'll come back at times and visit you."

"Friend, there's that word again," Howard muttered, staring at the tabletop.

With another long sigh, she slowly stood, walked around the table, and touched his shoulder. "I need to get home, but I'll be back soon. I'll let you know when and where I end up going. There's still time for a few more hot dogs before then." Out of sight of the stand, she pulled her phone out of her pocket and sent the text.

—He took the bait. The trap has been sprung.—

****

Melissa and John went to their favorite Chinese restaurant for dinner that night. They plotted the next step in their plan over egg rolls, pot stickers, and Mandarin crispy duck. "When I left him this afternoon, I heard him muttering about friends and great-grandbabies," she told John.

"Let's see how long it takes him to invite me over for a chess game. I imagine he's sitting by his fireplace, whiskey in hand, planning his next move. He told me I needed to think three moves ahead to keep you. We need to keep at least four steps ahead to pull this off."

She nodded. "I agree. I think we should let him stew for a few days, and then I'll announce my decision to take one of the offers. The question is, where? Do I go somewhere in California, where so many gaming companies are located, or all the way across the country to the East Coast?"

"I think it needs to be the East Coast." He twirled his chopsticks in his fingers. "He'll be convinced California isn't far, and there's no reason why you couldn't just commute occasionally. Or he might think I could do the reverse."

She nodded. "Makes sense. I think Florida is a good choice. It's as far away as I can get without going to Hawaii, and there's a good-sized gaming company in Orlando."

"Perfect. Oops, there's my phone." John pulled it out of his pocket and grinned. He rotated the phone to show her the name of the caller. "Just as expected—Pops. I'll let it go to voicemail and call him back later. I'm sure I'm being summoned to his lair."

****

The next night, John entered Pops's study, expecting to see the chessboard set up for a game. It wasn't. *So, this is going to be all business.*

Pops gestured toward the liquor cabinet. "Pour yourself a big glass. You're going to need it."

"All right, Pops. What's on your mind?" Pops fixed him with one of his most intimidating glares. John remembered what Melissa had said about Pops shifting into lawyer mode in their conversation and almost laughed. He was about to be given the same treatment—only worse. Sitting comfortably in the leather chair opposite Pops, he inhaled the earthy aroma, then slowly took a sip from his glass, waiting for the opening move.

"You know perfectly well what's bothering me." Pops jumped right in immediately. "Melissa sounds like she's about to make the biggest mistake of her life and leave."

"The biggest mistake of *her* life or *yours*?" John decided two could play this game.

"Don't get smart with me, young man." Pops shook his finger. "You know what I mean. The two of you are perfect for each other. If she leaves, then you might never get her back. You need to stop her."

John set his drink on the side table and made direct eye contact. "I told you before. It's her decision to make."

"Yes, but it's yours to influence. Why are you being so stubborn?" Pops stabbed an index finger in John's direction.

John almost laughed. Pops's eyebrows were crunched together like high-diving caterpillars. "I'm not being stubborn. I'm being realistic." John picked up his glass and sipped. "This is a huge opportunity, and I won't stand in her way. This isn't the caveman days. I can't just hit her over the head with my club and drag her back to my cave. She needs to, and has every right to, decide for herself what's best."

Pops scowled. He muttered inaudibly into his glass before speaking. "Let me ask you this. Do you love her?"

John winced at the question. It was not what he had been expecting. *Pops is really playing hardball.* With a mental shrug, he decided to be honest and see where Pops took the information. “Yes, and that is why I won’t pressure her one way or the other.”

Pops sloshed the liquid in his glass, then pointed it at John. “I don’t understand where you get these crazy ideas.”

“From you.” John raised his glass in a salute.

“What?” He shot his eyebrows up and gaped at John.

“I’ve watched you and Gramma all my life. I watched the two of you make decisions together. You listened and often acted on her ideas when she had an opinion. She said she wanted to go back to college and get her master’s degree in education, and you supported her. Even though it meant nights when she was too busy with her schoolwork to cook a nice dinner. You willingly picked up takeout from Mario’s when she was cramming for an exam or working on a paper. You helped her realize her dream.”

“Humph, that’s different.” Pops dismissed the idea with a wave of his hand.

John was on a roll now, relishing having the upper hand for once. “And then my mom said she wanted to complete her doctorate, and you also supported her decision. You told Dad to suck it up and order takeout, take his shirts and suits to the dry cleaners himself, and learn to run the vacuum cleaner occasionally. You told him they were partners, and she deserved to see her dreams come true.”

“Well, your dad was acting like a spoiled child.” Pops conceded the point with another dismissive wave.

John set his drink on the end table and leaned forward. “You taught me respecting the dreams of the person you love is important. In a good marriage, their aspirations must mean more to you than your own. Sometimes, you need to sacrifice what you think you want for what they need. That's what I want for Melissa and me. Even if it means letting her go if that's what she needs to do."

"Never quote an old man back to him. It's humiliating," Pops grumbled.

"But true. I love you, Pops, and I know you care for Melissa. So I know you also want what's best for her. We need to let her make that decision for herself."

"Pour me another whiskey and get the damn chess game set up. I might as well beat you at chess since I've lost this case."

Over coffee the next day, John told Melissa about his conversation with Pops.

"Maybe we should just tell him and stop this. I hate to see him so upset," Melissa fretted.

"Nah. By the time he beat me in chess, he was back to his usual self, crowing over his victory. I could see the wheels spinning in his head. He's planning his next move. I think this weekend you should tell him you're going to Florida at the end of the month."

Chapter 26

On Saturday, Melissa jogged to the snack stand. She sat at an empty picnic table and patiently waited until Howard had helped all the people clamoring for food. The winter weather had broken and was showing signs of spring. The sunshine brought people out, and the snack stand was busy again.

After the last order was filled, Howard turned the sign to *Closed.* Picking up two bottles of water, he joined her. "Have you made a decision yet?"

She gratefully took the bottle Howard offered. She needed something to hold to keep herself from fidgeting in her nervousness. "Yes, and I wanted to tell you myself. I've decided to accept the offer from the company in Orlando."

Howard fiddled with his water bottle, twisting the cap. "Oh." He didn't look up. He took a slow drink and stared out over the lake. "When will you be leaving?"

Melissa hesitated for a moment, concerned about Howard's reaction. With a sigh, she plunged on. "I said I'd be there by the first of next month."

"That soon?" Howard replied in a low voice. He stared her straight in her eyes with a small smile. "What are you going to do about your house?"

Melissa caught the "gotcha" moment and deftly sidestepped his move. "For now, I'll just leave it. I'll decide about selling it in a few months, once I know I'll be there permanently. I'll hire a company to check it frequently." The lies flowed easily.

"I see. How does your grandmother feel about this?"

He was clearly trying another tactic to show her the flaws in her decision. She studied his cocked eyebrow and half smile, guessing where Howard was going with his question. *He's hoping for an ally*. "She'll miss me, of course, but she understands my reasons. She agrees a change of scenery could be good for me."

"And what are your reasons exactly?"

The lawyer's voice was back. She sensed he was starting his cross-examination.

He sat straight and leaned forward.

Melissa paused for a moment. This conversation was getting more challenging than she anticipated. "It really came down to who has the greatest potential to help me reach the biggest market."

"So, this is about money?" Howard snapped.

"No. Money has nothing to do with my decision." She raised a hand in a stop gesture. "This company has the marketing power to make more people aware of the game. The more people who buy and play it, the more opportunity I have to educate them and do something positive for the environment. It's about honoring my Lummi heritage." She paused to take a quick sip of water. "I've talked it over with John and Dan, and they understand. They'll still market *Save Our Salmon*. This is about future opportunities." *Checkmate*. She stood to leave.

Howard just sat there, staring off into space.

Once she got a short distance away, she glanced over her shoulder to see he continued to sit there, apparently mulling over the situation. She knew he wouldn't leave this. She needed to warn John that he was plotting his next move and that John was the likely target.

****

That evening, Melissa and Karen drove together, laden with bags of baby gifts, to Jan's to see baby Katie. This time, they both summoned the courage to hold the baby and "oohed" and "aahed" over how adorable she was wrapped in her pink blanket.

Once Katie fell back asleep, Derrick took her to lay her back in her crib so the girls could talk.

"What's new?" asked Jan. "I haven't talked to you since you left for the gaming convention." She curled up in the corner of the couch and leaned forward.

Melissa updated Jan on the latest updates on *SOS* and Howard. She described Howard's reaction when she told him she was moving to Orlando at the end of the month. "But now, I'm a little worried. He seems so upset about my decision I want to end this."

"We need to hurry up and plan your going-away party," said Karen. "I'd offer to host, but my place isn't big enough for everyone."

Jan chimed in. "I'm afraid my place isn't much better with all the baby paraphernalia."

Melissa smiled at both. "No worries. I already decided to do it at my house. Sort of the opposite of a housewarming. It will be a house farewell."

"Perfect. Now, Jan, we're going to have to act really sad, so we don't give anything away," Karen warned.

Jan put on a fake pout. "No problem. My hormones are a mess. I weep at dog food commercials. I can tear up at the drop of a hat." Jan leaned forward, asking in a hushed voice. "So, now that we've taken care of Howard, tell me more about John. Has he told you he loves you yet?"

Melissa could feel the blush start to flare on her neck and cheeks.

Karen burst out laughing. "You go, girl. Right for the jugular."

Jan dismissed Karen's comment with a graceful wave of her hand. "Like you don't want to know. So, Melissa, tell all. I'm a sleep-deprived new mom, and I need to live vicariously through my still single friends."

Melissa pretended to fuss over refolding one of the outfits they had brought for Katie. "Well, we've been seeing a lot of each other. And it's been fun."

"I'm not interested in fun." Jan shook her head. "I want all the romantic details. Have you kissed? What does he say? Have you told him you love him?"

Melissa laughed at Jan's eagerness. "Yes, we've kissed…a lot." She grinned at Jan and Karen high-fiving each other. "Subtle, ladies. We talk, mostly about our families and *SOS.*"

Her friends groaned.

"And no, I haven't told him I love him. We agreed just to be friends for a while and see how the relationship progresses."

Jan leaned back with another groan. "Friends? It's so clear you have feelings for him. You always have. Even when you thought he betrayed you. You need to be honest with him."

Melissa sat quietly for a moment. "How did you know Derrick was the one? How did you know he was who you wanted to spend the rest of your life with?"

Jan fiddled with her wedding ring and glanced in the direction of the other room where Derrick had gone to study medical journals. “I didn’t at first. I didn’t give him a second thought when we were in high school. He was a science geek, and I was a cheerleader. Our paths seldom crossed. But then we became lab partners. I got to know him and thought he was funny. By senior year, we were dating. Then, poof, off to college for both of us.” She waved her hands in the air. “We didn’t reconnect until I was back home after college, and he was going to med school at UW. But the moment I saw him again, I knew. My stomach did this flip-floppy thing, and my heart raced. I know it sounds corny, but it’s true.”

“Sound more like the flu than love.” Karen made a face, scrunching her nose. “Maybe it’s a good thing you married a doctor.”

Jan held up a hand to ignore Karen and focused on Melissa. “How does John make you feel?

Melissa sighed. Slowly, she patted her stomach. “My stomach has been doing flip-flops since I met him. Lately, it does it even when I think of him.”

“It’s called love.” Jan gave her a satisfied smile.

“I don’t have time for love right now. I’m too busy with the launch of *SOS* and my going away part.” She made air quotes as she spoke.

Jan just grinned like the Cheshire Cat.

“Okay, you can protest, but you’re a goner.”

Melissa slumped back in her chair and groaned. “Enough of this, let’s plan this party.”

They decided to have the party the next weekend. After an hour of list-making, Melissa glanced up to see Jan had fallen asleep on the couch. “We’d better head out and let the new mommy get some sleep while she can," she whispered.

They tiptoed out of the room, meeting Derrick in the front hall. Holding their fingers up to their lips, they pointed to the sleeping Madonna in the living room.

Derrick smiled. "Thanks for coming."

Once back in the car, Melissa returned to the discussion of the pretend going-away party. "I'm glad we're doing it soon. I'm not sure how many more times I can see Howard and not break down and tell him the truth." Melissa clenched the steering wheel. "When we first came up with this idea, it seemed perfect to discourage him from meddling in other people's lives. But I don't like seeing him so upset."

"You said he's always plotting new ways to convince you to stay. My guess is he's already making his next move."

"You're right. We can pull this off for one more week. I just hope it works." She drummed her fingers on the steering wheel. "He's a tenacious fighter. Like a dog with a bone. I'm sure he's got a few more moves to make."

****

After answering Pops's call, John put his phone back in his pocket. As expected, he was again summoned to the lion's den. *I wonder what new move he's come up with now.* That evening, he found Pops sitting in his favorite chair in front of the fireplace, whiskey in hand. He headed to the bar and poured himself a glass before sitting in the chair across from Pops. "Okay. You summoned?"

"Your brother should be here any minute, then we'll talk. In the meantime, how is Melissa doing?"

John twirled the amber liquid in his glass, watching it coat the sides of the crystal glass before taking a sip. He could feel the warmth of the Irish whiskey slide down his throat. "She's doing okay." He took his time responding, letting the comment hang in the air briefly. "I think she's a little nervous about making such a big move, but she's very excited about the possibilities for expanding her environmentally themed games."

"Well, I see you have gathered the usual suspects, Pops. What's up?" Dan strolled into the room and headed directly to the bar. "Whatever the reason, I'm always happy to relieve you of some of your Irish whiskey." Drink in hand, he plopped into one of the overstuffed armchairs and raised his glass in a salute to Pops.

"I always knew my whiskey is what gets you here," Pops harrumphed.

"That and the chance to beat you in chess." Dan laughed.

"That will be the day," declared Howard.

"A man's got to have dreams. So, what's up? Why did you summon John and me here together?"

Pops set down his glass and stared directly at Dan. "We have a problem, and I fully intend to solve it. Melissa is leaving soon to move across the country. I can't seem to talk any sense into your brother's thick skull, so I need another tactic to keep her here. If John would do the right thing and propose, then she'd stay." He glanced at John and then shuddered. "But no. He's being all noble and letting her go without a fight. But not me." Pops thumped his chest.

John silently watched the interplay between Dan and Pops while he nursed his drink. He consciously chose to stay out of the conversation for a while to see where Pops was going. In the meantime, Dan could have some fun.

"Okay, what's your plan?" He gave John a conspiratorial wink.

"I talked to Melissa yesterday. She's moving because this other company could open her games up to a bigger audience." Pops spread his hands apart. "She's determined to reach as many young people as possible to turn them into warriors for her environmental causes. I said you two could do the same, but she said you didn't have the resources to reach a bigger market yet."

"She's right." Dan shrugged. "We all talked about it, and we agreed with her that going to the company in Orlando would enable her to reach a far bigger market than we can. Like you, I don't want her to go, but I realize we can't give her what she needs to make her dreams a reality."

John noted the glint in Pops's eye at Dan's statement. Pops was circling something, like a lion toying with his prey, watching and waiting for the right moment to come in for the kill. When he saw Pops look away briefly, John nodded to Dan to continue. They were getting close to the purpose of this meeting.

Pops eyed them both over the rim of his glass. "Cocky pock, you two are selling yourselves short. You could do this if you tried." Sitting up straight, he pointed a finger at them.

"It takes money we don't have right now. We'd need a much larger marketing team and the ability to hire a more experienced PR firm with a wider reach." Dan extended his arms to either side.

"So, it's about money?" Pops sat back. He steepled

his fingers under his chin and smiled.

Aha, now we're getting there. Here comes what Pops believes is his checkmate move. Need to play this cool. He leaned back, straightened his legs and crossed them at the ankles. "No, it's about helping Melissa see this grow the way she envisions."

Pops set down his glass with a thud. "Wrong, it's about the fact you're too stubborn to see the answer is right in front of you." Glaring at both of them, he bellowed.

John looked over at Dan.

Dan just shrugged. "What do you mean, Pops? I'm not at all sure where you're going with this."

Pops leaned forward. His gaze was laser-focused as he studied them both. "If you want Melissa to stay, then you need to provide her with the same opportunities these other guys can give her. That takes money. Money, I have. You wouldn't let me invest in your company when you started. You wanted to prove the two of you could do it without family help. Well, you did." He thumped the arm of his chair with his hand. "You built a successful company. Maybe not as big as others, but you two are smart and resourceful. You've accomplished a lot in just a few years, and I can see this will be huge one day." Slowly, he started to smile. "I can help you make that day come sooner. Let me give you the money to get the PR firm and anything else you need, so Melissa won't have a reason to leave." Pops sat back and picked up his glass again with a smirk.

John held up a hand to stop Dan's reply. He was ready. It was time to counter. "No, Pops. We told you when we started, we'd do this on our own. We'll grow as the business can support the growth."

"John, you're not being reasonable. I'm an old man. My money will go to you in time, so why not let me give you some of it now? It would make me happy in my final years to have helped you."

Pops quickly switched tone from lawyer to benevolent grandfather. John's reaction was immediate. He needed Pops to think this was a closed path to his attempts to influence Melissa's decision. He jumped up and pointed a finger. "Don't play the old man card. You're too stubborn to die any time soon. Besides, any money you have to leave will go to more than just Dan and me. Remember, you've got a few more grandchildren."

Pops lifted a hand, palm up. "Yeah, yeah. There's enough to go around. Don't you worry about that. Now, sit back down and be reasonable."

John continued to pace, playing at projecting his anger. Shaking his finger, he ranted. "You're the one not being reasonable. This isn't about helping Dan and me grow the business. I know perfectly well you're proud we've done this on our own. You've got this crazy notion you need to have great-grandbabies, and you've decided Melissa and I are the ones to give them to you. You're the one who needs to see this isn't your decision to make. You can try and manipulate us as much as you want, but it's not going to work, and I won't play your games anymore." John gulped the last of his drink and stopped short of slamming it down on the table. "I'm out of here. Come on, Dan, I'll buy you a beer."

Dan gazed at the whiskey left in his glass and took a large swallow. "Okay, bro. Make it another Irish whiskey, and I'll come with you. Night, Pops. Nice try, but as they say in the biz, no cigar."

At the door, John stopped briefly to look back. Pops was slumped in his chair, staring at the whiskey in his glass. *Melissa's right. We need to end this soon. We've tortured him enough.*

Out on the sidewalk, they both jumped into John's car. "Hurry, get us out of here. I'll get my car later," Dan called out.

Driving a block away, John pulled over to the curb, and they both exploded with laughter.

Still breathless from laughter, Dan punched John in the shoulder. "Wow, that was some performance, bro. I didn't know you had it in you."

John wiped his eyes on his shirt sleeve. "Me, either. I had to get us out of there fast. I was afraid one of us was going to crack and give it all away."

"Yeah. His face when you started ranting—you got him good. But you know, as soon as he finds out Melissa isn't moving, he's going to gloat. He'll insist he knew all along she wouldn't leave."

"I know, but at least for a few weeks, we've had him back on his heels."

"I sure hope he learns his lesson. I'm afraid I'm next on his list once he sees you happily married off. Speaking of marrying, have you asked Melissa yet?"

"What?" John stared, his mouth open. "What are you talking about? I haven't said a thing about marriage.

Dan just laughed. "Didn't have to. You've had this sappy look on your face for a week now. I know something's up. Melissa's party will need a new theme, and an engagement would be perfect."

John glanced over at Dan's smug expression.

"Keep it up, and I'm not buying you a beer, let alone another whiskey."

Dan just grinned.

I'll have to watch my step this week. Otherwise, Dan will try to worm his way into witnessing my proposal.

Chapter 27

Melissa readily agreed to have dinner with John on Wednesday night.

He picked her up at six and drove to the University of Washington campus.

Once parked, Melissa recognized where they were. This part of the campus was home to thirty Yoshino cherry trees gifted from Japan—just like the ones surrounding the mall area in Washington, D.C. In late March and early April, the quad was resplendent with delicate pink flowers and the intoxicating scent of cherry blossoms.

John took out a picnic basket from the back seat. "I thought we'd have a casual picnic to enjoy the trees."

Melissa glanced around, puzzled at the location. "Is it allowed?"

John just nodded, took her hand, and started toward the center of the quad. "Come, let's find a perfect spot to sit and enjoy the blossoms."

Still bewildered over his choice of location for a picnic, she took in the beauty of the cherry trees in full bloom. "John, this is beautiful. I haven't been here in years, and I forgot how incredible this sight is when the cherry trees are blossoming. It always reminds me of a Monet painting. If he had seen this, he would have been compelled to paint them."

"I hoped you'd like it here. I think it's beautiful.

Like you."

Her heart and stomach did a little flip-flop.

John let go of her hand to set down the basket and spread a plaid blanket on the ground.

Melissa sighed and slowly circled, arms out, taking in the beauty. "My mom did several paintings inspired by these trees. One of my favorites had the trees in full bloom, with a troupe of female dancers in floaty Grecian gowns, dancing barefoot on a carpet of pink petals."

John paused for a moment. "I know the painting. I saw it in the art museum with my mom. Is it still there?"

"No, it was a part of a private collection on display for an exhibit. I never knew who owned it." She glanced around at the nearly empty area. "Are you sure this is okay?"

John motioned for her to sit. "I'm sure. During college, we got food from the trucks lining the quad and had picnics here. On a nice spring day, this area would be jammed with students eating, studying, or just hanging out."

John busied himself opening the basket and removing a platter of cheeses, meats, fruit, and a variety of crackers. Next, he took out a bottle of champagne and two plastic glasses.

"Oooh, champagne. What are we celebrating?" Melissa looked to see if anyone was watching. *This is definitely more than a simple picnic.*

"Just us." John smiled and poured the bubbly into two plastic cups.

She relaxed against the trunk of one of the trees and nibbled on a piece of sharp cheddar cheese. Melissa scanned the nearby buildings. "You went to college here, right?"

"Yes, I spent four years here studying computer science. Did you ever consider going here? You told me you went to UC Berkley."

"No, I wanted to spread my wings a little. Besides, Berkley was my dad's alma mater, so it seemed appropriate. They have an excellent art school. At the time, I hadn't decided to focus on graphic design. I originally did more traditional art, such as painting and sculpting. After I graduated, I came back home."

"I, for one, am glad you did. Both that you decided on graphic art and returned to Seattle."

"Me, too." She smiled.

He leaned in to kiss her.

The same tingly feeling she experienced each time they kissed spread through her chest, and the taste of champagne on her lips only added to the experience. The sky briefly brightened with shades of magenta and coral as the sun dipped below the horizon. The full moon filtered through the lacy canopy of cherry blossom petals, and Melissa shivered a little in the chilling air.

"You're cold. Let me move the basket a little, and I can keep you warm." John shifted the basket and wrapped Melissa in his arms, gently rubbing her arms.

"This is perfect." Melissa sighed, wiggling farther into John's embrace. *And it is, sitting in a beautiful place, wrapped in John's arms. The moment is perfect.*

"I'm glad. I wanted the most romantic place I could imagine for this moment."

"What?" Melissa gasped and twisted in John's arms to see his face. "Why?"

John shifted to rise on one knee and pulled a small, dark-blue velvet box from his pocket.

She raised both hands to her mouth and gasped at seeing the box. Melissa could feel her whole body tingle in anticipation.

"Melissa, the moment you rushed up to Pops's stand, eyes flaming and ready to defend his property, I knew you were the woman I'd been waiting for my entire life. In that instant, I wanted to drop to one knee and ask you to marry me." He scraped his free hand through his hair and took a deep breath. "But common sense prevailed. I knew we needed to get to know each other first and give you time to hopefully feel the same about me. Since then, my love for you has only grown. I don't want another moment to go by without knowing we will share a life together forever." He paused and cleared his throat. "Melissa Anderson, will you do me the greatest honor of my life and say yes, you'll marry me?"

"Yes. Yes, a thousand times yes." She quickly got to her knees and cradled his face in her hands. "I love you, John McDonald, and I always will. Yes, I will marry you." The words tumbled out in a rush. Her heart raced, and her hands trembled. The rest of the world faded away, leaving only her and John in a cocoon of pure joy. Fireworks exploded in her brain when he leaned in and kissed her.

The sound of applause broke the spell. Startled, they stared at the strangers who had witnessed John's proposal.

"She said yes," John announced to the crowd. The applause continued when he opened the box and held it up. "I do have a ring." Smiling from ear to ear, he gently put the ring on her finger.

Both their hands shook so much, she was surprised he could manage it.

The crowd slowly dispersed with shoutouts of congratulations.

"That was cool, man," yelled a male student out with a couple of buddies.

"Beautiful, what a romantic proposal. I wish you all the best." An older woman stood with her husband's arm around her shoulders. "Almost as good as yours, George." She reached up to stroke his face.

Laughing, John and Melissa collapsed back onto the blanket. "I didn't mean to put on a show. I was sure by now the area would be deserted," John declared.

Melissa smiled through the tears that flowed down her face. "It's perfect. I say we pack up this food and head somewhere to celebrate. Hopefully, somewhere with more light so I can admire this ring." She quickly wiped away the tears and held her hand up to gaze at the ring he placed there.

Still laughing at the memory of the crowd's cheers, they packed up the food and champagne and ambled together back to John's car.

Melissa waited while John put the basket in the car, then gripped his hands and swung them around in a circle. "I want to shout this to the world. I want everyone to know I'm in love with the most incredible man."

John pulled her in close. "We need to keep this quiet for a few days if we want to trick Pops."

Melissa felt like she was floating. She placed her hands on his shoulders to steady herself. "You know he's going to take full credit for this."

John nodded. "Oh yes, he'll gloat all the way to our wedding day."

"We need to keep this quiet until Saturday. We can't tell anyone."

"Your grandmother kind of already knows. I asked for her blessing when we visited her."

Melissa stopped in her tracks and poked John in the arm. "So, that was why the sudden interest in her tapestry."

"Yes, I had been trying all day to find a moment alone with her. I was running out of time until you said you wanted to walk on the beach to look for shells. However, I still had her show me her tapestry because she said you'd ask me what I thought. And you did on the way home."

"So, I can tell her?" Her breath quickened at the thought of Grams's reaction. *She likes John, so she'll be happy for both of us.*

He smiled and nodded. "Yes, and Dan sort of knows. I didn't tell him, but he accused me of being up to something. He said he could tell by the sappy way I was mooning around the office all week that I was going to propose."

"I'm surprised he wasn't part of our audience." Melissa laughed.

"That's because I told him I hadn't figured out when and where yet, and I was careful not to say I was seeing you tonight. I wouldn't have put it past him to have followed us."

"I'm glad we don't have any meetings scheduled in your office for the rest of the week. I don't think I could hide my smile. I'd better not go see Howard either."

"Good idea. And I hope he doesn't plan one of his emergency meetings to convince me to throw you over my shoulder and prevent you from leaving."

Melissa laughed at the image. "He seriously suggested that?"

"Not exactly, but the sentiment was there. Now, let's go to your place and plan the rest of our lives together."

Our lives. The sound of that had her tingling all over again.

Chapter 28

For Melissa, the next two days crawled by. She stared at the clock as if, by sheer force of will, she could make it move forward. On Saturday morning, she woke up filled with anticipation.

Grams arrived mid-morning, ready to help prepare for the party.

Melissa had called her Thursday morning to tell her about John's proposal. So far, Grams was the only person she told.

At lunchtime, Karen showed up loaded with decorations. She had streamers, balloons, noise makers, and a banner that read, *We'll Miss You, Melissa.*

After a delicious meal of cheesy chicken enchiladas made by Grams, the three tackled transforming the living and dining rooms into a festive setting. By five, they had hung all the streamers, anchored balloons around the rooms, and arranged fresh flowers on the dining room table and fireplace mantel.

Melissa had made arrangements with Mario for various Italian dishes, including her favorite fettuccine *alfredo*.

Once everything was ready, Karen headed home to change.

Melissa and Grams hurried upstairs to get ready, too.

Melissa was checking her hair one more time when

the doorbell rang.

John stepped in, lifted her, and swung her around in a circle. “Soon, we will tell everyone you’ve made me the happiest man on earth by agreeing to be my wife.”

“I have your ring in my pocket and can’t wait to put it on and never take it off again.”

At that moment, Grams came down the stairs. She hurried over to John and took his face in her hands. “You have made me so happy to know my granddaughter will have you by her side from now on. You have filled the hole in her heart with joy, and I love you for that.”

John took Grams’s hands in his. “I promise you she will always be loved and cherished by me. I know things won’t always be sunshine and roses, but she will be my partner in life, and we will face whatever life has in store together, hand in hand.”

“That is all I can ask for.” Reaching for Melissa’s hand, Grams placed her hand in John’s. “Remember the love you feel for each other in this moment, and you will always find the right path to travel together. I love you both.” Grams embraced them both. “Now, we have a party to get ready for, which will be even more joyous once everyone knows the real reason they’re here.”

The three bustled about arranging a variety of beverages on a side table, along with bottles of wine ready to open.

John pulled a bottle of Irish whiskey from a bag. “Pops is going to need this tonight.” He winked at Melissa as he put the bottle on the beverage table.

In a few minutes, the doorbell rang again.

Mario hustled in, followed by his grandson

carrying trays of covered dishes.

The tantalizing aroma of tomato sauce and cheese wafted behind him all the way to the kitchen.

Once all the food had been carried in from his van, Mario shooed them out of the kitchen. "I will take care of all this. You get ready to greet your guests."

"Mario, thank you so much for agreeing to make the food for this." Melissa gave him a quick hug.

"*Mia cara,* I will cook for you anytime. Next time, I want it to be for a happier occasion. Now, go before you make me cry and ruin my sauce." Mario wiped his eyes on the corner of his snow-white apron.

They all left the kitchen in Mario's capable hands.

He began barking out orders to his grandson in Italian.

For the next thirty minutes, Melissa was busy greeting her friends, John's family, and colleagues from Brothers at Play.

Everyone expressed their dismay that she was leaving them.

John nudged her when Howard came in with John's parents. Melissa had met them a little while ago over dinner, but John hadn't filled them in on their plan.

His mother, Natalie, rushed over, taking her hands in hers. "I can't believe you're leaving. I was hoping for a different ending to your relationship with John. He's been so happy since meeting you."

Melissa had to turn away for fear she'd say something to reassure her and give their secret away prematurely.

Jan saved her when she came over and wrapped her arms around her. "I can't believe you're leaving just when I need you most. I had visions of you, Karen, and me taking baby Katie out for strolls and to the beach for picnics." Jan's eyes misted over, and she hugged Melissa tight.

"You have a new baby?" Natalie patted Jan's arm sympathetically.

Jan continued to wipe away the tears that were forming in her eyes. "Yes, and this is my first time leaving her with someone else. Derrick's mom is watching her, but I'm heartsick she might smile and I'm not there to see it."

Melissa silently thanked her friend with a smile for distracting John's mother and slipped away. *Good tactic, Jan.* She spotted Howard looking on sourly.

John poured him a generous shot of Irish whiskey.

"I'm not talking to you," Howard grumbled as he took the drink. "I still can't believe you're letting this happen and even helping to throw a party to celebrate it."

John just shrugged, and when Howard looked away, he winked.

Howard stood there for a moment, muttering to himself. "Well, I'm going to talk to someone with more sense." With that, Howard headed across the room toward Grams.

Melissa hurried over to John and linked arms just as Dan approached.

"Boy, that was rough, bro."

John faced his brother and smiled. He gave Melissa a nudge, pointing his chin over Dan's shoulder. The pretty barista from their favorite coffee shop was talking to John and Dan's dad, Paul. He gave his brother an inquiring look.

Dan grinned. "Yes, I finally got up enough nerve

and asked her out. We've only been out a few times, but I really like her. Her name's Jennifer, and she's amazing. Did you know she graduated from Harvard Law School, clerked for a judge in Boston for a few years, and is working as a barista while studying for the Washington State bar exam? I think she and Dad are talking torts or some such thing."

"That's awesome. I'm proud of you for finally asking her out." John slapped Dan on the back.

"I also wanted to let you know I stocked Melissa's fridge with a few bottles of the bubbly for later." Dan gave them both a conspiratorial wink.

"What makes you think we're going to need champagne?" John whispered, glancing around the room.

Dan continued to grin. "Bro, you are so transparent it's fun. I love seeing this goofy side of you. Don't worry. Pops is so busy trying to devise a new plan to keep Melissa here that he's blind to anything else. But I'm not." He leaned in to give Melissa a quick kiss on the cheek, "Congrats, my new fu-sis." Laughing, Dan strolled away to reclaim his date.

Melissa gestured at Dan's retreating form and raised one eyebrow.

John chuckled. "Don't bother trying to figure it out. Dan speaks his own language."

Glancing around, Melissa noted Howard had found Grams and maneuvered her off to the side so they could talk privately. With the excuse of needing a glass of wine, she inched closer to Howard and Grams, eager to eavesdrop.

"Why are you letting Melissa make such a horrible mistake with her life?"

"What mistake is that?" Grams tilted her head to one side.

"Leaving us, leaving John. He thinks he's being noble by letting her go, but I think he's just being bullheaded. I told that boy he needed to propose, but he wouldn't listen. He says Melissa needs to make her decision without complications."

Melissa put a hand over her mouth to keep from laughing out loud and give herself away.

"That's very supportive of him." Grams nodded.

"Love isn't a *complication.*" Howard went on as if Grams hadn't spoken. "It's a necessity of life, and they're in love with each other. That's so obvious, even a blind man could see it."

"I agree with you there, but still, it's their lives." Grams laid her hand on Howard's arm to console him. "They need to figure out the best way forward."

Melissa continued to slowly open the wine bottle, straining to hear what Howard had to say next. Seeing John approach, she put her finger to her lips and nodded in Howard and Grams's direction.

He mouthed a silent *Oh?* and grinned.

Howard leaned in closer to Grams. "So, you're not going to play the grandmother card to get her to stay?"

"The grandmother card? Whatever do you mean?" Grams raised a hand to her cheek.

"You know, tell her you're an old lady, and it would mean so much to you to have her here in your waning years."

Melissa stole a quick peek to see Grams softly bite her lip.

"Ah, you mean use guilt. Sorry, Howard. That's not my style. Her parents and I raised her to be independent and to find her own path in life. I won't stand in her way." Grams put her hands in her pockets and smiled.

Howard stared at Grams for a moment, shaking his head.

"Humph, no one sees the urgency I do. You were my last hope to set things right and end this foolishness on their part."

Grams softly patted his arm again. "I'm sorry, Howard. I know you will miss her. You've been a dear friend, and I will be forever grateful for the love and support you gave her this last year. Don't worry. She'll be back to visit as often as she can."

Howard gazed down at his glass, muttered that he needed more whiskey, and walked away, sulking.

Grams came over to Melissa and John. "I assume you heard. I think it's time for you to make your announcement. I don't think Howard can get any more despondent. Time to end his misery."

Melissa caught John's eye. "It's time."

Nodding, he took her hand and strode to the center of the room. He clinked his glass with a fork from the buffet to get everyone's attention. Once the room quieted, he raised his glass. "Thank you all for coming to celebrate everyone's favorite graphic artist. I know this means a lot to her. I'll turn this over to Melissa so she can tell you herself."

She gave him a little smile and faced her friends and family. "Thank you for coming. Part of tonight is to celebrate the success of *Save Our Salmon*. You all know the story, so I won't bore you with the details. Suffice it to say, we premiered it at a gaming expo to rave reviews, and I'm confident it will be a huge success when it hits the market next month. Now, I'm committed to expanding this concept to other environmental challenges."

A general murmur of dismay sounded amongst the group. They all anticipated what she'd say next.

Arabella stepped forward. "But we really, really want you to stay and do it with us."

Melissa smiled at Arabella. "I'm grateful so many of you don't want me to go. One person, in particular, has been working very hard to keep me here."

Everyone turned expectantly toward John.

He just smiled and gestured for her to continue.

Melissa made sure Howard was in her sights. "Howard, I know you have been working diligently, attempting to influence my decision."

"You've been playing the chess master, attempting to manipulate both of our moves for a long time," John added. "From the moment you woke up from your hip surgery, you plotted to get Melissa and me together. Don't think for a minute I didn't figure out why you insisted I take over your snack stand. You knew Melissa would show up one day, and we'd meet."

Everyone in the room shifted their attention toward where Howard was standing.

He straightened and stepped closer to John and Melissa. He pointed a finger at them both. "It was for your own good. Both of you needed a little maneuvering to discover you're perfect for each other. But somehow, you still managed to botch up all my hard work, and now she's moving across the country. I told you to propose. That would keep her here."

"This is just so you can have great-grandbabies, right?" John countered. "This is all about what *you* want."

Howard just grunted. "What I want is for the two of you to be happy. As happy as I was with your grandmother. A woman like her only comes along once in your life. If you won't do it, then I'll do it for you." Howard reached out to take Melissa's hand. "Melissa, I know you two love each other. It's easy to see whenever you're together. I know marriage can be scary, but I promise you'll be surrounded by people who love you both. For John's sake, would you please do me the honor of marrying my grandson—even if he is an idiot?"

Everyone in the room gasped. In the silence, all gazes pivoted back toward Melissa.

Melissa had been confident Howard had one more move to make, but this was a shock. And to do it in front of everyone. He clearly was desperate. She scanned the room, taking in the expectant looks.

Melissa glanced at John, who shrugged, and she burst out laughing. "Howard, that is the most unconventional proposal I've ever heard of." She withdrew her hand from his. "But yes, I will marry your grandson." She paused briefly, watching Howard's stunned reaction. "Actually, I already told him so the other night when he proposed." With that, she pulled her left hand out of her pocket to show the ring John had given her Wednesday night.

John pulled her in for a kiss while the room erupted in cheers.

Howard stood there, blinking rapidly. A grin slowly formed.

People began to rush up to John and her, shaking hands, patting John on the back, and admiring her ring.

For a few minutes, the room resounded with a cacophony of happy chatter.

Working her way through the throng, John's mom, Natalie, reached her. "But what about you moving to Orlando?"

Melissa took Natalie's hand and answered loud enough for everyone to hear. "I'm not moving."

Again, the room fell into silence.

Melissa slowly circled and once she spotted Howard she continued in a louder voice. "In fact, I was never moving. This was all a ruse to teach Howard his meddling in people's love lives could backfire. I did have offers from other gaming companies, but even without John's proposal, there's no way I'd desert my co-workers at Brothers. We're a team."

The team from Brothers all cheered and hugged each other, jumping up and down.

"I knew she wouldn't leave us. We're family," shouted Davey.

"It's time to change this banner," Grams spoke over the din of cheers. "Karen, Dan, would you please put this one up instead?"

Karen and Dan hopped onto chairs to pin up the new banner—*Congratulations, Melissa and John.*

The room continued to erupt.

Howard gawked at the banner. "You knew? All the time I was asking you to intervene and stop Melissa, you knew?" He poked a finger in the direction of Grams.

Grams just smiled and nodded.

Howard glared around at the assembled group. "Who else knew? Was I the only one who was duped?"

Karen and Jan both raised their hands.

"We knew about her not leaving, but not the engagement," Karen replied.

Dan didn't hide his smug expression when Howard glared. "I figured it out."

"And I knew," added Mario, following his grandson to the dining room table, where he placed a large sheet cake with candles and *Best Wishes, Melissa and John* written in royal blue letters on the white icing.

Melissa glanced at John.

"I called Mario and asked him to make this in secret."

"And I brought more festivities." Dan re-entered the room, holding chilled bottles of champagne in both hands. "Time to party."

The group hurried to fill glasses to toast the couple.

Natalie gave Melissa a huge hug. "I'm so thrilled. You've made John the happiest I've ever seen him. That's all a mother could want for her child. I know no one can ever replace your mother, and it pains me she isn't here for you. But I hope you'll let me help you with the wedding plans and everything else in life."

"I would really love it." Melissa returned Natalie's hug. Her chest tightened and then relaxed as she sank into Natalie's embrace. She blinked back tears and smiled.

Howard slowly approached Melissa and John. "I suppose you expect me to say congratulations," he grumbled as he continued to nurse his drink.

John put his arm around Howard's shoulders. "I love you, Pops. But I had to do this my way."

Howard slapped John on his back. "All's well that ends well. Don't forget, you never would have met her if I hadn't meddled."

Melissa stared at Howard, "But…"

John stopped her by putting an arm around her. He pointed his finger at Howard. "That might be true, but you were lucky this time. It's time to stop meddling in other people's love lives. It could be dangerous. This time, you had to break a hip to get what you wanted."

Howard waved a hand in front of his face. "No need for anything that drastic again. Now that you're taken care of, I think I see my next mission. Excuse me, I believe there's someone I need to meet." Howard swaggered across the room to join Dan and Jennifer.

Melissa wrapped her arms around John's waist. "Howard didn't seem to take our trick too hard. Do you think he'll stop meddling?"

"Oh, he's a resilient old coot. And no. It seems he's already spotted his next victims. He's planning his moves as we speak."

He directed her attention to Howard, chatting animatedly with Dan and Jennifer.

"I wish them luck. It looks like Howard is determined to continue his quest for great-grandbabies. I just hope their story has fewer bumps in the road than ours did."

John leaned back to study her face. "Bumps in the road? So, it wasn't love at first sight?"

"Maybe second or third," she teased. She looked around the room at her friends, Grams, and her new family-to-be celebrating John and her. A year ago, she was immersed in grief and couldn't have imagined a time when this house would ring with joy and laughter again. Glancing at John, she laid her head on his shoulder. *In a year, I've found confidence in my art, developed* SOS, *and fallen in love. What's next?* Taking

John's hand, she headed back into the thick of the party.
What's next is a wedding.

A word about the author…

After retiring, I turned years of writing training presentations and scripts for computer-based training programs to my love of sweet romance. I was introduced to the world of romance by my mother at an early age, and to this day, my favorite thing is to curl up with a good book, glass of wine, and maybe some dark chocolate.

When the pandemic struck, I took my love of books one step farther and began writing my own, leading to my first novel, Rapunzel's Escape.

When not writing or thinking about potential story lines, I love to cook, especially Thanksgiving dinner for my extensive family. I also write poetry and do photography. I had the privilege of traveling all throughout the USA and Europe with work, and now, I live in Seattle, WA, surrounded by close family members and friends.

Find me at booksbybeth.org or at my Facebook page by the same name.

Thank you for purchasing
this publication of The Wild Rose Press, Inc.

For questions or more information
contact us at
info@thewildrosepress.com.

The Wild Rose Press, Inc.
www.thewildrosepress.com

www.ingramcontent.com/pod-product-compliance
Lightning Source LLC
Chambersburg PA
CBHW072106020726
47501CB00003B/729
* 9 7 8 1 5 0 9 2 6 0 8 0 5 *